Gypsy Rock

OTHER TITLES BY ROBERT D. MCKEE

Killing Blood (2016)
Dakota Trails (2017)
Out of the Darkness (2017)

A BILLY YOUNG AND
HUGO DORLING NOVEL

GYPSY ROCK

ROBERT D. MCKEE

FIVE STAR
A part of Gale, a Cengage Company

Farmington Hills, Mich • San Francisco • New York • Waterville, Maine
Meriden, Conn • Mason, Ohio • Chicago

LIBRARY OF CONGRESS CATALOGING-IN-PUBLICATION DATA

Names: McKee, Robert, 1948- author.
Title: Gypsy rock / Robert D. McKee.
Description: First edition. | Waterville, Maine : Five Star, a part of Gale, Cengage Learning, 2018.
Identifiers: LCCN 2018013041 (print) | LCCN 2018014281 (ebook) | ISBN 9781432843113 (ebook) | ISBN 9781432843106 (ebook) | ISBN 9781432843083 (hardcover)
Subjects: LCSH: Frontier and pioneer life—Fiction. | GSAFD: Western stories.
Classification: LCC PS3613.C55255 (ebook) | LCC PS3613.C55255 G97 2018 (print) | DDC 813/.6—dc23
LC record available at https://lccn.loc.gov/2018013041

First Edition. First Printing: September 2018
Find us on Facebook—https://www.facebook.com/FiveStarCengage
Visit our website—http://www.gale.cengage.com/fivestar/
Contact Five Star Publishing at FiveStar@cengage.com

Printed in Mexico
1 2 3 4 5 6 7 22 21 20 19 18

For Mom

CHAPTER ONE:
GET 'IM

Billy Young stayed with the horses and watched as his friend, Deputy United States Marshal Hugo Dorling, climbed the small, grassy rise, dropped onto his belly, and extended his spyglass.

"See any signs of life out there, Hugo?" Billy asked, but Hugo didn't answer. He kept his glass leveled at the abandoned, ramshackle remains of what once had been the stage station west of Casper, Wyoming.

After giving the place a look-over, Hugo shoved the telescope closed with the heel of his hand and pushed to his feet. "It's Ben O'Dell, all right," he said as he trotted back to Billy. "I recognize his roan. They got their animals tied over next to the pile of lumber that used to be a barn."

Hugo slid his glass into a small felt sack. "The old station's in pretty bad shape," he said, "but at least it's still got a roof. All that's left of the barn is one rickety-ass ol' wall."

Rickety-ass or not, Billy told himself, it was enough to give the outlaws' horses a little protection from the icy wind, which was a lot more protection than he and Hugo had. Billy shoved his gloved hands deeper into the pockets of his sheepskin jacket.

"I didn't see Ben," said Hugo, "but I gotta quick glimpse of Dim Sam through the front window." Dim Sam was Samuel J. Marsh, a riding partner of O'Dell's, and a man who was every bit as mean as he was dumb. Along with his meanness and ignorance, Dim Sam was also short-tempered and quick to use a gun, all of which made for an unpleasant combination.

Hugo tucked the sack holding his spyglass into his saddlebag and pulled out a set of hobbles. "Let's fetter the horses," he said, "and try to get a little rest. We'll move in on 'em after sundown."

Billy dropped from Badger, his big gray, and wished he'd remembered to put on his long johns before he talked Hugo into letting him tag along on this manhunt. Billy was already so chilled it was all he could do to keep his teeth from clacking together. He hated to think how cold it would be once the sun went down.

"I guess Connie was right," offered Billy as he opened a saddlebag and took out his own set of hobbles. "She said we'd find O'Dell holed up here at the old station."

Connie was a working girl at the Half-Moon Saloon down on the west side of Center Street in Casper. She had once been O'Dell's woman, but those days were over. Connie had informed Hugo that Ben told her he'd killed the elderly Gypsy woman, Gwenfrei Faw. As a rule, murder wasn't in Hugo's jurisdiction, but this one had occurred on federal land southeast of town. Billy didn't know what Ben had done to sour Connie, but whatever it was, Ben would've been wise to think twice before he did it. The girl was the sort to carry a grudge.

Billy hobbled the gray, untied his bedroll, and tossed it to the ground.

"I wouldn't be gettin' too comfortable," Hugo said. "We ain't takin' a nap, you know."

Billy knelt and unrolled his blankets. "I doubt there's much chance of getting too comfortable on this damned freezing prairie." He sat and threw a blanket around his shoulders. "But if we're going to sit here 'til dark, I'm at least going to wrap up a little."

"How long've you lived in this country, Billy?" Hugo asked.

"You know as well as I do, Hugo. Mama and Pa brought us here sixteen years ago when I was four and Frank was eight."

Billy's brother, Frank, had been murdered in a train robbery a year and a half before, and it still caused an ache in Billy's heart every time his brother's name came up.

"Seems to me," said Hugo, "any fella who's been living in the middle of Wyoming since he was four years old oughta be able to handle the crisp climate better than you do."

Billy shrugged. "Pa always said I had thin blood. He figured that's the way some folks're built." Billy pulled his blanket tighter around his shoulders.

Hugo spread the two long tails of his heavy duster and plopped down, too. He brushed his bushy mustache away from his lips and dug out his tobacco and papers. "I kinda like the chilly months myself," he said. He rolled a thin, tight cigarette as he spoke. "Folks get into less mischief when the air's a little on the frigid side, which tends to make my job some easier." He struck a match, and as he lit his smoke, he cupped his hands to protect the blaze from the wind.

"Maybe you should explain your opinions on cold weather and crime to Mr. O'Dell," Billy suggested. No matter the season, Ben, his brother Thatcher, and their gang of ruffians were eager to cause trouble. "Killing an old woman just because she's a Gypsy sounds like mischief to me."

"Well," Hugo said as he flicked away the spent match, "Benjamin O'Dell is worse than most."

The wind let up a little once the sun set, but the temperature was dropping fast. Billy took a long drink of water from his canteen and wedged the side of it beneath his saddle blanket. He figured Badger's body heat might keep it from freezing. If there was one thing Billy hated, it was having to chew his water.

"Now, you don't have to come along on this chore, Billy,"

Hugo said. He untied a two-and-a-half-foot-long piece of rolled-up canvas from the back of his saddle and shook out a sawed-off, double-barreled shotgun. The deputy always maintained a man needed the right tool for the job, and there was nothing better for indoor fighting than a couple of feet of shotgun. "It ain't your job to catch O'Dell," he added. "It's mine."

Hugo thumbed the lever, and the shotgun's barrels dropped open. He inserted two twelve-gauge shells into the chambers. Billy knew the shells were loaded with double-aught buckshot; it was all Hugo ever used. "Why even bother to carry a shotgun," Hugo was fond of saying, "if you don't wanna blow the shit outta somethin'."

"You're right, Hugo," Billy said. "It's not my job to catch O'Dell, but it is my job to see you don't get yourself killed."

The deputy lifted a bushy eyebrow and fixed his young partner with a hard glare. "Why, you little pup. I was bustin' in unannounced on desperate men long before you was ever born."

"I expect that's true, Hugo."

"And I ain't got myself kilt yet."

Billy felt himself smile. "Well, sir, it might be you aren't as quick and clever as you once were, and you need the assistance of a younger, more capable man who has a mind more agile than your own."

Billy enjoyed the scowl his comment brought to Hugo's face, but he knew, even at forty-one, Hugo Dorling was as competent a lawman as anyone at any age. The deputy was a bit on the vain side, however, and Hugo's vanity made for a fine target.

Billy offered Hugo another smile, but the smile was not returned, which made Billy's smile stretch even wider.

The rising moon provided enough light they had no trouble making their way down to the station, about three hundred yards from where they left their hobbled horses. Through the window, Billy could see the yellow blot of a kerosene lamp, and the aroma of woodsmoke, coffee, and frying bacon was inviting.

"You figure they have enough bacon for us, too, Hugo?" Billy asked.

"They might, but I doubt they'll be willin' to share."

When they were fifty feet from the station, Hugo told Billy to stay put, and, in a crouch, the deputy sneaked around to a side window. Removing his hat, he peeked over the windowsill. After studying things inside awhile, he turned to Billy and motioned in the direction of the front door. The two met at the rough-planked porch.

"They're both in there, all right," Hugo whispered. "Dim Sam's by a rusty ol' pot-belly on the left-hand side of the room. He's frying up the bacon and boiling some coffee so his back's to the door. O'Dell's sitting with his feet propped on the table by the far-side window. The lamp's on the table, so O'Dell has plenty of light on him. When we get inside, you cover him with that." He nodded to the short-barreled forty-five Billy held. "It's a little darker and harder to see over where Sam is. I'll cover him with this." He lifted his scattergun.

In the confines of the small station, Billy doubted the load from Hugo's shotgun would have the time or space to do much scattering. If the twelve-gauge was fired in there, the shot would travel in a grouping about the size of a large man's fist, and hit with the force of a locomotive.

Hugo jerked a thumb at the porch planks. "When we step on them old boards, they're gonna creak like bastards, so we'll have to move across 'em fast. You kick in the door, and I'll go in first. You come in behind. Sam's wearin' his gun, but O'Dell's shooter's hangin' from a peg on the near wall by the door. Since you'll be between him and it, I'm thinkin' O'Dell won't be causin' you any trouble."

"You be careful with Dim Sam, though, Hugo. The fella's a

11

dullard, but he's also quick and tricky."

"They're both the sort to be reckoned with," Hugo said. He patted his shotgun and winked. "But I ain't concerned."

Billy could tell Hugo's excitement was building. Hugo loved this sort of thing. He took real pleasure in confrontation. Billy had seen that in the deputy before, but he still found it odd, especially when the confrontation involved gunfire.

"Are you ready?" Hugo asked.

Billy tugged off his right glove and shoved it inside a jacket pocket. He nodded to his partner, and feeling a sudden bit of excitement himself, he answered, "You betcha."

Billy leapt onto the porch, and in two steps he crossed to the door and kicked his boot an inch to the right of the knob. In the same instant, there was the crash of Billy's kick and the screech of the door bursting open and sweeping around on rusty hinges.

The door was still in motion when Hugo crossed the threshold. "Hold it, boys," he shouted. "Don't even blink."

Billy ran in behind Hugo and found O'Dell with his boots still on the table. Hugo's shotgun was aimed at Dim Sam. As Billy leveled his Colt at O'Dell, from the corner of his eye, he spotted Sam whirl and slap at his holster. With amazing speed, Sam cleared leather, but that was as far as it got. His shooter was not yet cocked when Hugo's sawed-off roared. The blast caught Sam in the chest, and amid bone and gore, he was airborne. He smashed into the station's back wall and tumbled to the floor like a pile of bloody laundry.

In the split second Billy's attention went to Dim Sam, Ben O'Dell's feet came off the table, and in one scooping arc of his right hand, he grabbed the lamp and threw it at Hugo. It hit at Hugo's feet and shattered, sending flaming kerosene across the station's floor, up the wall to Hugo's left, and onto the long tails of Hugo's duster. In a flash, the coat was ablaze.

"Oh, *shit!*" Billy screamed. And as he did, O'Dell dove through the window beside the table. Billy fired but missed. He spun to help Hugo, who was struggling with the duster's buttons.

"Here, Hugo," Billy shouted, dropping his pistol, "let go." With both hands, Billy grabbed Hugo's lapels and ripped the coat open, sending its buttons flying. He peeled the flaming duster from Hugo's back and threw it in the corner.

Both cuffs of Hugo's jeans and the lower portions of his boots were afire. Billy tore open his own jacket in order to use it to beat out the flames, but Hugo shouted, "Never mind me. I can do this. Don't let the son of a bitch get away."

See page 14

"But Hugo—"

"Get 'im," Hugo shouted, and he dashed across the room. He grabbed the coffee pot from the top of the stove and poured the scalding coffee over the tops of his boots and pants. "Goddamn it, Billy, don't stand there. Go get O'Dell."

Billy ran onto the porch and looked toward the leaning wall where the outlaws had their horses tied. Both animals were still there, but O'Dell was nowhere to be seen. Billy sprinted around the side of the building to the window O'Dell had escaped through, and there he was, seventy-five yards away, running for all he was worth into the safety of the dark prairie. Billy squared his hat and took off after him.

At first Billy was gaining—cutting O'Dell's lead by half, but O'Dell must have heard him coming. He looked back over his shoulder, saw Billy, and increased his speed.

Billy sped up, too, but not enough. The distance between them grew.

The outlaw was three or four years older than Billy, and his legs were three or four inches shorter, but thick cords of muscle spanned O'Dell's lean frame, and it appeared the outlaw was built to run. Billy redoubled his effort and narrowed the gap between them to forty or fifty yards, but no matter how he poured on the steam, he couldn't get closer. O'Dell was no longer extending his lead, but neither was Billy gaining.

Billy dropped his right hand and felt for his pistol, but with disappointment remembered he'd let it fall to the floor back at the stage shack. That was bad. A shot from the forty-five—whether he hit O'Dell or not—would likely bring this foot chase to a quick end.

Billy soon realized there would be no quick end. He and O'Dell were not running a sprint.

O'Dell was no longer bothering to look back. Instead, he continued to pump his arms and legs, heading deeper into the dark, windswept prairie.

It had been a while since Billy had run at all and even longer since he'd run the way he was running now, but he settled into it, making a conscious effort to control his pace and breathing. He timed his breath with the movement of his arms and the smack of his boot soles hitting the ground.

When they were boys, he and Frank would run for miles along the base of Casper Mountain where the Young family ranched. Most times, a dog or two scampered beside them, and boys and dogs would go until Billy feared his lungs might explode. But, he recalled, never did he pull up before Frank. That, Billy hoped, would be the case tonight.

At least he was no longer cold. Sweat beaded all over his body, and soon the heat was stifling. He batted away his hat and felt the wind ruffle through his wet hair. He undid the buttons of his sheepskin jacket, pulled the jacket from his shoulders and let it fall away. The cold air felt good as it hit his sweat-soaked shirt.

O'Dell was running with a smooth rhythm. His strides were long, strong, and sure, but Billy was determined. He was the cause of O'Dell getting away in the first place. O'Dell had thrown the lamp in the half second Billy had turned his gaze

14

toward Dim Sam.

If it weren't for pure luck, Hugo would be lying back there burned to ashes. The thought was painful. Billy had seen too many people he cared for die.

Sara Young, Billy's mother, had been killed in an Indian skirmish two years after they moved to Wyoming. Three years ago, his father, Joshua, was hit by a stray bullet as he walked down the street in Casper. A couple of wild cowboys had gotten into a gunfight in the barber shop as Josh walked by outside. A bullet blew through the shop's thin clapboard siding and killed him on the spot.

Billy swallowed hard and ran his sleeve across his wet face.

He'd been only half joking when he said he'd come along to make sure Hugo didn't get himself killed. Billy refused to let Hugo die a violent death like the others, although it was his own carelessness that nearly got Hugo fried tonight. Billy knew he'd spend a good piece of the next few days rehashing that fool's blunder, but there was no time for it now.

He fixed his eyes on Ben O'Dell's broad back and focused on the chase.

O'Dell began to slow. Not much. At first Billy wasn't even aware of it, but then he noticed the distance between them had dropped to thirty yards. It held at thirty until the outlaw tripped. He hit the ground in full stride, rolled once and came back to his feet in a run. He did it with grace, but it cost O'Dell more distance, and Billy continued to close.

At ten yards, he could hear O'Dell's wet, labored breathing. Billy was outrunning this son of a bitch. Billy dug down inside himself and found enough still there to move a little faster.

When the gap was at five yards, O'Dell skidded to a stop and spun around. His eyes bulged, and his dirty, sopping hair clung to his head and the sides of his face like a greasy scarf. He gasped for air the way a banked fish will gasp for water, and even in the moonlight, Billy could see the man's cheeks and neck were scarlet.

Never slowing, Billy ducked his shoulder, plowed into O'Dell's chest, and they both went sprawling. Too exhausted to raise his hands to break his fall, O'Dell landed face-first. Billy winced as he watched him grind across five feet of rough ground. Once he skidded to a stop, O'Dell attempted to get up, but his legs no longer worked.

Billy made it to his feet, though. He lifted the outlaw by the hair and looked into the man's empty eyes. A half-dozen jagged cuts crisscrossed O'Dell's face from where he'd hit the ground, and his expression was blurry with exhaustion. The outlaw was finished, but Billy didn't care. With all the strength he had left, he balled his fist and drove three quick punches—*whap, whap, whap*—square into the point of Ben O'Dell's nose. Blood exploded, and Billy felt the satisfying snap of cartilage.

O'Dell didn't seem to notice. His glassy stare never altered as he fell to his back and rolled onto his side, gagging, and vomiting into the gray dirt. O'Dell's wasted body stiffened and shook all the way from his feet to the top of his head.

Billy watched him flop about but soon realized he wasn't feeling so great himself. Drained and breathless, Billy dropped to all fours and gulped in the cold night air.

As Billy stared at the dirt, trying to collect himself, O'Dell continued his weird convulsions. For a while, Billy guessed the man was dying, but after a few minutes, the outlaw's thrashing let up. Even so, Billy guessed O'Dell would not be causing trouble anytime soon. His eyes were still glassy, mucous and blood bubbled from his nostrils, and strings of saliva leaked from the corners of his twisted mouth.

Once Billy was breathing easier, he looked back in the direction they'd come. He could see a glow in the far distance, but his vision was blurred, and it was hard to make out what it was. He sat up straighter, rubbed his eyes, and looked again. The glow was the burning station. It looked as though the building was engulfed in flames, but it was hard to tell for sure because the tiny bright spot had to be at least four miles away.

In the near distance a rider approached, leading a couple of horses. It had to be Hugo, which meant the old coot hadn't burned up after all. Billy felt relief.

By the time Hugo arrived with the horses, O'Dell had come around, and although he still retched and sputtered a bit, it appeared his soured guts were empty at last.

"So you ran 'im to ground, eh?" Hugo said as he trotted up. "Good work." He dropped from the saddle, grabbed his canteen, and crossed to Billy. "You thirsty?" he asked with a smile.

"A little." Billy took a sip from the canteen. He let it settle into his own sour guts and took another. Checking Hugo out, he said, "I guess you didn't burn up after all. What's the story? Are you fireproof?"

"Could be. My brand new coat's a loss, though, and my jeans and boots were a little charred. I expect if I hadn't been wearing them big ol' tall boots my leg hairs mighta got a bit singed, but as it was, I didn't suffer much damage. I dragged Dim Sam's body out of the building before the place went up completely, and since he was about my size, I borrowed his coat, jeans, and boots. I figure they'll do me until we can get home."

"I doubt he'll be needing them," Billy said.

"My shirt was okay," said Hugo, "which is lucky for me since Dim Sam's was full of pellet holes."

Not to mention covered in Dim Sam's gore, Billy recalled, as he took another drink. "Looks like his stuff fits you pretty good."

"Not bad. It's all a bit stinky, though. I reckon ol' Sam was a little inattentive to his personal hygiene."

Hugo motioned toward O'Dell, who was ten feet away, lying on his side with his knees pulled up tight against his chest. "Let's put a little water in this one and get back to the station. We'll camp there." He looked up at the sky. "Sleepin' next to them hot coals oughta take the bite outta what promises to be a chilly night."

"Did you happen to spot my coat?" Billy asked. The sweat had dried, and he was ready to put on his sheepskin.

"I saw it. We'll pick 'er up on the way back."

Hugo went to his horse and pulled out a set of handcuffs. He crossed to O'Dell and locked the killer's wrists behind his back. Holding the canteen for O'Dell to take a drink, Hugo noticed his face. "Damn, Billy, ol' Ben here ain't lookin' so good." He nodded to the scrapes and deep cuts. "Did you do that to 'im?"

"I kind of bumped him, I suppose," Billy said. "He got banged up when he fell."

"Musta been quite a fall. Looks like it damned near broke his nose clean off."

"Well," Billy conceded with a shrug, "I guess I did do the nose part."

"Lift your head up here, Ben, so I can see it better." Hugo scrutinized the outlaw's injuries, and said, "Ah, hell, it ain't so bad. Besides, it serves you right, takin' off the way you did, makin' folks run for miles through the cold and dark havin' to chase you down." The deputy was never one quick to offer sympathy to outlaws, but he did take off his kerchief and blot away some of the blood covering O'Dell's face. Lifting his canteen, he took some water for himself, and asked, "Connie down at the Half-Moon says it was you who kilt the Gypsy Gwenfrei Faw. Is that so, Ben?"

O'Dell shrugged. "Yep."

The deputy looked perplexed. "That poor old woman couldn't't've meant one thing to you, Ben O'Dell, and I sure doubt she had much worth stealin'. Why in the world would you want to kill her?"

"I don't know, Hugo. I can't believe you're making such a big deal out of it."

"You can't, huh?"

"No, she was just a dern ol' Gypsy. Who cares?"

"Well, as far as I know, the law don't say it's a crime to kill ever'body except for Gypsies. I could be wrong there, I guess, though I doubt it. Here, have another slosh-a water." He held the canteen.

"Thanks," O'Dell said. He sounded grateful, and the water perked him up. "Any chance I can get you to take the cuffs off?" he asked. "They sure ain't comfortable."

"Hell, boy, you're under arrest. Them cuffs ain't supposed to be comfortable." Hugo seemed to give it some consideration. "Though I suppose we might loosen 'em a little once we bed you down. We'll see how she goes." Hugo looked back toward the still-burning stage station. "I expect after your lengthy run you'll sleep solid tonight, Ben, which is a good thing."

"Why d'ya say that?" Ben asked. "What's it to you how I sleep?"

" 'Cause bright 'n' early in the morning, we'll be headin' back to Casper. There's no time to waste. We'll want to have your trial so we can string you up as soon as possible."

"C'mon, Hugo," O'Dell said with the sound of confidence, "they ain't no jury gonna hang a fella for killing a Gypsy. It'll never happen." He offered Hugo a wide grin. "You wait and see."

CHAPTER TWO:
BAKER'S DOZEN

Enos Woodard slapped down an ace and said with a chuckle, "That makes thirty-one for two, and last card is three, which puts me out. And, Deputy Dorling, unless I'm wrong, I believe you got double-skunked." Enos made a big show of sticking a tiny peg into the last hole on the polished oak cribbage board between Hugo and him. "If we were playing for dollars instead of mere pennies, I would now be a rich man."

"You're already a rich man, you faker," Hugo responded, "but you're one poor winner. Don't you know gloatin' is a sign of bad character?"

Billy, who had been sitting at the table all morning watching these two friends play cribbage, could tell waiting for the jury was wearing on Hugo's patience, and spending four or five hours getting whipped at cards was doing nothing to improve his disposition.

Billy was feeling pretty low himself.

"Gloat?" said Enos. "I guess maybe I am gloating a bit, Hugo, but when it comes to you, I can't help myself. I sometimes think the good Lord's sole purpose in putting me on this Earth was to whack you down a notch or two every chance I get."

Hugo frowned, and Enos tossed back his head and came out with his loud, friendly laugh. He licked the tip of his pencil and did some calculating on a tablet. "It now comes to four dollars and ninety-seven cents you owe me. I would like it in hard cash, American money, if you don't mind." He turned to Billy and offered a sly wink. "Knowing you as I do, I cannot allow credit."

"Considering your low skill at cribbage, Hugo," Billy pointed out, "if the jury doesn't come back soon, I expect you'll end up indentured to Mr. Woodard here for the next twenty years."

The date was Thursday, November twenty-fourth, and a large portion of the town's population was congregated in Casper's Community Room—or CR, as the townspeople called it—waiting for both their Thanksgiving dinner and for the jury to return a verdict in Ben O'Dell's murder trial.

United States District Judge Thomas Reed had finished charging the jury at three o'clock the previous afternoon and sent them out to deliberate. When midnight rolled around and the jury still wasn't back, the judge allowed them to go home to sleep on it. As every President had done since the time of Mr. Lincoln, President Harrison had declared today a national holiday, but even so, Judge Reed told the jury to return to the courthouse at seven o'clock and get back to work.

"Sorry, Enos," Hugo said, "whether you want to or not, you're gonna have to provide credit on my losses. I handed over my last six bits to your sister for my turkey and fixin's. If you insist, though, I could get the money back and give it to you as payment against what I owe."

Reverend Abner Sewell and the Lutheran Women's League were raising money for the church by providing a Thanksgiving dinner here in the CR. Billy doubted the stone-faced Sewell did any of the work. Apparently his function was nothing more than to stand at the front of the room and look sanctimonious. The women, however, had been working for days, baking cakes and pies and making preparations. Enos's sister, Stella, was collecting from everyone as they came through the front door.

Earlier, Enos had confided to Billy and Hugo that the women had put Stella at the door to get her out of the kitchen. Billy knew Enos loved his younger sister. He doted on her in every way, but it was clear Enos recognized the young woman's limitations.

As poor luck would have it, Stella had been cursed from an early age with what the doctors called a nervous condition. "She's always been a little edgy, you might say," Enos had told them one late night a year earlier when he, Hugo, and Billy were working on the dregs of a bottle of Scotland whisky. "But the worst of it is her mood changes. It's hard to understand. Sometimes she can be as giddy as a schoolgirl, and other times a deep melancholia can hit her so hard she'll not leave her room for days. In those times I fear for what she might do. None of the docs can figure it out, not here, Cheyenne, or even down in Denver. We've been to them all. It's a sad mystery that I fear has me beat."

Now as they waited in the CR, Enos said, "Don't bother to retrieve the money for your dinner, Hugo. I could never live with myself if I was the cause of you missing a meal."

"My, ain't you generous," Hugo said, but he did not sound sincere.

The way Billy saw it, if anyone in Casper could afford to be generous, it was Enos Woodard. Enos was from the East and had attended school at Dartmouth College, where he received a degree in geology. He had come to the Wyoming Territory because, as he put it, there were more interesting rocks around this place than anywhere in all of North America. But he soon developed more interest in the territory's—and later the young state's—business potential than its rocks.

Three years ago, Enos had purchased a ranch southwest of town that was twice the size of Billy's at the foot of Casper Mountain. Later, Enos bought the largest feedlot in central Wyoming. Early last year, he acquired Casper's finest haberdashery.

Eventually, Enos brought local bigwig Avery Sloane and

Sloane's younger brother-in-law, Scott Parrish, in as investors, and most folks expected the three would own the entire county before they were done.

"How 'bout you, Billy?" Enos asked as he rapped the deck on the table. "Care for a game?"

Billy enjoyed cribbage, but he didn't feel like playing cards. He was anxious over the length of time it was taking the jury to finish its deliberations. "No, sir. I think I'll pass."

Enos looked surprised. "Why, Billy Young, I don't recall you ever saying no to a game of cribbage."

"Maybe you should go ask Lawyer Hawthorn over yonder if he'd like to play," Hugo suggested. "His mood seems to be as jovial as your own." Hugo nodded toward Miles Hawthorn, a distinguished-looking middle-aged man sitting with a group of people a couple of tables away.

Enos glanced in Hawthorn's direction. "His spirits are high, aren't they?"

"They ought to be," said Billy. "He's got a client who confessed to me and Hugo that he murdered a woman in cold blood, yet the jury's been deliberating now for—" He looked up at the Regulator on the back wall. "—almost fourteen hours, and we still don't have a verdict."

He tossed back what was left in his coffee cup, but he'd allowed the coffee to get cold, and he grimaced when the bitter liquid hit the back of his throat. Shoving the cup away, he added, "And it's all my fault."

"It ain't your fault," said Hugo. "If you ask me, it's the fool judge's fault."

Enos placed the deck of cards on top of the cribbage board and leaned back in his chair. "Now, don't take this the wrong way, boys. I'm on your side. You know I am." He tapped his chest with an index finger. "You don't have to convince me Billy would never do what Miles Hawthorn is saying he did, but

I can also see how Judge Reed would feel obliged to let Hawthorn argue his position to the jury."

"Why?" asked Billy. "People around here know me. Anyone who'd think I'd ever beat a confession out of a man is out of his mind."

"I know, but you have to admit it didn't look very good, you fellas dragging O'Dell in all busted up the way he was. I mean Doc Waters had to put a couple of dozen stitches in his face, and his nose—" Enos shook his head. "—well, sir, his nose was pretty near mush."

"He's no uglier now than he ever was," Hugo said.

Enos ignored the remark and continued with the point he was trying to make. "I don't like that federal judge any more than you fellas, but in all honesty, what's the man to do? We know it's a lie, but still, O'Dell tells everyone he only confessed because he figured you two wouldn't be satisfied to hear anything else. He was terrified of you. You busted into the stage station and started shooting the place up. You killed Sam Marsh, and then when O'Dell ran for his life, Billy chased him down and beat him senseless. It comes to your word against O'Dell's that it didn't happen in just that way."

"If we'd been able to get to Connie," Billy said, "she could've told everybody O'Dell had also admitted to her that he'd killed the old woman."

"She lit outta here fast, all right," said Hugo. He looked across the room at Ben O'Dell's brother, Thatcher. Thatcher had come into the CR a few minutes earlier. He had no doubt been over at the jail, waiting for the verdict with Ben. Now he sat at a corner table, laughing it up with a bunch of his pals. "I'd bet Thatcher O'Dell had something to do with Connie leavin' so sudden."

Billy looked at Enos and jerked his head toward Hugo. "Hugo here figures Connie must've gone down to Cheyenne."

"We know she left for Cheyenne," said Hugo. "I expect she's at her parents' farm a couple of miles this side of the Colorado line. Wherever she is, though, I know we could've found her if Judge Reed would've postponed the trial date, but he wouldn't even consider it. The man wouldn't even give us one more day."

Enos shrugged the shoulders of his handsome gray suit. "I hate to say it, boys, but with no direct evidence that it was Ben who killed the woman, plus the accusations of a coerced confession, and Connie leaving the country, I guess I can see how the jury might have some problems reaching a decision."

"Horseshit," said Hugo, and he didn't whisper when he said it.

Enos blanched and looked around. "Watch your language, there, Hugo. We're surrounded by Lutherans."

"I don't give two farts in a windstorm if we're surrounded by Jesus Christ and all the holy saints. The jury's havin' problems, all right, because, thanks to Miles Hawthorn, the jury's stacked with the twelve dullest morons in all Natrona County. With the help of Judge Reed, Hawthorn was able to get anybody with any brains off the panel. Hawthorn knew he had to do it, too, or his client's goose was cooked for sure.

"Another problem is the jury can't see the truth past that judge. Every ruling he made, he made in Ben O'Dell's favor. I've been testifying in trials now for a couple of decades, and I ain't never seen anythin' like it."

"Well, sir," Enos said, "I guess you're not the first fella I've heard question the competence of Thomas Reed."

"Reed's performance in this trial was poor, even by his usual low standards," said Hugo.

"I'd hate to think this of him," said Enos, lowering his voice, "but it could be he doesn't like Gypsies."

Hugo nodded. "I expect you're right. There's sure been plenty of that sorta thinkin' ever since those Romanies set up camp out by the big rock. But there's gotta be more to it. Some of the things Reed's done in this trial were plain crazy."

"It is hard to figure," said Enos.

"Lots of things are hard to figure," Billy said. "Like where did Ben O'Dell ever come up with the money to hire Miles Hawthorn in the first place?" He turned his gaze in the lawyer's direction. "That pettifogger's as expensive as any attorney north of Denver."

Before Enos or Hugo could respond, a boy of ten or twelve burst through the front door, bolted past a flustered Stella Woodard, and shouted above the chatter in the Community Room, "Hey, everybody, get over to the courthouse quick. The jury has reached a verdict."

By the time Billy, Hugo, Enos, and Stella walked into the courtroom, the place was almost full. A half-dozen thirteen-year-old boys were sitting on the bench right behind the prosecutor's table, and since that was where Hugo always sat, Billy knew those kids were in for trouble.

"Unless all you urchins wanna get your ears pinned back," Hugo said as he walked toward the young teens, "you'd best—" But before he could finish, the boys hopped up and scooted to the back of the courtroom. "Damned kids," Hugo muttered under his breath as he dropped onto the bench.

Most of the participants had taken their places on the other side of the bar. Dan Higgins, the deputy federal prosecutor, was at his table. Miles Hawthorn sat at the defense table next to Ben O'Dell, who slouched in his chair, wearing his usual smirk. Billy and Hugo's friend, Walter Cosgrove, the court stenographer, was flipping through his shorthand tablet at his desk in front of the bench.

Hugo's boss, Webster Pierce, the United States Marshal, stood next to the bench, looking as self-important as ever. He wore jeans so crisp and neat they appeared to Billy to have been pressed with a hot iron. Strapped across his hips was a ridiculous two-gun get-up. The fancy rig looked as if it might have been borrowed from a Bill Cody trick shooter. Pierce's black hair was combed high in a shiny pompadour, and Hugo maintained the man colored it with mail-order hair dye he bought by the case from a place out of Chicago. Hugo said it was a known fact told to him by the janitor who cleaned the federal offices down in Cheyenne.

The spectator's section was made up of twenty benches—ten to a side—and people were packed onto them as tight as steers in a boxcar. Everyone was squished so close to the person beside them that Billy was embarrassed. His right hip was shoved next to Hugo, a bad enough situation, but what was even worse was having Stella Woodard shoved against him on his left.

He had no dislike for Miss Woodard. At twenty-four, she was young and pretty, and in her way, she had always been pleasant. But even before he learned of her afflictions, Billy had considered her a strange one, and she made him uncomfortable. She always seemed preoccupied or distracted by things only she could see. She sat next to him now, not speaking, staring across the courtroom's bar at the back of Dan Higgins's pockmarked neck.

"How are you feeling, Stella?" Enos asked. "Is there anything I can get you?" Enos was fifteen years older than his sister and acted more like her father than her brother. "A glass of water, maybe?"

"No, Enos," she answered. "Thank you, but I'm fine." Her expression never changed.

Miss Woodard's behavior had become even odder in the last couple of months, ever since her fiancé, Philip Pritchard, was killed in a riding accident north of town. Pritchard had been a friend of Enos's. Both Enos and Stella were grief-stricken by the man's sudden death. Now, though, Enos was at least trying to put Pritchard's death behind him. Clearly, his sister could not.

Billy felt awkward snuggled against her the way they were. He searched for some topic of conversation but could come up with nothing. When Thomas Reed's chambers' door opened and the robed judge stepped into the room, Billy was relieved.

"All rise," shouted Webster Pierce in a booming voice. And the courtroom was filled with the thunder of a hundred people coming to their feet.

Judge Reed assumed the bench, looked down at Pierce, and said, "Bring in the jury, Marshal."

Pierce nodded and walked around Walter Cosgrove's desk to a door on the far side of the bench. He knocked on the door and disappeared inside. A few seconds later, the door reopened, and Pierce came out, leading the jury.

Once the twelve men were in the box, Judge Reed said, "You may be seated," and Pierce resumed his position next to the bench.

"Has the jury elected a foreman and reached a verdict?" the judge asked.

Arthur Hinds, an older man, who once had been a farrier on Tom Sun's ranch down by Devil's Gate, stood and said, "Yes, sir, we sure have."

From the corner of his mouth, Hugo said to Billy, "The fact they elected Arthur to be the foreman oughta tell ya somethin'." Arthur was a well-liked, affable sort, but his intellect was of the dubious variety.

Reed shoved his spectacles down to the tip of his nose and took Arthur in over the rims. "Mr. Foreman, in the matter of the United States of America versus Benjamin O'Dell, how does the jury find, guilty or not guilty?"

Arthur swallowed, and when he did, his Adam's apple

bobbed. "We find the defendant—" He looked first to the prosecution and then to the defense. "—not guilty." As soon as he said it, he dropped into his seat as though saying those six words had tuckered him out.

When the verdict was announced, the spectators began to stir and talk among themselves. Hugo muttered a curse and smacked his hand onto the top of his thigh, but all in all, Hugo took it better than Billy might have predicted.

"Hold the noise down out there," ordered Judge Reed. He turned to the jury and said, "I want to thank you gentlemen for your service over the course of the last few days. You've all done a fine job. I sat here on this bench and listened to the very same evidence you fellas've listened to, and the way I see it, there is no way you could've come to any other decision. You have every right to be proud of the verdict you've rendered this morning."

"What a pile," Hugo said.

"Quiet, Hugo," said Billy. "Not another word." When Billy said it, he whispered, but he tried to make the admonition firm.

"And," the judge went on, clearly enjoying the sound of his own voice, "your verdict could not have come at a more appropriate time: Thanksgiving Day. Along with the right to vote for our elected representatives, jury service is the hallmark of free men. Sitting on a jury is not only a duty, it's a right and a privilege. It is an honor to be called, and it is an honor to serve. It is, in fact, the very thing that Americans have died for since the birth of our great nation."

Before Billy could stop him, Hugo was on his feet and leaning over the bar. "Another thing Americans've been dyin' for the last hundred and sixteen years," he said, "is to have the right to say what they think. And I'm gonna tell you what I'm thinkin' right now." He pointed to Billy. "When me and this fine young fella sittin' here got on the witness stand and said on our oaths—"

"Sit down, Deputy Dorling," the judge said.

But Hugo ignored him. "When we said on our oaths that Ben O'Dell, by his own free will, confessed to us he had murdered a poor, defenseless old woman—"

"Sit *down*, deputy," repeated the judge, "or I will hold you in contempt."

Billy stood and grabbed Hugo's sleeve. He tried tugging him toward the door, but Hugo would not be tugged, and he would not be silenced.

"Since you fellas sittin' up there in the jury box *still* saw fit to find O'Dell not guilty in spite of what Billy and me swore, then I gotta think you are about the twelve dumbest sons-a-bitches God ever let breathe air."

Now Judge Reed was also on his feet. "That'll be fifty dollars, Deputy Dorling," he shouted. "Fifty dollars payable immediately."

Billy pulled on Hugo's arm for all he was worth, dragging him out in a jerky, stop-and-go fashion. As Hugo was pulled toward the courtroom door, he jabbed his finger at the judge. "And as far as dumb sons-a-bitches go," he shouted back, "you, Reed, make it a regular baker's dozen."

"A hundred dollars," screamed the judge, spittle flying with every word. "One hundred dollars, Dorling, payable before you leave this building, and if you utter even one more syllable, I swear to you upon my *own* oath you will find yourself in jail."

Billy clamped his hand around Hugo's mouth and dragged him in a headlock from the room.

Enos said, "I assume, Roger, you're willing to accept my personal check in payment for the deputy's fine." The Woodards, Billy, and Hugo were in the office of the Clerk of the U.S. District Court.

Roger Keyes, the clerk, nodded. "Of course, Mr. Woodard.

That'll be no problem at all."

Enos wrote the check, signed it with a flourish, and presented it to Mr. Keyes. "Considering Deputy Dorling's temperament," Enos said, "maybe it'd be more convenient, Roger, if I deposited some funds here with your office, and every time the deputy opens his mouth, you can withdraw whatever amount the judge orders paid."

The clerk smiled. "It'd sure make it easier, wouldn't it, sir?"

"Very funny," Hugo said. "Maybe you two fellas could form a comedy team and go on the vaudeville stage."

"They're both already employed, Hugo," said Billy. "If you don't watch yourself, it'll be you who ends up looking for a new line of work."

Roger placed Enos's check in a steel lockbox and dropped the key in his pocket. "If that's all, fellas, I'm going to close up and head over to the CR. Today is a holiday, you know."

"Oh, sure, Roger," Enos said. "We were headed back over there ourselves."

They left Roger to close his office and stepped into the cold November afternoon. Although it hadn't started yet, it appeared as though it might snow. Thick folds of gray clouds hung low in the sky.

"I wasn't kidding about you losing your job, Hugo," Billy said as he buttoned his jacket and pulled it tighter. They headed down First Street toward the CR. "I was watching Webster Pierce back there when you were making your big speech. He looked to be about as perturbed as Judge Reed was."

Hugo nodded. "Pierce don't have a mind of his own. If Reed's riled about somethin', you can bet Pierce'll be riled about it, too. But I doubt he's got what it takes to fire me. If he did, he might have to do some work. Most folks know between Pierce and me which one of us does most of the marshalin' around Wyomin'." He took off his hat and ran his hand through his hair. "But you're right, Billy. I need to watch myself. It rarely accomplishes much for a fella to lose his temper the way I sometimes do."

Enos pulled his watch from his vest and checked the time. "The train back to Cheyenne won't be leaving for another two hours. I expect the judge and marshal will be joining us for Thanksgiving dinner."

"My, my, what good news," said Hugo.

Billy jabbed an index finger toward the old deputy's chest. "You'll need to be careful with what you say. Even if you're right about Pierce not firing you, I doubt you can afford too many more fines from the judge."

"That's for sure," Hugo conceded. "By the way, Enos, thanks for paying for me back there. I got some money in a savings over at the bank. I'll get you your hundred dollars."

They started to cross the street, and as they did, Enos reached down and took Stella's elbow. "There's no rush, Hugo," he said. "Pay me whenever you can. Of course, you know a hundred dollars isn't enough."

"What d'ya mean?"

"A hundred and four dollars and ninety-seven cents is what you owe. Part due to your poor skills at curbing your surly tongue, and the rest due to your poor skills at cribbage."

CHAPTER THREE:
TALKING TO HIS EMPTY PLATE

Billy glanced up as Walter Cosgrove, the court reporter, and his wife, Millie, finished filling their plates at the long food table. "Say, Walt," Billy called, "come on over. We're about done, but you and Millie can join us while we polish off our coffee and punkin pie."

There were a couple of free chairs at the table Billy and Hugo shared with the Woodards, and Billy motioned for the Cosgroves to have a seat.

"Thanks, Billy," Walter said. He carried both his and his wife's plates, and it wasn't hard to tell which was his. One was piled high with thick slices of turkey and huge portions of dressing, cranberries, green beans, and corn. It held more Thanksgiving fare than Billy and Hugo had put away between the two of them.

Hugo watched as Walter set the plates on the table. "I'm sure glad we made it through the line before you showed up, Walt. There might not've been anythin' left." To Millie he added, "I reckon it keeps you busy both night and day cookin' for this fella, don't it, young lady?"

Millie looked at her husband and smiled. "That's about all we ever do," she said. "I cook, and Walter eats." Judging by the round swell of belly beneath the young woman's frock, Billy doubted cooking and eating was *all* they did.

Walter Cosgrove, who was not quite four years older than Billy, was a big, muscular man. He stood over six-feet-four and weighed close to two-forty, which put him more than three inches taller and thirty-five pounds heavier than Billy. In the summers, Walt played first base for the Casper Red Stockings, and he was the team's best player. He had finished the previous season with thirty-eight home runs and a batting average of better than four hundred. Millie, on the other hand, was tiny, barely more than five feet tall, and her bones were as a thin as a sparrow's. But even with the difference in their sizes, Billy had the young woman pegged as the boss in the Cosgrove household.

"Before you sit down, hon," she said, "would you get us some punch?"

"Sure thing, Mill," said Walter in an eager-to-please voice. He scampered over to the table that held a half-dozen pitchers of red punch, poured two glasses, and scampered back.

"Thank you, dear," said Millie, as Walt set the punch down next to her plate.

Billy knew these two were in love, and he was happy for them, but at the same time he was envious. Not so long ago, Billy had fallen in love himself. The girl's name was Jill Springer. She lived in the town of Probity, a few miles down the North Platte River from Casper. The year before, Billy had helped her out of an unpleasant situation. For a while, it had been his hope he and Jill would one day marry and raise a family, but it had not happened, and Billy knew it never would.

"You've sure had a busy week, haven't you, Walter?" said Enos, once the Cosgroves were settled in.

"It was something, all right." Walt had a court reporting business and made verbatim transcriptions of depositions, various sorts of public hearings, and the court proceedings in Judge Aaron Bishop's state district court. When the federal judge, Thomas Reed, came up from Cheyenne to hold court in Casper, Walt reported for him as well. "Did you watch the trial, Mr. Woodard?"

"Some. I was in and out. Stella here watched it all from beginning to end."

"What did you think of the verdict, Miss Woodard?" Millie asked as she cut a slice of white-meat turkey into a half-dozen pieces no bigger than the tip of her finger.

Stella, who had been chewing on her thumbnail, gave a shrug and furrowed her brow. "I don't know much about such things," she said, glancing at her brother. Her voice was soft and difficult to hear in the noisy room. "I didn't like what Mr. Hawthorn said about Billy and Hugo." After making this comment, she went back to her nail.

Soft voice or not, Hugo had heard what she said about Hawthorn, and he let out a growl.

In what appeared to be an afterthought, Stella added, "I feel Mr. O'Dell is quite capable of murder."

"No doubt about it," Hugo said.

Billy decided another woman joining them must have made Stella feel more comfortable. It was the most she had spoken at one time during the course of the entire meal.

"What did you think of the trial, Walt?" Hugo asked.

The big court reporter shoved a glob of dressing into his mouth, chewed a couple of times, and swallowed. "To be honest with you, Hugo, I wasn't surprised by the verdict." He held his palm out to stop Hugo before he jumped to some hasty conclusion. "Now that doesn't mean I think it was right, but I wasn't surprised. Once Judge Reed let Hawthorn present evidence that O'Dell's confession might've been given under duress, it tossed enough reasonable doubt into the mix that the acquittal wasn't much of a shocker."

"Do you think Reed should've let it in?" Billy asked. Billy felt odd about the whole mess. Of course, O'Dell had lied about his confession being coerced, but Billy had to admit O'Dell was so used up from the chase that he wasn't going to cause any trouble. Mostly, Billy hit him because he was furious at the man for damned near burning Hugo to a crisp and forcing Billy to run for miles in the cold and dark.

"No," said Walter in answer to Billy's question, "Reed probably shouldn't've let it in, but whether he should or shouldn't have isn't the point. The way he did it was backwards."

"What do you mean?" Enos asked.

Walter looked around to see who was near them. When he spotted Judge Reed and Marshal Pierce sitting at a table on the far side of the room, he turned back and said, "The way Judge Bishop would've handled it in a case in his court would be to have a hearing prior to the trial, before the jury was ever picked. He would've listened to what both sides had to say about O'Dell's confession. If he believed the confession had been coerced, he would not have let the prosecution use it. If he didn't believe it had been coerced, he would've let them use it. It's my guess ol' Judge Bishop would not have found Ben O'Dell very believable."

"So you don't figure," asked Hugo, "Bishop would have let O'Dell tell the jury the confession was beat out of 'im?"

"I doubt he would have," Walt said.

Hugo smacked the table hard enough to rattle the dishes. "By God, that is how the damned trial should-a been run."

"Language, Hugo," said Billy. "Ladies at the table."

"Sorry," Hugo said.

Billy finished off his last bite of pie. "I expect if the trial had been run the way Bishop would've run it, things would have turned out different." The pie had lost its flavor.

"Not much doubt about it," agreed Enos.

"There's no fixing it now, though," Walter said. "Even if Ben climbed onto one of these tables and told the whole town he really had killed that poor ol' Gypsy, it wouldn't change a thing."

"Because," said Enos, "he can't be tried twice for the same crime."

"That's the way it works," Walter said.

Millie nodded toward the front of the room. "Look who came in," she said.

They all turned to see a smiling Ben O'Dell step through the doorway.

He scanned the room and headed for his brother's table. After he said a few loud hellos and shook hands all around, he crossed to the food line and started filling a plate.

Earlier, once all the food was set out, Stella had been given permission by Edith Baldwin, the woman in charge of the Lutheran Women's League, to leave her money-collecting post at the front door and join her brother and his friends.

"I don't believe Mr. O'Dell paid his seventy-five cents," said Billy.

With a chuckle Walt suggested, "Maybe you oughta run over there and arrest him, Hugo."

Hugo's dark eyes fixed on the man, and for a second, it appeared the deputy was giving Walt's joke some real consideration.

"Stealin' turkey 'n' stuffin' from the Lutherans," Hugo said, "ain't no federal offense. Though I wish it was. I wouldn't mind gettin' my hands on that skunk one last time."

Billy didn't care to speculate on what Hugo meant by the "one *last* time" remark.

O'Dell carried his full plate to the beverage table and poured himself a glass of punch. As he headed to where his brother and their cronies were sitting, he spotted Billy and Hugo and came toward them sporting a broad grin.

"Now watch yourself, Hugo," Enos said. Hugo didn't respond.

"Howdy, Billy, Hugo." O'Dell said this as though they were

all the best of pals. Nodding to the others at the table, he said, "I'd shake hands, folks, but—" With a shrug, he lifted his plate and punch. "—as you can see, I'm all loaded up."

"Loaded up with food you didn't pay for," Hugo pointed out in a cold voice.

O'Dell gave them all a look of clearly feigned surprise. "Why, Hugo, you mean this Thanksgiving dinner ain't free? I figured it was."

"Free only to thieves," Hugo answered.

The smile melted from O'Dell's face, but before he could reply, Enos sat forward in his chair and said, "The ladies have stopped collecting, Mr. O'Dell, so you go ahead. Enjoy your meal. It'll be on the house." He added with a quick laugh, "Or I guess I should say it'll be on the church."

While Enos spoke, O'Dell's eyes never left Hugo's. "Well, ain't that charitable. I'll have to go back to the kitchen and give a special thank-you to all them nice ladies." His smile reappeared, and as he turned toward his brother's table, he said, "Judging by your sour tone, Hugo Dorling, I'm thinking you must be a poor loser." He started walking away and added in a voice loud enough to stop all other conversation and jar the room to silence, "I reckon you're perturbed 'cause the jury as much as called you and Billy Young a couple of dirty liars."

Hugo came to his feet. "Hold where you are, O'Dell."

O'Dell stopped, but he didn't turn around.

Billy reached for Hugo's arm, but Hugo shook him off.

"I ain't fond of bein' called a liar, mister, 'specially not in front of the whole town. Now offer me an apology or be ready to regret you didn't."

"No, deputy," Webster Pierce called from the table where he sat with Judge Reed. The marshal stood and made his way between the tables to O'Dell and Hugo.

The CR was not so well lit as the courtroom, but even in the dimmer light, Pierce's high, black hair was shiny. Comb marks lined the top and sides, and every strand was in its proper place.

At first glance, Pierce had the appearance of a man in control, but a closer inspection revealed his tension. Billy suspected it was not the marshal's idea to butt into this quarrel. No doubt the judge had sent Pierce over to deal with yet another unpleasant situation provoked by the willful deputy.

To O'Dell, Pierce said, "It'd be best, Mr. O'Dell, if you apologized. I'd say it's likely Hugo will carry this argument further if you don't."

It appeared Ben gave consideration to the probability of the marshal's comment. He chuckled a friendly laugh and said, "Why, hell, Hugo, I was only making a little joke. I wasn't trying to get you mad nor hurt your feelings none."

The room was quiet for a long moment. Billy guessed O'Dell and Pierce were waiting to see if Hugo would accept Ben's feeble apology. Hugo, who Billy knew was about at the end of his rope after days of fretting over the trial, was no doubt trying to decide whether to let O'Dell live or kill the son of a bitch where he stood.

Hugo offered O'Dell a long, hard stare. "You got away with it this time," he said, breaking the silence, "but you best hope them Gypsies are as acceptin' of the jury system as the rest of us are."

O'Dell frowned as if his machinery was not well-oiled and he had trouble running Hugo's comment through his sluggish gears. "What's that supposed to mean?" he asked.

But Hugo didn't elaborate. All he said was, "Go on over yonder and sit with your brother."

After a bit, O'Dell responded with a grin. "Why, sure, Hugo. That's where I was headed in the first place." He walked away, turning once and glancing over his shoulder.

Hugo could have let it end there, but he didn't. Instead, he turned to face Pierce, and Billy felt himself wince.

"And you, *Marshal*, why don't you toddle on back over and nuzzle up to that sad excuse of a jurist you like so much?"

Enos and Billy shared a quick look, and in unison they shouted, *"Hugo!"* But Hugo ignored them.

"What was that?" Reed called from his table. He came to his feet, and in seconds he was standing next to the marshal. "What did you say?" he demanded.

"You heard me," Hugo said. "You're an embarrassment to the judiciary of this state. You were a poor lawyer, Reed, and you're an even poorer judge. You ought to be sent packin' for the stunts you pulled in O'Dell's trial. Everythin' Miles Hawthorn asked for, you gave him, and you was trompin' on the prosecutor's neck at every turn. You're a disgrace. You've been afforded a position of trust, and you've shamed it."

The more Hugo spoke, the more sanguine Thomas Reed's already ruddy complexion became. By the time Hugo shut up, Reed was only a shade or two less red than the Thanksgiving punch. The judge took in a deep breath, and through clenched teeth, he squeezed out, "I don't believe, Marshal, Hugo Dorling has the sort of disposition needed to wear a deputy's badge. What're your thoughts on that?"

"What're my thoughts?"

Reed turned to Pierce and glared. "What are *your* thoughts?"

After swallowing hard, Pierce nodded. "Why, I-I agree. I-I r-reckon you're right, Judge."

"Well, then," said the judge, turning back to Hugo, "do something about it."

Pierce, looking sheepish, cleared his throat and said, "You best go ahead and give me your star, there, Hugo. It looks like you're through."

Hugo nodded, curled his lip, and unpinned his badge. Tossing it over, he said, "Fine, Pierce. I never was real fond of workin' for a bootlicker like you. But I'm gonna tell you boys one more thing before I call 'er a day."

"You probably shouldn't, Hugo," Billy said, though he couldn't imagine what it would hurt now. He closed his eyes and pinched the bridge of his nose between his thumb and forefinger. "I expect you've told them enough," he added, but even as he said it, he knew he might as well be talking to his empty plate.

"Nah, it's okay, Billy. I'm 'bout done."

"He sure is," said Judge Reed.

"You know, Judge, there's some who figured your poor behavior in this trial was because you didn't like Gypsies, and you didn't give a damn if some derelict scum like O'Dell killed one of 'em. Which is true, I suppose. But a-course it's also true you don't give a damn about the likes of Ben O'Dell, neither. We both know you'd as soon see O'Dell hang as squish a bug." Hugo pulled a toothpick from his vest pocket and slipped it into his mouth. "No, sir," he went on, "there's gotta be somethin' more to all this that would somehow explain your peculiar behavior in this case." He smiled and offered the judge a little wink. "And I'm lookin' *real* forward to the time when whatever it is sees the light of day."

Hugo's comment caused the puffy flesh on Thomas Reed's face to droop.

Still holding his smile fixed on the judge, Hugo reached behind him and lifted his coat from the back of his chair. As he pulled it on, he added, "You two fellas have a real nice trip back to the capital." And he headed for the door.

CHAPTER FOUR:
THE SORRY NEWS

Billy carried a sheaf of hay from the barn into the corral and dropped it to the ground. A couple of years earlier, he and Frank had purchased one of Mr. McCormick's reaping machines, and it not only made the harvesting easier, but the sheaves made winter feeding easier as well. He pulled a pair of cutters from his hip pocket and snipped the center cord that held the small bale together. As he kicked the hay loose, he heard someone coming into the yard, and he turned to see Hugo riding up.

" 'Mornin', Billy," Hugo called out. He came to a stop next to the corral and swung a leg over his bay's rump. As he dropped to the ground, he said, "I see you're already hard at work." Beneath his bushy mustache, Hugo wore a wide grin. "With an early bird like you out 'n' about, the worm population 'round here must be plenty nervous."

"Just doing the morning chores," Billy said. "For a fella who's without a job, you are in mighty high spirits."

Hugo rubbed his gloved hands together. "You're right, Billy-boy. My spirits're soarin'. How could they be anythin' less on a nice, crisp mornin' like this?"

Billy gave a snort, and when he did, he saw a couple of plumes of steam shoot from his nostrils. "You might call it crisp, Hugo." He reached down and used the cord cutters to break the thick crust of ice in the horse trough. "I call it colder than a penguin's balls."

"Now what do you know about a penguin, Billy Young, or his balls?"

"Hell, I read, Hugo. You oughta try it sometime." He lifted an eyebrow and offered Hugo a questioning look. "You can read, right?"

Hugo looked hurt. " 'Course I can. You know that."

Billy knew Hugo could read, but he also knew reading wasn't one of the things Hugo did best. "I meant something besides those girlie books you order from Brooklyn, New York. Of course, I guess it's mostly the pictures you're interested in, anyhow."

"You can be smart-alecky all you want, boy, but I've seen you sneak a peek or two at my library when you figured I wasn't lookin'."

Billy smiled and shrugged. When Hugo was right, it was hard to argue. He shoved the cutters back into his pocket and closed the barn door that led into the corral. "What brings you out this morning?" he asked. He returned to where Hugo stood and vaulted himself over the corral's top rail. "If you're looking for work, you've come to the wrong place. There's nobody around here who needs beat up or shot."

"I ain't lookin' for work. No, sir, and if I was, I wouldn't come here. I'd sooner cook Chinese food for a livin' than work for you."

Billy smiled. "Chinese food, huh?" Sometimes Hugo could come out with something strange even for him.

"I come for two things," Hugo said. "First, I'll take a cup of coffee, and then I thought maybe you and me could ride over to visit the Gypsies."

"What're you headed over there for?"

The smile Hugo wore earlier was gone. "As much as I hate to, I figure I'd best tell Pov Meche about the verdict. I'd rather get a tooth pulled than do 'er, but since Gwenfrei Faw was his grandma, he'll be wonderin' how things turned out. I might as well be the one who breaks the bad news since I'm the one he's been talkin' to ever since the old woman was kilt."

Pov Meche was the *Kapo,* or leader, of the group of Gypsies camped by the big rock located on federal land a few miles to the south and east of Billy's place.

"Maybe I can head off Pov from doin' anythin' rash," Hugo added.

"Come on inside," said Billy. "There's a pot of coffee that's been simmering on the stove for about three hours. It oughta be thick enough by now to suit your tastes."

Hugo liked his coffee robust.

Billy led the way across the yard to the woodpile. "As long as you're here," he said, "you can give me a hand hauling in some wood." He and Hugo each picked up an armload of split cotton-wood and carried it in.

Billy's house was large. Built by his father a dozen years earlier, it was constructed of pine logs hauled down from the broad-shouldered mountain that loomed to the south. The place was home, but it was much too big for Billy, especially now that he was the last of the Youngs.

They crossed the entryway and went into the kitchen, where they dropped the wood into a large box beside the cookstove. "I reckon I could make time to ride over to Gypsy Rock with you," he said.

"Good. I could use the company, and besides, I had the idea you might be eager to go, since it'll give you a chance to see Deya Andree."

Deya Andree was a Gypsy girl a year or so older than Billy. He had met her when he accompanied Hugo a couple of times early on, when Hugo was first investigating the murder. Hugo made it his mission to find Billy female companionship, which Billy found a real annoyance.

He ignored Hugo's comment about Deya and pulled a couple of cups from a cabinet. Pouring the coffee, he said, "I got some cattle wintering around there. It wouldn't hurt to check on them."

"You don't need to invent excuses for my benefit." Hugo's thick eyebrows bobbed a couple of times, and he gave Billy a knowing smile.

Billy couldn't understand why Hugo insisted on playing his matchmaker game. For one thing, the Gypsy tribe camped by the rock would never allow one of its own to be with an outsider. Besides, Hugo knew Billy was still reeling from having been jilted by Jill Springer.

After his brother's murder, all Billy could feel was the need for revenge. Once he had gotten his revenge, he had allowed himself to fall in love. Billy had believed Jill loved him as well, and maybe she did for a while, but, in the end, she rebuffed him—told him she wanted no part of him, that she never wanted to see him again. Her manner of saying it was not so blunt, but still . . .

Hugo took one of the cups and crossed to the table in the center of the room. Billy stayed next to the stove where it was warmer.

"So you're thinking once Pov hears about the verdict, he might try something with O'Dell?" Billy asked.

"Oh, you know, I only said what I did to O'Dell yesterday 'cause I wanted to nervous him up some. Pov doesn't strike me as a fella much prone to violence, but a-course you can never be sure about that sort of thing."

"Why would it matter to you if Pov and his boys did do something, Hugo? I mean, as of last night, you're not a deputy anymore."

"True, and personally I wouldn't give two hoots if Pov was to slit O'Dell's throat from lobe to lobe; but if the Gypsies did go after 'im, somethin' bad would come down on 'em for sure. Peace officer or not, I'd like to stop it before it happens."

Billy had to agree. "I don't reckon Thatcher and all his friends would appreciate Ben's getting his throat cut," he said.

Hugo nodded and took a gulp of coffee. "Neither one of them O'Dell boys've ever been worth a damn, but if it comes down to it, I expect Thatcher's even worse than Ben."

"I'd say he's harder to get along with," said Billy. "At least Ben pretends to be sociable. Thatcher doesn't even try. He's just mean—a sick, crazy kind of mean."

Hugo took off his hat and ran stubby fingers through his hair. Though it showed some gray around the edges, it was still mostly dark and as thick as a bear's. "I wish them Gypsies would-a kept on headin' west," he said. The *Kapo* had mentioned the band planned to meet with another group of Gypsies in California somewhere south of San Francisco. "I had a feelin'," Hugo added, "them decidin' to stick around for a while was gonna end poorly. Them Roms are a different kind-a folk. And I feared that difference could get 'em into trouble."

Billy had already put sugar in the bitter coffee, but he spooned in a little more. As far as he was concerned, it was impossible to use too much sugar. "Trouble because of the way they dress? Their customs?" Billy slurped in a sip. The sugar made it better.

"For sure, there is that," Hugo allowed. "Some citizens around here aren't so tolerant as you and me."

Billy had never considered Hugo tolerant, but he had to admit, Hugo did seem open-minded when it came to the Roms.

"What worried me most, though," said Hugo, "is they're a buncha thieves and bunco artists, who I figured would be workin' their shenanigans on us dumb, unsuspectin' rubes. And I feared once they did, bad things would happen."

Thieves and bunco artists. Billy might have been too hasty with

46

the whole open-minded thing. "Are you calling those Gypsies out at the Rock a bunch of thieves?"

"Well," said Hugo with a shrug, "most times generalities about the races don't mean too much, but I've known a few of the Roma in my day, and every one of 'em's been a thief."

"Every one?" Billy asked. He found it hard to believe. Despite what Hugo said, Billy was not sweet on Deya Andree, but even so, he couldn't picture Deya stealing anything. "I can't believe they're *all* thieves, Hugo."

"Then you're wrong," Hugo said. "Them Gypsies figure pilferin' is their birthright."

Billy laughed. "Their birthright, huh? Well, if they have the *right* to do it, then I guess that makes it okay."

The coffee was still hot enough to steam, but Hugo polished his off and told Billy to do the same. "We're wastin' daylight here, boy. Let's saddle your horse and get goin'."

They returned to the corral, and Billy led Badger into the barn. He shook out a saddle blanket, and as he smoothed it over the animal's back, he said, "So go on with what you were saying about the Gypsies figuring they have a right to steal."

Hugo leaned against a wall and pulled out his makings. With a laugh, he said, "That's what they believe." He rolled a cigarette and tucked his tobacco and papers back into his coat pocket. "By the way, when you're trying to sweet-talk little Deya, you might avoid usin' the word 'Gypsy.'"

Billy'd had enough. He stopped what he was doing and turned to Hugo. "I'll not be sweet-talking Deya," he said. As soon as he said it, Hugo laughed again and gave him a wink. The gesture made Billy stiffen. "Goddamn it, Hugo. I'm not joking here."

Hugo held up his hands. "All right, all right. Don't get ruffled. All I'm sayin' is they ain't fond of bein' called Gypsies, though I reckon they've pretty much got used to it since folks've been callin' 'em that for a few hundred years now. And I believe I've heard 'em call themselves that from time to time. Still, it ain't polite." He struck a match on the rough barn wall, lit the cigarette, and let the smoke leak out as he spoke. "They move around a lot, you know, and they got the name Gypsy because from what I hear Egypt was the last place they lived before they come rollin' into Europe."

Billy lifted his saddle off a rail and snugged it onto the gray. "What was it you called them back at the house?"

"Roma. That's what they call their ownselves, Roms or Roma or Romani."

"Romani, yes, now that you mention it, I guess I've heard Deya use that word, too."

"I don't know how they got them names 'cause I'm sure they don't come from Rome, neither. What I was told by the few I've known was they figure they started out two or three thousand years ago in India or Siam or one of those other damned foreign lands on the far side of the world. They lit outta there for some reason, and they've been travelin' this direction ever since."

Billy finished cinching the saddle, pulled off the gray's halter, and replaced it with a bridle and bit. "You still haven't said how they figure they have the right to steal."

"They say the right was give to 'em by God."

"God?"

"Well, Jesus, to be exact."

Billy snickered. "Nice of him to do it, I guess, but why in the world would he? I figured stealing to be one of the things Jesus was dead-set against."

"The Gypsies say that on the afternoon of the crucifixion, one of their ancestors was so troubled by the whole mess he decided to steal the nails they was gonna use to hammer poor ol' Jesus up on the cross. Now, it could be this little Gypsy wasn't the brightest star in the firmament 'cause I guess he figured if he stole the Romans' nails, them boys'd forget about the whole thing and let Jesus head on down the road, which I doubt would-a been the way it turned out, nails or no nails."

"I expect those Romans could be pretty determined fellas," Billy agreed.

"Yes, sir, the way I hear it, once a Roman got somethin' in his head, there was no stoppin' 'im. Anyhow, this little Gypsy tried his dead-level best to swipe all four of them nails that'd been set aside for crucifyin' the Nazarene, but for some reason he could only snatch one. The Gypsy took it, though, and shoved it down deep into his pocket and made out to be as innocent as a lamb when them hard-lookin' soldiers come around with their hammer. Once the Romans figured out one of their nails'd gone missin', they searched everywhere they could think of, high 'n' low, but, damn if they could find it. After a while, they give 'er up and decided to tack both of Jesus' feet down using one nail. That'd still leave 'em two to use on his hands, and things should work out all right. It made the chore a little harder, but with some effort, they was able to get 'er done. Even as awkward as it was, I guess they figured in the long run it was easier than hikin' all the way back down the hill to the fort to fetch one measly nail. Though this Gypsy fella was a bust when it came to nail stealin', Jesus figured it was pretty nice of 'im to even give 'er a try. So in gratitude, he said it was okay by him for all the Gypsies 'til the end of time to steal whatever they wanted whenever they wanted it."

Once Hugo finished his story, Billy led the gray out of the barn and across the yard to the house. When he got there, he flipped his reins around the porch rail and started inside.

Hugo had come out of the barn at the same time and crossed to his bay. As he climbed aboard, he asked Billy where he was going.

Billy pulled his watch from his pocket and said, "Since we're headed to Gypsy Rock, I think I'll leave Pa's timepiece here at the house. I'd sure hate to lose it."

Hugo smiled. "You're bein' awful cautious, ain't ya, boy? I mean, hell, you've worn that watch over there ever' time we've gone."

"You're right, Hugo, but that was before I learned Jesus had given those folks the go-ahead on thievery."

Billy and Hugo had no trouble spotting the livestock Billy knew to be on this section of the ranch. They milled about in a wide meadow below a stand of aspen and were wintering well. Though it was cold, so far there had been very little snow and the grazing was still easy. Plus, these white-faced cattle his father had brought onto the ranch were of a hardy breed.

Billy had always enjoyed the cattle business. Ranching was all he knew, but now that both his father and Frank were gone, he liked it much less. He was toying with the idea of leasing or selling the cattle operation to Orozco Valdez, the Youngs' longtime friend and foreman. Orozco was spending a month this winter down in Coahuila, Mexico, visiting his family. When he returned, which should be any day now, Billy thought he might talk to him about it. Rosco already ran some of his own cattle on the place. What Billy hadn't figured out was what he would do for a living if he did let Rosco take over.

"If you're satisfied your animals are thrivin'," Hugo said, "let's get on to Pov's and tell 'im the sorry news."

Billy knew one of the reasons Hugo was dreading this job was he had given the Gypsy leader his word that Ben O'Dell would hang. Hugo had been foolish to make such a promise, and when Hugo was foolish, he didn't like to be reminded of it. He wasn't a man fond of crow.

They loped the mile to the Gypsy camp. As they approached the camp, they brought their horses down to a trot and slowed to a walk as they rode in.

The rock rose to the south of the camp like a monolith. It was big, about the size of three or four barns stacked atop one another. Though a local landmark, it never had a name. Now, since the Gypsies had rolled in and set up camp at its base, folks had taken to calling it Gypsy Rock, and the name had stuck.

When they came in, a half dozen of the smaller kids ran toward them, laughing and cavorting and hopping about. Billy gave them a smile and waved, but they were soon scooped up by their mothers. Though Pov Meche and the young Deya Andree had always been cordial, the rest of the tribe, unless they were engaged in doing business with an outsider, stayed to themselves and made sure their children did the same.

Billy scanned the camp and spotted a group of older kids hiking down the hill from the large rock rising behind the ten or fifteen wagons scattered about. As Billy suspected, Deya was leading the pack.

Deya had been married at the age of fourteen, as was the Romani custom for girls, but four years into the marriage, her husband had taken sick and died. His death was more than three years ago, and Deya still had not remarried.

Now that she no longer had a man, and since she and her husband had not had children, Pov made it Deya's job to be in charge of all the kids older than five or six. As early as his first visit to the camp, Billy could tell Deya loved her wards and they loved her.

He watched now as the pretty girl led the children down the long, narrow path. Deya was not much more than five feet tall, but the way she carried herself made her appear taller.

Hugo stood in his stirrups and squinted out across the camp. Billy knew without his spyglass, Hugo's vision got a little fuzzy when he looked at anything farther away than fifty yards or so.

"Ain't that Pov over yonder?" Hugo pointed toward a wiry man in his late forties who was pulling a wheel off a brightly painted wagon, or caravan, as the Romanies called them.

"What's that?" Billy asked. He forced his attention away from the little group coming down from the rock and followed Hugo's squinty-eyed gaze to where a hatless man worked in the wintry gray light. The man wore a brown corduroy jacket, heavy wool pants, and thick-soled brogans. "Yep," Billy answered. "It looks like it."

Pov was on the far side of the camp. The trees began fifty feet farther on. Coming out of the trees, fifteen yards beyond Pov's wagon, ran a small creek. This whole area was nestled into the foothills of Casper Mountain, and ever since his childhood, Billy had liked the place. At this time of year, the creek was no more than a narrow strip of water, but it still had enough flow for the needs of this small band of Gypsies.

Billy and Hugo rode up a little closer, dismounted, and led their horses the rest of the way.

The camp was a busy place. A couple of men were splitting wood. A couple more were butchering a deer. A half-dozen women sat about one of the many fires, sewing pieces of clothing and weaving baskets to sell to the townsfolk.

Five or six men worked at a large wagon in the center of the camp, applying copper to pots and pans. Tinsmithing was a profitable enterprise for the tribe. A huge, stern-faced man named Baul Emaus ran the operation, and he moved about the workers, keeping a sharp eye on their efforts.

Off to Billy's right, an old grandfather with silver hair pulled into a tight bun sat on the tailgate of one of the caravans, coaxing a lively ditty out of a mandolin.

Music was everywhere. Besides what the old man played, Billy could hear the lilt of a violin. He couldn't tell from where it came, but its sound flitted through the camp like a bird.

Another of the Gypsies' businesses was raising horses—a few saddle horses, but mostly vanners or draft animals used for pulling their caravans. Their stock was strong and healthy.

"Let's stick our horses in with theirs," Hugo suggested. They led the bay and gray into a large rope corral. The boys took the bits out of the horses' mouths, and the animals went to munching grass with the others.

Once the horses were taken care of, Billy and Hugo turned and looked out over the bustling camp, taking it all in. The community was small but well-run. Everyone had a job, and everyone did it. Hugo once said he admired the kind of close life they shared. Theirs was the sort of life the old lawman had never enjoyed. Billy had often heard his father describe Hugo Dorling as a very lonesome man.

They were closer now, and Hugo could see things better. His eyes narrowed and focused again on *Kapo* Pov Meche, who was using a foot-long slat of wood to slather thick, black grease onto his wagon's axle.

With a groan, Hugo rubbed the back of his neck. The high spirits he had shown when he first rode into Billy's yard now were absent. He let out a steamy breath, and with a grimace, he said, "All right, Billy-boy, I reckon there ain't no way around 'er. It's time to get this damned chore done."

CHAPTER FIVE:
DEYA'S LITTLE RUSE

When Pov spotted the boys coming his way, he called out, "Ah, look who is here." He greeted them with a wide smile. His square, white teeth were bright in contrast to his berry-brown skin, which was at least a shade or two darker than most of the other members of the group.

Pov dropped the greasy slat of wood into a bucket at his feet and stepped out to meet them. "Good morning, Deputy Dorling," he said. His hand didn't appear dirty, but he wiped it on his pants anyway before extending it toward Hugo, who took it and gave it a shake. Pov grabbed Billy's hand and shook it as well. "Billy," he said with a smile. Billy returned the smile. It had taken considerable effort over the last several weeks to convince the *Kapo* to call him by his Christian name. Pov Meche was a formal man.

"Come by the fire," he said, "and let's be comfortable." He led them to a fire pit a dozen feet from his wagon and called to his wife, "Tasar, we have guests."

A covered two-wheeled cart stood next to the caravan, and a hefty, round-faced woman poked her head through the cart's rear door. She wore a green scarf on her head and a heavy shawl about her shoulders. "I will bring cups." She spoke without enthusiasm and disappeared into the cart.

Billy suspected Pov's owning both a caravan and a cart was a sign of the Meche family's status in the group.

After a bit, Tasar came out carrying three porcelain cups,

which, without making eye contact, she handed to Pov, Billy, and Hugo. By then the men had settled in at the fire, and instead of going back into the cart and resuming her work, Tasar folded her formidable arms beneath her bosom and watched the men through the narrow slits of her eyes.

"It is good to see you fellows," Pov said as he lifted a pot from a grate at the edge of the fire and filled their cups with steaming, fragrant tea. "I was thinking of going to town today and looking you up, Deputy."

Pov's first language was Romani, the traditional Gypsy tongue, and he spoke English with the hint of an accent; but Billy recognized Pov's English to be at least as good as his own and a damned-sight better than Hugo's.

Billy took a sip of his tea and watched as Hugo blew across the top of his cup and slurped some in. After one of their earlier visits, Hugo had said that it was all he could do to force the herbal-scented brew down his gullet. Polite behavior, though, demanded he drink it with a smile. Billy liked the stuff himself. Of course, he took little pride in being more willing to try new things than Hugo Dorling.

When Hugo set his cup down and looked across the fire at Pov, Billy figured Hugo had finally screwed up the courage to tell the Gypsy what had happened. But as Hugo opened his mouth to speak, Pov lifted his hand and said, "Don't worry, Deputy. It is all right."

Hugo looked perplexed. "What's all right, Pov?"

A lock of coal-black hair had flopped across Pov's forehead, and he lifted a hand and shoved it back. "I get the feeling you are troubled."

Well, Billy found that interesting. He wasn't sure how Pov knew Hugo was troubled, but he had sure gotten it right. Hugo was damned troubled.

In one of their conversations when Hugo was first investigating the murder, Deya had mentioned to Billy that Pov Meche, in addition to being *Kapo*, was also a *Chovihano*, which was a kind of sorcerer. Billy didn't think Deya put much stock in it herself, but she said all the Romani believed they were in touch with the Otherworld, as she called it, but a *Chovihano* like Pov, or a female *Chovihani* like Pov's grandmother, Gwenfrei Faw, had special skills and often seemed to know things impossible for them to know. Deya had never used the word "magic," but Billy had guessed magic must be what she was talking about, although he wasn't one to believe in that mumbo-jumbo.

"I reckon you're right, Pov," Hugo said. "I'd have to admit to being troubled."

Pov pulled a clay pipe from his jacket pocket. The pipe was already loaded with short-cut tobacco. He took a burning stick from the fire and held it to light the pipe. As he puffed, he watched the flame bounce over the bowl. Once the pipe was going, he tossed the stick back into the fire. "I'm sorry to hear it. Finish your tea. It'll make you feel better."

Hugo looked skeptical, but he picked up his cup.

"I'm guessing, now," Pov explained, as he blew a stream of smoke at the sky, "but I believe I know the reason you're feeling so low."

"You do?" Hugo asked.

"It could be," suggested Pov, "you are upset because the jury let Ben O'Dell go free."

Hugo drew back, and after blinking a couple of times, he shifted his eyes across the fire toward Billy. "Looks like passin' on the bad news ain't gonna be so hard as I feared." He turned back to Pov and asked, "How in the devil did you know 'bout it already? Have you or one of your boys been into town?"

Pov shook his head. "No, but I knew the trial should be over by now, and when it was, you'd ride out to let us know what happened. Your sorrowful face told me plenty." Pov took another puff on his pipe and looked across at Billy. "There wasn't any magic to it, young fella."

Billy was taking a sip from his cup and had to make two or three hard swallows to keep from choking. He tried to think of something to say in response to what appeared to be getting his mind read, but Pov had already turned his attention back to Hugo.

"So, Deputy, one of my people is murdered—my own grandmother—and no one is brought to justice?"

"Well, first off," Hugo said, "you don't need to be callin' me deputy no more. Hugo'll do. I had a little run-in with my boss yesterday, and I'm now what you might call between positions."

Pov was a nomad who had never held a regular job in his life, so losing one didn't impress him much. He pointed the stem of his pipe toward the large caravan in the center of the group. "You can always help Baul Emaus with the pots and the pans." There was a twinkle in his eye when he said it.

Billy smiled. He knew there was never a man less suited for such work than Hugo, and he figured Pov knew it as well. Billy had looked at a few of the pots the Gypsies produced. They were of high quality, but the only sort of cooking utensil Hugo knew anything about was the tin can that held his pork and beans.

Hugo shook his head but answered as though he assumed Pov was serious when he made the offer. "I'm afraid I wouldn't be much good to you there, but thanks anyhow." He shoved his hat back a notch. "I'm sorry 'bout what our fool jury done with O'Dell, Pov, but as far as gettin' justice is concerned, it's a tricky thing. Justice is supposed to happen in courtrooms. That's the idea, anyhow, but it ain't always the way she works. Sometimes it happens out in the street or the prairie long before it ever gets to any courtroom, and sometimes it doesn't happen at all."

"Are you saying maybe this is one of those times it doesn't happen at all?"

"It's a real possibility. There's a couple of things about all this I don't understand, and I plan on snoopin' around a little more before I let 'er go, but no matter what, O'Dell can't be tried again. That's the law."

Pov stared into his teacup. "America has many laws," he said. The tone of his voice was flat. "I reckon sometimes they even enforce them, eh?"

Billy appreciated Pov's implication, but the Gypsy's irony was lost on Hugo.

"Even though O'Dell's out loose," Hugo said, "I'm hopin' none of you Roms decide to go after 'im yourselves. If he was to turn up dead, I figure Gypsy Rock here'd be the first place folks'd come a-lookin'. O'Dell's brother Thatcher and his friends are a hard crowd, and they wouldn't think twice about killin' ever' man, woman, and child among you."

"And," a voice behind Billy added, "they'd get away with it, too, wouldn't they, Deputy Dorling?"

Billy turned to see Deya walk up with all of her little chicks scurrying along behind.

"No, Deya," snapped Tasar Meche from beside the cart. "It is not your place. When will you learn?" The older woman brought her hands to the sides of her face and rocked back and forth in a gesture more dramatic than Billy figured was necessary.

Deya gave Tasar a quick glance, frowned, and shook her head. Billy suspected Deya considered Tasar's comment—and maybe even the older woman herself—ridiculous.

"I'll never learn it's not my place to say the truth," Deya answered, but she said it to Pov, not Tasar. "We all know the *Gaje* would much rather see us dead than alive."

Billy had been told the *Gaje* was anyone who wasn't a Rom.

"I don't believe," Pov pointed out, "what you say is true of the two men at my fire, Deya."

Although Pov had not said it in a stern voice, his comment did bring the young woman up short. Her eyes cut to Hugo and then to Billy. An awkward smile tugged at the corners of her full lips. "I'm sorry," she said in a voice much meeker than her usual bold tones. Billy would have never believed the self-assured Deya Andree could become rattled. "Of course, I didn't mean Billy or the deputy." She straightened herself and looked again at Pov. "But they're two among how many?" It hadn't taken long for her to regain her composure.

Pov took in a breath, nodded, and gave a shrug. "Too many for an unschooled ol' Gypsy like me to ever count."

Though the word "Gypsy" might be considered less than polite, Billy noticed Hugo was right when he said the Rom sometimes used it to describe themselves.

Deya turned to the children behind her and clapped her hands three times. "All right, *Manusha*, listen," she said. "It's time for you to return to your caravans and do your chores." She said this in English rather than Romani. Although in their travels the Rom kept themselves separate from the local population, Billy knew they felt it was necessary to learn the language of whatever country they passed through. And most felt it was rude not to speak English when Billy and Hugo were in camp and within earshot.

Laughing and shouting, the children scampered off.

Deya spun back to the men, and when she did, her hair swirled about her shoulders, and her skirt swirled about her legs. The movement was as graceful as any dance. "I wonder," she said to Pov, "if I could borrow Billy Young. This morning I found a kind of moss I've never seen growing on a stand of trees in the forest. Perhaps Billy could tell me about it. Our *Patrinyengri* might be able to use it in her medicines."

Tasar made a disgusted sound, pulled her shawl tighter

around her plump shoulders, and climbed into the cart. Billy guessed everyone, especially Madam Meche, could see through Deya's little ruse, but the girl's pretty smile was guileless and hard to resist. After a bit, Pov nodded his permission. Even though he allowed it, the *Kapo* appeared reluctant, and because of that, for a moment Billy considered declining Deya's invitation.

But, instead, he pushed to his feet and followed the girl away from the fire. Saying no might make the situation even more uncomfortable.

Billy had learned early in their acquaintance that Deya Andree lacked whatever skill was necessary to take no for an answer.

CHAPTER SIX:
THE *Chovihani* AND THE LUTHERAN

As Billy and Deya left, he noticed Hugo stifling his chuckles. There was no doubt Billy would have to suffer the older man's gibes once he and Hugo were out of the camp.

"Come along, Billy, it's this way," Deya said, and although Romani women never walked ahead of a man, she led Billy past the last wagon and into the copse of pine and aspen.

Billy could feel the sting of a couple of dozen sets of eyes burning into his back as they walked away. Once he was sure they would not be overheard, he asked, "Why do you do it, Deya?"

"Do what?" She spoke as if she had no idea what he was talking about.

"Try your best to rile them up."

"I don't know," she said with a smile. "It's fun. The old ways have a place, but they take them much, much too seriously, if you ask me." She led him to the creek bank, where she located a rock large enough for them both to lean against. She sat down with her legs extended. Patting the ground next to her, she said, "Have a seat."

Billy looked back over his shoulder to see if they could be seen by anyone in the camp. The trees were thick enough, he doubted they could be, but even so he decided sitting next to Deya was not a good idea. "I'll stay right here," he said, squatting beside the creek. The bank was covered with gravel, and he picked up one of the small stones and tossed it into the water.

"Sometimes I think you're afraid of me, Billy Young."

"I am, Deya. I'd say you're about the scariest unarmed person I've ever run across."

"But I am armed," she said, spreading her arms like wings.

Billy gave her a frown, "You know what I meant," he said, tossing another rock into the stream. Deya's brain tended to work a lot faster than his, and sometimes it was hard to know what to say.

"Scaring you is what I had in mind," she said.

Despite what Hugo wanted to think, and as appealing as Deya was, there was nothing between Deya and Billy. Billy had no room left for that sort of thing. He told himself his love for Jill had been nothing more than his effort to stop the pain and anger of Frank's murder. But he knew that was a lie. He *had* loved Jill, and a little more than a year ago he had lost both his brother and the woman he had wanted to become his wife.

Then something smacked him hard on the temple.

Deya had hit him with a rock. "Stop daydreaming, Billy," she scolded.

Deya did not like to be ignored.

"We seldom have the chance to visit by ourselves, and I'll not spend what little time we get watching you gather wool." She tucked her legs under her hip, and with the palm of her hand, she ironed away a nonexistent wrinkle where the skirt covered the curve of her thigh.

Though she was an irritation, Billy had to admit Deya was a beauty. Her intelligent, wide-set dark eyes appeared to take in everything around her. Her smooth olive skin had no blemish. Her straight nose was narrow and her jawline firm. There was the hint of a cleft at the tip of her chin, and when she smiled, which was often, dimples framed her full mouth.

Deya's hair had been the first thing he had noticed about her. Little of the gray morning light could find its way past the canopy of evergreens; still, Deya's thick mane of black hair glistened.

"I don't think, Deya, just because I happened to look at something besides you for a second, it gives you any right to clout me with a rock."

"Oh, don't be such a baby. The rock was small. Tell me about the trial."

"Not much to tell. They found Ben O'Dell not guilty even though Hugo and I climbed onto the witness stand and testified on our oaths he had admitted doing the killing."

Deya turned away and said, as much to herself as she did to Billy, "They'd never convict one of you of killing one of us."

Billy remembered O'Dell had said pretty much the same thing the night he and Hugo captured him.

"At first we figured it that way, too," said Billy, "and it did seem the judge was doing all he could to make the trial go O'Dell's way." Billy explained how Hugo had pointed that out to the judge at yesterday's Thanksgiving dinner, and as a result, Hugo was no longer employed.

"I'm sorry about the deputy's job, but *Gaje* judges are no different than anyone else. They'd never let a jury convict someone of murdering a mere Gypsy."

Billy knew she could be right, and he told her so. "But," he added, "this judge made rulings that ignored the testimony of both a respected Deputy United States Marshal and a fella who has at least a little standing in the community. I can't believe he'd go so far to save a scum like Ben O'Dell."

Deya seemed to ponder what Billy said. "So why'd he do it, then?"

"No way to know for sure. Could be you're right. Maybe he dislikes the Roms more than he dislikes O'Dell, but Hugo figures there's more to it. I tell you, Hugo's fire is pretty stoked about all this."

"What does he plan to do?"

"Hard to say. I don't think he knows. And there's not much he can do. He'd like to investigate, except he's not sure where to start."

"But you said he's not a deputy anymore."

Billy laughed. "Well, there is that," he agreed.

"I heard him warn Pov not to go after O'Dell."

"Hugo thinks there's a chance you Romanies might decide to provide O'Dell with the punishment he should've gotten from us."

"Well," Deya said, "we've been traveling through other people's lands for centuries. We learned long ago any blood we might spill often causes our own blood to be spilled a hundred-fold. Still, the *Kapo* loved Gwenfrei very much. His wish is we pass through here in peace, but—" she paused and then repeated "—he loved her very much."

"So you think there's a chance he will look for revenge?" Billy asked.

Deya shrugged and answered, "I don't know."

Billy wondered if she was telling the truth. For all her flouting of the old ways, Deya was still loyal to who she was and the people she cared for.

Billy wished she would tell him for a fact that Pov and his people would not do anything. But it was clear Deya could not or would not.

"Pov Meche," she said, "has not been the same since Gwenfrei's passing. He hides it from you and the deputy, and even from us most of the time, but I can see it. He has not been the same man these past months."

"I'd hate to see anything bad happen to you, Deya," Billy said.

Deya's eyes moved to his. Much to the dismay of the older women in the group, Deya made her fondness for Billy no secret. By anyone's standards, Deya was a flirt, but by the strict standards of the Romani, the girl was brazen. And she was a puzzle. Billy knew she loved her heritage, and in some ways she was a Rom to her bones. She was like no woman Billy had ever run across. Deya Andree, Billy had decided, was much too complicated for a simple Wyoming cattleman to ever understand.

"We're worried what might come about if anything happened to O'Dell," Billy said straight out.

Deya gave no response, and the moment became a little somber in an uncomfortable way.

Billy tossed another pebble into the creek and added, "Too bad O'Dell doesn't have anything of any value. Maybe you could swipe it and teach him at least some kind of lesson that way." He smiled at his little joke, but Deya did not.

"Swipe it?" she asked, lifting her chin. "Oh, I see. You think we are all of us thieves."

Her hard tone made Billy feel as uncomfortable as her flirting had earlier. "No, no, but Hugo told me a story this morning about—"

"The nail thief."

He nodded. "Yes."

"Don't believe everything you hear, Billy. The story started back in the old country long, long ago. And yes, there might have been some pockets picked from time to time, but it was only to survive. The way the story got started was some clever Romani was caught lifting a purse, and he convinced the none-too-bright villagers that he'd been given the right to do it by the Savior. It's a good story, but there's no truth to it. You've seen our camp. You know how hard we work. Do thieves work so hard?"

"Well, I guess it made sense the way Hugo told it, but I only believe about half of what he says anyway." He looked back in the direction they had come. "I reckon I'd better go. Hugo'll want to be getting back to town."

"Back to town to do what?"

"Good question. I guess what's bothering me the most right now is Ben O'Dell and what might happen if some harm came to him. It's not *only* concern about what Pov might do."

"What do you mean?" she asked, but before Billy answered, she added. "You mean no matter what it might be, if something happened to Ben O'Dell, the townspeople would think we did it even if we didn't." There was no surprise in her voice.

Attempting another joke, Billy said, "To keep him safe, maybe Hugo and I should hire on as Ben O'Dell's bodyguards."

Deya didn't smile at this joke either.

"What kind of man is Ben O'Dell?" Deya asked.

"A healthy one, I hope. Maybe that's what Hugo and I should do in town—check on Ben's health."

Another one Deya didn't smile at.

"Hugo calls Ben a scum and a scoundrel."

"I would like to talk to O'Dell. I'd at least like to see him." Deya let out a tiny sigh of frustration. "I wish there was something I could do to help in all this," she said. "I loved Gwenfrei too. She was Pov's *Puri Dai,* his grandmother, but really she was *Puri Dai* to us all."

"What can you tell me about her?" Billy asked.

Though there was very little sun, a shadow passed across Deya's face. Her full lips thinned, and she looked away. "Gwenfrei was a wonderful woman," she answered. "Gentle and loving. She was the oldest among us. And the kindest. All of us had known her our entire lives. Now that she's gone, the camp is different. Pov is different. Everything is different. She was our teacher." She paused, then added, "Gwenfrei was familiar with the old ways."

"Old ways?"

Now the girl did smile. "She had a crystal ball," Deya said.

"She did? Could she see things in it?" Billy had heard about crystal balls, but he had never seen one.

"She said she could. She claimed to be able to tell a person's future with tarot cards or tea leaves. She could read palms. Some believed Gwenfrei could call up the souls of those who had passed over, but she would never do such a thing."

"Why not?"

"First, it's impossible."

Billy smiled. "Well, there is that, I suppose."

"But even if it weren't, disturbing the dead would be dangerous. Gwenfrei would never attempt it. But she was very skilled in the arts." Deya held out her left hand and ran the fingers of her right hand over it. "Would you like me to read your palm, Billy? Gwenfrei taught me." Her smile was warming.

"Er-a, no." He gave an embarrassed chuckle. "No, thanks," he said.

"Why not?"

"I don't want to know about the future. I have enough trouble with the present and the past."

Deya studied him for a long moment, and she said, "Anyway, that's what Gwenfrei had been doing on the day she was murdered."

"What?"

"Telling fortunes. She had a fine little business going. She always did readings for the townspeople wherever we happened to be."

"I wouldn't've guessed there'd be much call for such a thing around here."

"Ah, then you'd be surprised, Billy Young. Here, as in every place, there's always a call for it. Gwenfrei was walking back to the Rock from Casper where she'd been reading palms on the day she was killed."

Billy knew the woman had been killed on the road from Casper, but this was the first he had heard about palm reading. "Whose fortune had she been telling?" he asked. "Do you know?"

"Lots of people's," said Deya.

"Can you remember any names?"

"No, I was never given a name, and even if I had been, it's not something I should tell."

"Why?"

"Because looking into a person's life is personal. It's private."

Billy wondered if she was teasing him. Sometimes it was hard for him to know. "I thought you didn't put much store in those superstitious ways," he said.

"Maybe I do; maybe I don't. Do you put much store in your religion, Billy?"

Billy and Frank had been raised strict Lutherans—going to services every Sunday of the year and every Wednesday night during Advent and Lent—but when their father died, the Young brothers had become lax in their attendance.

"Sure, I put lots of store in it," he said. "Of course, I do." The words sounded a little hollow when he said them, but he wasn't sure why.

Deya must have heard the hollowness, too. She looked doubtful.

He didn't disbelieve, but he felt many in the local congregation wore their righteousness like a sign around their necks. Although he had not attended services since the Gypsies had arrived, he knew the stony Reverend Sewell had spent more than one Sunday morning ranting against the evil devil worshipers camped below the Rock. To even gaze upon them, Sewell had shouted from the pulpit, was sinful. Billy had never liked the self-righteous man.

"Which is your church, Billy?" Deya asked.

His head jerked up. As with Pov Meche, it was almost as

though she had read his mind. He wondered if Deya had a little *Chovihani* in her as well. "I'm a Lutheran," he answered. "Most folks around here are."

"Then," Deya said, "you'd know the names of many of the people whose fortunes Gwenfrei told better than I would."

"Why? What're you saying?"

"For a while, not long after we stopped here, Gwenfrei told me she was reading the fortunes of at least a dozen women in the Lutheran Women's League."

Chapter Seven:
Milwaukee Beer

Billy had expected Hugo's guffawing about Deya Andree to begin as soon as they rode out of the Gypsy camp, but to his surprise, Hugo was quiet. After a half mile or so, Billy asked, "So what's on your mind, there, Hugo?"

"What makes you think I got something on my mind, boy?"

"Because you haven't been your usual hard-to-abide self, and the only time you're not is when something's weighing on you."

"I don't recall you bein' so sassy when your pa was alive."

"And I don't recall Pa ever hesitating to point out your rude behavior, neither," Billy added, with a smile he made sure Hugo couldn't see. "In fact, it's my memory he always took great pleasure in pointing out all of your tacky ways."

Hugo snorted, and they rode on without conversation. After a while, Hugo straightened himself in his saddle and asked, "Have you come to an opinion on whether ol' Pov back there might try anything with O'Dell?"

"I figure it's possible," Billy said and related some of his conversation with Deya on the subject. "So, yep, Pov sure might do something."

Hugo agreed. "I'd say it's possible, too. Maybe even likely. If it was my ol' granny who'd been shot down like a coyote, I expect I'd be lookin' to see the fella who did it got his due."

"There'll be hell to pay if the Gypsies do go after Ben."

"It has me worried. Like I said before, I don't give two farts in a sandstorm 'bout Ben O'Dell, but I'd hate to see a massacre. I've kind-a taken a likin' to them Roms, and I don't wanna see anythin' bad happen to 'em."

Hugo reached in his coat pocket for his makings. He had rolled a couple of cigarettes earlier and stuck them in his tobacco pouch. Billy had never seen any man more capable than Hugo Dorling at rolling a cigarette while riding horseback in the Wyoming wind, but sometimes Hugo rolled one or two before a ride to avoid the inconvenience. He stuck the shuck in his mouth, and as he dug for a match, he said, "Looks like you've developed a fondness for at least one of them Roms your ownself."

Here it comes. "I was wondering when you were going to get around to it," Billy said.

Hugo laughed, lit his smoke, gave the match a shake, and flicked it away. "I knew you were. That's why I waited." He laughed again, harder this time.

Billy was not going to give the old coot the satisfaction of explaining himself. Instead, he asked, "What do you figure on doing to head off the massacre if some misfortune does befall Ben O'Dell?"

Hugo's laughter went silent, and his smile disappeared. "If somethin' happens to Ben O'Dell, there ain't no headin' off what comes next. The dern fool could be struck by lightnin', and his brother and his brother's pals'd go after them Gypsies. They'd kill 'em one and all, and by the looks of things, there ain't a soul anywhere around who'd give a damn one way or the other."

As crazy as it was, Billy knew it was true. "None of this makes sense," he said, as much to himself as Hugo. "It never has. Not the jury verdict, not the way the judge handled the trial. Not the very fact that Ben killed the old woman in the first place. No, sir, none of it makes one bit of sense."

Hugo nodded. "I don't know where to start to get to the bottom of it all. What I'd like to do is beat the truth out of O'Dell." He hawked up something from deep in his lungs and spit. The wind was picking up, and it caught the spittle and carried it an impressive distance. "That's what I'd like to do." Hugo wiped his mouth with the back of his gloved hand.

"Everyone thinks we already tried."

"Then there ain't much to lose in the doin' of it now, is there?"

"Nothing to gain either, except for getting ourselves tossed in jail. I don't suppose you'd fare too well behind bars. You're probably the reason most of the inmates are in there themselves."

"I ain't gonna beat nothin' outta Ben O'Dell even as much as I'd like to. But it would be a pleasure to beat the truth outta the Honorable Thomas Reed."

Billy nodded. "I'd like to hear him explain a few things, but if you did that, they wouldn't even bother to stop at the jailhouse. They'd haul you right off to prison. Or maybe shoot you outright and save the warden the trouble of putting up with you for the next ten years, or however long it is these days a fella gets for beating the hell out of a judge."

Hugo let out an exhausted-sounding breath and said, "Well, the one and only thing we know for certain is if them Romanies do anything at all to Ben O'Dell, bad things are gonna happen."

They rode in the general direction of town, but Billy wasn't sure what they'd do once they got there. Hugo was more or less leading the way, but Billy doubted Hugo had a plan.

"Maybe," said Billy, "that's where we should start." Thinking back on his conversation with Deya had given him an idea about what they should do and where they should begin.

"What d'ya mean?"

"If the Roms are planning to do something to Ben, there's no way we can talk them out of it—"

"That's for sure," agreed Hugo.

"—and if Ben gets killed or even injured, Thatcher O'Dell and his bunch'll go after the Roms." The conversation paused as Billy sorted through his thoughts. Buying time to think, he reached forward and gave the gray's neck a gentle rub. Settling back into the saddle, he said, "The way I see it, there's only one choice we have."

There was another lull in the conversation. A long enough lull to cause Billy to glance across the gap between them. The ex-deputy wore his brooding expression, and Billy assumed Hugo was having no luck coming up with what the only choice they had might be.

"All right," Hugo said, looking toward Billy. "I give up. What are you gettin' at?"

"Ben needs to stay healthy. The only way to make sure he stays healthy is to locate him and the two of us keep him safe—safe from the Gypsies or any other misfortune he might encounter."

Hugo gave Billy a soft laugh that held more scoff than humor. "How do you suppose we do it?"

"Well, I'm not too clear on the particulars myself, but we have to find him and hole him up somewhere."

"What? Are you saying we whack Ben O'Dell over the head and kidnap 'im?"

"No, not kidnap him, Hugo. Offer to let him stay with us awhile for his own well-being."

"And what if he ain't inclined to accept our cordial invitation?"

"Well, then, I guess we'll have to give him a whack."

Though cold even by late-November standards, the weather hadn't been too bad at Gypsy Rock; but the closer they got to Casper, the stronger the northwest wind became. By the time

73

they rode into town, it was blowing hard enough they had to screw their hats down a few more threads to keep them from sailing off to Nebraska. Casper was noted for its old fort, for the Mormon Crossing over the North Platte River, and for the wind that blew pretty much nonstop every year from the first of January right on through to the end of December.

"Let's head to the westside-a Center," Hugo shouted over the gusts. "I figure Ben'll be drinkin' in one of them saloons. He's a big celebrity now, and there'll be folks around town willin' to buy 'im whiskey. He wouldn't want to miss an opportunity of free drinkin'."

Hugo was cheerier since they'd devised a plan, even if the plan was not a very practical one.

They went first to the Half-Moon, which was still one of the O'Dell boys' regular haunts, even though it was where Connie worked before she left the country. The prospect of going into this place made Billy uneasy. Hugo was accomplished at attracting trouble, and the Half-Moon was noted for its rowdy ways.

When they arrived, it was still early. The place was empty except for Charlie Martin, the establishment's owner and operator, and a few of the house's girls, who were playing hearts at a table in the corner.

Despite the Moon's rough reputation, Charlie himself was an affable sort, but he was a man fond of a penny and was willing to allow his clientele to behave however they pleased as long as they paid him to keep their glasses full.

When he saw them come in, Charlie's lips peeled back into a wide smile. "Well," he said, "lookie here, if it ain't Hugo Dorling and his young shadow, Billy. How you doing, boys?"

Billy wasn't sure he liked the "young shadow" remark, but all in all Charlie was a good enough fella, and Billy let it slide.

"Doin' fine," said Hugo as he strode to the bar. "How 'bout you, Charlie? How's business?"

"Pretty slow after the holiday. I figure folks had enough fun yesterday they're taking it easy today. So far, anyhow," he added with a note of optimism. "What can I get you fellas?"

It wasn't yet noon, but Hugo would not consider walking into a saloon without ordering a drink no matter what time of day it was. He leaned his forearms on the bar and said, "How 'bout a couple of them bottle beers, the kind you import all the way from Milwaukee? That sound good to you, Billy-boy?"

"Sure," Billy agreed, although, even as he said it, he chided himself for drinking alcohol this early. Maybe he was picking up too many of Hugo's bad habits, and Charlie's jape about being a shadow wasn't far off the mark.

Charlie put the bottles in front of them, and Hugo slid two bits and a dime across the bar. A high price, in Billy's opinion, for a couple of beers, no matter where they came from.

Hugo's throwing his money around was proof he intended to squeeze Charlie for information; otherwise the miserly Hugo would never pay a cent more than a nickel for any beer brewed anywhere on Earth. Hugo was by nature tight-fisted, but he was quick to spend in order to get his way. To Billy's amazement, Hugo's not-very-subtle ploy worked more often than not.

"Heard there was a little bit of a ruckus over at the Thanksgiving dinner yesterday," said Charlie as he scooped up the coins and dropped them in his till.

"Where'd you hear somethin' like that?" asked Hugo, taking a long pull on his costly lager.

Charlie shrugged. "I don't know. A few of the boys were talking, I guess."

"Could-a couple of them boys've been named O'Dell, perchance?"

"I reckon. It ain't much of a secret, though. The whole town knows about the to-do you got into with the judge—both in the courtroom and at the dinner. Heard it cost you a hundred dollars and your job." Charlie winked at Billy and nodded to the bottle in Hugo's fist. "You sure a fella with no visible means of support should be indulging in Milwaukee beer?"

"You let me worry 'bout that, bartender." Hugo pointed toward a jar of pickles at the end of the bar. "How 'bout you give me and Billy here a couple of them big dills."

Charlie slid the jar over. "Well, sir, I won't be giving you any, but I'll let you dig out as many as you please for two cents apiece."

"Damn, Charlie, but you are one money grubber, ain'tcha?"

"I didn't go into the pickle-selling business so you could eat them for free, Hugo."

Hugo unscrewed the top on the jar and dug inside.

"You only need to pull out one of them things," said Billy. "I'd rather take a bullet than eat a dill pickle."

"Spoke like a fella who never took a bullet," observed Hugo. He handed Charlie a nickel and said, "Go ahead and charge for two, you bushwhacker. I expect I'll be going back for seconds. Unlike my young friend here, I have always had a soft spot for the dills."

Again, Billy was amazed at how Hugo was spending his money.

As Hugo crunched into the pickle, he said, "I reckon them O'Dells was whoopin' 'er up last night, weren't they?"

"They had reason to celebrate." Charlie reached under the bar for a rag and wiped up the mess Hugo had made when he fished out the pickle.

"It was sure Ben's lucky day when they drew that dim-witted jury and that fool of a judge," said Hugo.

"Now, now, Hugo, don't be a poor sport." Charlie gave them both another of his wide smiles. "It was my lucky day, too. Ben O'Dell being in jail for a month or so cut pretty deep into my whiskey profits. I was afraid I'd have to take out a loan so's to get by."

Hugo returned Charlie's smile, which meant he must have considered the comment pretty funny. Talk about the O'Dells seldom made Hugo smile. "Yes, sir, I can see how Ben's absence could've been a problem. I expect he'll be makin' up for lost time, though, so it'll all work out for you in the end." Hugo finished off his first pickle and dug into the jar for his second, sending another splash of pickle juice across the bar.

"Damn, but you're slovenly," Charlie said, cleaning Hugo's mess once again.

Hugo ignored Charlie's remark. "Fact is, Billy and me figured ol' Ben'd be so eager to make up for lost time, he'd already be in here this morning poundin' 'em down."

"Well, sir, I suppose he would be," Charlie allowed, " 'cept unlike you, Ben O'Dell is now a fully employed, contributing member of Casper society."

Hugo gave a little jerk of surprise. "The hell you say."

"Nope, believe it or not, it's the truth."

"Who'd be fool enough to give that misfit a job?"

"Don't know for sure," answered Charlie, "but since he's gone to work for the city, I reckon that fool'd have to be the mayor."

Chapter Eight:
A Stony Few Seconds

The boys finished their Milwaukee beers, bid Charlie farewell, and left the Half-Moon Saloon. Billy went first, and Hugo followed, neglecting, as was so often his way, to close the door behind him. Charlie Martin, when provoked, was an accomplished practitioner in the fine art of profanity, and even from the boardwalk, the boys could hear Charlie let loose a string of obscenities capable of curling the bark off a cottonwood.

"Wait up a minute, there, Hugo," said Billy, and he went back to pull the door closed. He stuck his head in before he did and said, "Sorry, folks." The Wheeligo girls playing hearts all gave him hard scowls. Billy assumed their skimpy dresses were poor protection against the nippy November wind whirling about the barroom. As he shut the door, he touched the brim of his hat and gave them an apologetic smile.

When he came back, Hugo was muttering to himself.

"What did you say?" Billy asked.

"I said I can't picture that loafer Ben O'Dell with a real job."

"What I can't picture," said Billy, "is the mayor finding a reason to give him one."

"True," Hugo agreed. He buttoned his coat and said, "C'mon, boy, let's go make a call on the mayor."

They unhitched their horses from the Moon's rail and led them the four blocks to Enos's haberdashery. Billy, being a cowboy, was not fond of unnecessary walking and figured it was rarely better to lead a horse than to be astride one. Hugo, though, when in a pensive mood—which is what he was in now—liked to walk, and they made their way afoot and in silence to Woodard's Clothiers.

Once there, they had to tie their animals in the alley because there was no hitching rack in front of the store. The store management wanted to discourage the possibility of tracking horse apples into Casper's finest clothing emporium.

A tiny bell above the door jingled when Hugo and Billy went in, and Theodore Hart, the town's mayor, approached from somewhere in back.

The position of mayor was not a full-time job, and when there were no council meetings or city matters to attend to, Mayor Hart spent his workdays as manager of the haberdashery.

"Good morning, gentlemen," Hart said with what, for him, passed for a smile. As he said it, the wall clock chimed out twelve, and he added, "Or I should say good afternoon?" He chuckled, and tugging on a gold chain, he lifted his own timepiece from the pocket of his brocaded silk vest. He popped the hunter-case open and compared his time to that of the Regulator. Snapping the lid closed, he dropped the watch back into his pocket. His movements appeared rehearsed, like an actor's on a stage.

"Now then," he said, rubbing his hands together as though it was time to get down to business, "what may I show you gentlemen?" He eyed them both up and down, taking them in from the scuffs on their boots to the sweat stains on their scruffy hats.

"Ain't interested in buyin' new duds," answered Hugo.

"Oh, *really*?" The snooty tone in Hart's voice did not escape Billy; although Billy could tell it did escape Hugo—or at least Hugo showed no sign of noticing.

"Nope," Hugo said, "we stopped in to talk to you 'bout your

mayorin' duties."

"Well," said Hart, his back stiffening, "I don't discuss those sorts of things here at Woodard's. I always keep my professional life and my political life separate."

"This won't take long," countered Hugo.

Hart raised his index finger to the side of his head and shook it a couple of times as though he had come to realize something he should have known before. "Why, you're Hugo Dorling." Hart then turned to Billy. "And you, sir?"

Billy was about to give his name when Hugo said, "He's with me."

Either intentionally or out of habit, Hugo had slipped into his deputy marshal demeanor, and when he was marshaling, it was important to him everyone around knew who was in charge. It appeared, though, Mayor Hart was at least as accustomed to being in charge as Hugo. He turned again to Billy. "If he's Dorling, you must be Billy Young." He thought about it for another second and said, "Why, yes, of course you are."

"Word is," Hugo said, "you gave Ben O'Dell a job of work for the city."

"Indeed? Is that 'the word'?"

Hugo didn't respond. He asked questions; he didn't provide answers.

After a silence long enough to make Billy squirm even if it didn't appear to bother the other two, Hart, who was a man fond of speeches—at least his own—said, "I'll tell you what, Mr. Dorling, a jury determined Ben O'Dell was wrongfully accused of a heinous crime. As I understand it, the evidence showed Mr. O'Dell had been intruded upon in the dark of night. His companion was killed, and O'Dell was forced to run for his life. He was then chased down like an animal, and severely beaten. He stood incarcerated for many weeks before, thank God, justice prevailed. So, yes, to answer your question, after the behavior of some members of local law enforcement—" He paused for that to sink in. "—I felt, in fairness, this community owed Mr. O'Dell something to make up for what he'd been through, and I provided him employment."

Without a smile, and in a dry, even voice, Hugo said, "You're a saint."

Hart cleared his throat but otherwise made no response.

"Where's he workin'?" Hugo asked.

"I have no idea. I told the clerk to give him a job, and I assume he did. Where O'Dell was assigned, I wouldn't know."

Hugo stared at the man for a moment, and without further conversation, he turned on his boot heel and headed for the door.

Hart called after him. "What business is it of yours, anyway, Dorling?"

Again, Hugo ignored the man's question, opened the door, and stepped outside.

Billy started out, too.

"How about you, young man? Are you going to tell me what your interest in all of this is?"

Billy stopped, turned toward Hart, and said. "We want to do O'Dell a favor."

"A favor?" Hart laughed. A thin line of gold rimmed the edges of his right front tooth. "Aren't you the one who beat the living devil out of the poor man at the old stagecoach stop?"

Like Hugo, Billy didn't answer the man's question. He turned and walked outside, not bothering to close the door.

"What're your thoughts on Mayor Hart?" Billy asked Hugo as they led their horses out of the alley.

"He thinks pretty high of his self, I reckon—one of those who figures he knows a whole lot more about whatever topic's bein' discussed than whoever it is he's talkin' to knows, but I

81

expect mostly he's a harmless blowhard. Why? What're your thoughts?"

Before Billy offered an opinion, he said, "I'm not sure where we're headed, Hugo, but wherever it is, I'm riding, not walking." Billy flung a leg over Badger and dropped into the saddle.

"We're headed to city hall, a-course, to visit with the clerk. Looks like he's the fella to tell us where we can find O'Dell." Hugo climbed atop his own horse. "Wouldn't hurt you to walk now and again, Billy. I hear it's good for both the health and the disposition."

"If you're an expert on healthy living, I guess you must think whiskey, cigarettes, and late nights with loose women are good for the health too."

"Well, sure, they are," said Hugo. He cocked his right arm and made a muscle. "Look at me. I'm fitter'n a fiddle, and my disposition is always cheery." He pulled his tobacco pouch and dug out what looked to be the last of his already-rolled cigarettes.

Billy knew playing word games with Hugo was difficult, not because Hugo was so good at them, but because he was so bad.

Shaking his head in frustration, Billy provided Hugo his thinking on the mayor. "I don't know Hart myself, but I hear that all his mayoring chores ever add up to is him doing whatever the money boys around town want him to do. Which includes your pal Enos."

"S'long as Hart does whatever he's told at the haberdashery, I doubt Enos much cares what the preenin' jack-a-dandy does at city hall."

"Could be," said Billy, though to his thinking, even as much as Billy liked him too, Enos Woodard was a smart man who had opinions—lots of them—and he expected folks to heed what he had to say.

They were riding at a walk down First Street when Thatcher

O'Dell and eight or ten of his buddies stepped out of Armstrong's pool hall. Billy could not figure this bunch. Here it was the middle of the day, and none of them was working. He knew a few hired out for day work at some of the local ranches from time to time, especially during roundup, calving, and branding. Billy's family hired the bulk of their hands each year during those times as well. Now and again, Thatcher was a bouncer at some of the seedier joints around town.

How they came by their whiskey money was hard to say. They were all suspected of the bank robberies done the year before in Lander and Rock Springs, but there was no proof, and the idea never got past the suspicion stage.

"Well, well," called out Thatcher with a laugh when he spotted Hugo and Billy, "take a look, boys, it's ex-Deputy Dorling in the flesh. Have you beat any poor law-abiding citizens senseless yet today, Hugo?"

The cronies seemed to think Thatcher was pretty funny, all except for Hank Green, a tall, steely-eyed man who was a recent transplant from Montana. He stood away from the group, watching without expression.

Billy figured Green for an odd sort even by the curious standards of the O'Dells' crowd. Most were disheveled slobs, but Green was a fancy dresser. Billy had never seen the man wear anything but black—black boots, black hat, and black everything in between. Everything, that was, except for the light tan gun belt and holster he wore slung low on his hip. The gun the holster held, though, was a midnight blue Colt Army with onyx grips as black as an undertaker's necktie. The fanciest thing about Green's get-up was his hat. It bore a flat crown, a wide brim steamed into upward curves on both sides, and a long stampede string. Goddess of Liberty quarters circled the crown, and on a dry, sunny day, the glints shooting off the band looked to be powerful enough to kindle a grass fire.

But Green's manner of dress wasn't the oddest thing about him. As far as Billy knew, he never laughed or smiled, either one; and now that Billy thought about it, it was rare the man even spoke.

"I have not," was Hugo's answer to Thatcher's question about beating up citizens. "But," he added, "the day is yet young."

A couple of Thatcher's boys laughed at that one too, but their chuckles trickled off pretty fast when they noticed they were the only ones in their crowd who found it amusing.

"Me and the fellas're headed down to the Moon for a noontime pick-me-up if you and your pup Billy Young'd care to join us. Lester here was the big loser shooting pool so it'll be his treat." Thatcher slapped the lantern-jawed, low-browed Lester Warbler on the shoulder. Billy knew Lester to be a poor loser with a hot temper, and he didn't look pleased when Thatcher invited two more to a party he was paying for.

"Thanks, but no thanks," said Hugo. "We were just there. Had us a couple of beers and a fine conversation with Charlie."

"That so? What did the ol' fibber have to say?"

"Not so much. He told us you fellas was whoopin' 'er up last night celebratin' your brother gettin' away with murder."

"So he said that, did he?"

"Well, sir, he might not've put so fine an edge on it. Some of it might be my own poetical way of phrasin'."

Thatcher raised his right hand, and with a smile he jabbed all four fingers at Hugo a couple of times. "Why, I do believe you're trying to provoke me, aren't you, you old fool?"

Hugo smiled, too, although it was clear this was not a friendly exchange.

"What's to keep me 'n' my friends here from dragging you two fellas off them horses, thrashing you into unconsciousness, and leaving you lay right here in the middle of First Street?"

"I don't know. What is?" asked Hugo. "I'd doubt it's good

sense, since you ain't got none."

After a beat, Thatcher laughed, and after another beat, so did his boys, except for, again, Hank Green. Thatcher moved in closer to Hugo's horse and gave the animal a gentle scratch on the nose. "You know something, Hugo," he said with a smile and in a congenial tone, "someday I might decide to kill you."

Hugo leaned forward, and said, "I'm eager for you to try 'er, Thatch. Promise me when you do give it a go, you'll bring along ol' Ben. Killin' two O'Dells instead-a just one would more than double the pleasure."

Their eyes locked, and they shared a stony few seconds, but to Billy's surprise, it didn't go any further.

"C'mon, boys," Thatcher said. "Let's get us a drink."

C.Q. Carlson was way too old to be city clerk. At least Billy thought so. C.Q. had been a man on the shady side of forty when he took a ball at Gettysburg. Fortunately, the ball didn't hit any of C.Q.'s moving parts, and in time, he made a full recovery. Still, Billy figured a wounded veteran deep into his seventies should be sipping tea or maybe whiskey on a porch somewhere, not shuffling papers in a dingy office in Casper, Wyoming.

The old clerk was a little deaf and didn't hear Hugo and Billy come in. He had his back to the counter where the boys now stood and was typing away on a fancy Densmore typewriter. There was a bell on the counter, and Hugo gave it a smack, but the bell's tinny little ding wasn't enough to get C.Q.'s attention. Hugo tried again, and after pounding a few more times, the old man turned in his chair. When he recognized who was doing the bell ringing, he gave a smile that deepened in a pleasant way a dozen of the more pronounced wrinkles on his cheeks and around his eyes.

"Why, Hugo," said C.Q. "I haven't seen you in ages. How

you doing, boy?"

Billy guessed it had been a while since Hugo had been called "boy." Maybe it was the last time he'd run into C.Q.

"Just peachy, C.Q. How 'bout yourself?"

"Don't like the winter weather," answered the old man. "Makes my bones hurt. I swear it even makes my hair hurt, if you can believe it." He rubbed the top of his head.

"My young pal Billy here doesn't care much for this frosty climate neither. Maybe you two fellas should head down to Texas till springtime."

"I like Texas," offered C.Q., "but I never had a fondness for Texans."

"That could pose a problem," Hugo said. "I hear they got a bunch of 'em down there."

"Yep, I expect they do. What brings you gents around on such a chilly day?"

"Well, sir, we're lookin' for Ben O'Dell, and we hear, as of today, like yourself, he is now a gainfully paid employee of the city of Casper. Can you tell us where you got 'im workin'?"

"I was going to have him doing odd jobs here at city hall, maybe some cleaning, some painting, but the rascal hasn't showed up for work yet."

"He hasn't showed up? Hell, C.Q., the day's half over."

"I noticed that, too. Looks like Ben O'Dell might be a gold-bricker."

Hugo provided C.Q. with an expression Billy read as an I-could-a-told-you-that-before-you-hired-him look, but all Hugo said was, "Could be the case, all right. You got any idea where Billy and me could locate the man?"

"Dan Higgins, the Deputy U.S. Attorney, said something about once O'Dell got out of jail, he'd be staying in the old shack behind the White Star Livery over on David Street. Maybe he's there still sleeping off the drunk I expect he pulled after the jury came back."

"I bet you're right," said Hugo. He turned and started for the office door. Billy could tell Hugo had the information he came for and was eager to get going. "Thanks, C.Q. We'll be seein' you."

"Here fellas, I'll see you out. It does me good to move my legs from time to time." The old man shuffled around the counter and walked them down the short hallway between his office and the front door. "You take care, now, boys," he said once they were on the stoop outside. "And give the shack behind the White Star a try. I expect you'll find that layabout O'Dell in there sound asleep and smelling of whiskey."

"We'll do 'er, C.Q.," said Hugo. "And thanks again for the help. You stay warm now, you hear?"

The old man pulled the sweater he wore tighter around his shoulders and glanced up at the low, gray clouds scudding by. "A thing hardly possible in this cold-ass country."

Hugo laughed. "At least we ain't got us very many Texans. There's always that."

The White Star Livery sat on the corner of Second and David streets and took up most of the block. The retail portion of the business was conducted in the main building, where the owner, Theo Parker, sold feed, tack, and various tools. Out back was a barn and stable, a couple of work sheds, a large privy, and two corrals. One corral held horses. Another held between fifteen and twenty cattle. Mr. Parker appeared to have started a small cattle-feeding operation over the winter. Parker's operation was nothing like the huge feedlot Enos owned, but this one looked to be doing all right. The area carried the smells common to all places where animals are held in tight quarters, but Billy knew the odor now was nothing compared to what it would be when spring came and four or five months of frozen cow shit began to melt.

An old hammered-together shack stood between one of the work sheds and the livery's main building. Billy and Hugo figured this to be a likely spot to locate the Gypsy-killing weasel Ben O'Dell. They rode down an alley and came at the place from the rear. Dismounting, they flipped their reins around the top rail of a corral and started for the shack. The small building had neither windows nor a back door, so they went straight for the front.

"We'll knock first to be polite," said Hugo. "We wouldn't want ol' Ben to consider us rude."

Billy would rather they kick the door in with sidearms drawn and at the ready. He figured it unwise to give O'Dell time to think. The last time they met like this, even with surprise on their side, O'Dell was still fast enough to set Hugo on fire and almost get away.

As he lifted his short-barreled revolver from its holster, Billy said, "If it's all the same to you, I think I'll keep my Colt handy. I don't care one bit if O'Dell thinks me rude."

Hugo scoffed at his young partner's caution, but Billy didn't much care in matters like this. "Go ahead," he said, nodding toward the door, "give it a knock."

Hugo provided two solid raps to the rotting old door, hitting it hard enough to send gray dust floating from its dry pine planks. "Ben O'Dell," he called out, "open up. It's Hugo and Billy. We mean you no harm. Let us in." When he received no response, he pounded on the door again, even harder. Still there came no answer or even the sound of movement. Hugo sent Billy a questioning look, which Billy answered with a shrug. "I reckon we've gone about as far as polite behavior demands we go," Hugo said. "With any one of them O'Dells, we need to be cautious bustin' in. It's probable their first reaction'll be one of violence." He pulled his own piece and added, "I sure wish I'd remembered to bring along my sawed-off."

He reached for the knob, turned it, and gave the door a push.

It didn't budge. Not an inch. Something on the other side was blocking it closed. Hugo gave another shove, putting his shoulder into it this time, and the door began to open, pushing aside whatever was in the way. When Hugo had it ajar a couple of feet, he and Billy slipped into the dark room.

When Billy was convinced they wouldn't get shot on the spot by a trigger-happy Ben O'Dell, he said, "Damn, it's darker than the inside of a goat."

Hugo took a match from his vest pocket and popped it alight with his thumbnail. As the match's flare settled into a yellow glow, Hugo lifted it higher. When he did, they could see what they had dreaded. Ben O'Dell lay against the door with his throat slit open from one ear all the way to the other.

Chapter Nine:
Clanging Bells

Hugo carried the match to a lamp atop a table on the far side of the small room. After lighting the lamp, he sucked in a deep breath, blew out the match, and turned to face Billy. "Looks like our worst fears came to be," he observed as he dropped into a rickety chair next to the table.

Billy, who still stood beside the body, didn't respond. All he could do was stare into Ben O'Dell's clouded-over, cross-eyed gaze. Judging by the expression frozen onto Ben's face, whatever he was looking at with those poor, ruined eyes must be a real horror.

Ben O'Dell's lifeless body was not Billy's first encounter with a dead man. He had seen plenty of death at the train robbery the year before. He had also encountered death on La Prele Creek in a rough cabin not so much different from the one they were in now. He himself had put an end to the second of the three killers from the train—wrapped a rope around his neck and hanged him from a hook.

So, although death was not a new thing to young Billy, it still left him shaky.

"What now?" he asked. He heard the hint of a quiver in his voice.

Hugo jerked his chin toward another chair at the table where he sat.

Billy crossed the room, making sure to step over the trail of blood ending at O'Dell's body and beginning in the darkness somewhere beyond Hugo's light.

The second chair at the table was wobbly, and Billy sat down carefully until convinced it would hold his weight. He took off his hat and shoved his hair back. "What now?" he repeated, but Hugo still didn't answer. Instead, he rolled a cigarette and lit it with the flame of the lamp. Exhaling a stream of smoke toward the floor, he sat forward and leaned his forearms on his knees. He sat for a long moment, not speaking or even smoking, just watching the red glow of his cigarette turn to gray ash.

He allowed the shuck to burn down almost to his fingers before he sat up, took a last drag, and dropped the butt to the floor. He ground it with the heel of his boot and stood.

Hugo took the lamp from the table and lifted it above his shoulder, casting its light into the cabin's corners. The blood trail began in the far northwest corner. The attack had taken place there. Billy imagined Ben cowering in the gloom, trying without success to make himself invisible to his killer or killers. Even before he murdered Gwenfrei Faw, Ben O'Dell had been a bad man. Maybe he got what he deserved, but, even so, Billy figured a fella getting his throat sliced open in a smelly, dilapidated livery shack was a hard way to go out.

After the attack, Ben had crawled from the corner to the door.

Hugo walked to the body and squatted down, placing the lamp on the floor so it lit Ben's grisly face and upper chest. Ben was dressed in nothing but his long johns, the top of which was soaked in crimson. The floor surrounding the body, too, was covered in a dark, viscous goo.

Watching the way Hugo stared down at what remained of Ben O'Dell, Billy knew Hugo was slipping into his deputy marshal's manner of thinking.

"Maybe we should get the hell out of here, Hugo," Billy suggested. "If anyone should walk in, it might be hard to explain what we're doing."

Again, Hugo ignored Billy's comment, and Billy was finding Hugo's rude behavior irritating. He was about to point out how irritating it was, when Hugo began to run his fingers over the flesh around Ben O'Dell's eyes, down along his jawline, and onto his neck, making a point to avoid the deep and gruesome gash.

Billy didn't know what Hugo was up to, but it was a fascinating thing to watch. In the years he had known Hugo Dorling, Billy had witnessed the man exhibiting strange behavior many times. Billy doubted, though, he had ever seen Hugo doing anything so strange as running his fingers over the face of a dead man.

Hugo avoided touching any of the gore, but when he was finished doing whatever he had been doing, he wiped his hands on his jeans. Still staring at O'Dell's ashen face, Hugo sat back on his haunches and said, "Judgin' by the rigor around his eyes, jaw, and neck, I figure he was kilt three or four hours ago, maybe a little more." Again avoiding the blood, he reached over and felt Ben's left arm. He must have found the arm pliable because he added, "For sure no more than six."

"That puts it at, what, eight, nine o'clock this morning?"

"Probably a little earlier," said Hugo. "I doubt it was done in the daylight, so that'd put 'er closer to seven. And I expect the chill in this room would've slowed the rigor down some."

"It looks bad for Pov and his group."

"Yep," Hugo agreed, "it does." He picked up the lamp and took it back to the table. "Also if Ben was kilt even before we went out to the Rock this mornin', maybe there was more to Pov's figurin' out why we were there than those reasons he gave us."

"If," said Billy, "the Roms did have a hand in this, when Pov first saw us, he might've figured we rode out to accuse him of murder. It must've been a relief when he saw we didn't know anything about it."

"Well, whether they did it or whether they didn't, no matter how you look at 'er, it's bad news for the Gypsies."

Hugo set the lamp on the table and blew out its flame. The hot tip of its wick glowed for a moment and vanished in a swirly wisp of smoke.

The boys made their way through the alley and out to Second Street without being seen—a lucky break, thought Billy. From their first minutes in the shack, he imagined someone barging in on them and he and Hugo being charged with killing Ben themselves. Not until they were headed away from the cabin and well down the street did Billy begin to feel better. Once they were past the edge of town, he reined in and repeated his still-unanswered question. "What now, Hugo?"

Hugo pulled rein as well and, still without answering, reached into his saddlebag and dug out a bottle of Kentucky whiskey. He pulled the cork and tossed back a slug. Extending the bottle to Billy, he asked, "Care for a snort?"

"No," said Billy.

Hugo's bushy left eyebrow went up an inch or so. Billy recognized the gesture as one Hugo often used to telegraph his aggravation for any one of a few hundred daily annoyances. "Suit yourself," he said and took another pull from the bottle. He wiped his mouth and added, "As for me, cut throats make me thirsty."

"It had to be Pov or one of his people who did it. Don't you think?" asked Billy.

"I don't know what to think. It looks like it, though. And it's sure easy to figure what the town's gonna think." Hugo might have had the same discomfort Billy felt back at the shack because Hugo went on to say, "Folks're gonna figure either the

Gyps killed ol' Ben or you and me did, one or the other." He took another pull on the bottle.

"So if you were still a marshal, Hugo, what would you do next? Since we know we didn't kill him, would you go after whatever Gypsy did it and bring him to justice? Or would you figure Ben got what he deserved and tell Pov he needs to get his people out of here before all hell breaks loose?"

"Well, Ben's murder didn't happen on federal land, so it wouldn't've fallen into my jurisdiction anyhow. If some fella did get brought to justice for killin' Ben O'Dell, the task would have to go to the high sheriff."

Dale Jarrod was the county sheriff. He had been voted out of office in the election a couple of weeks earlier, but he would continue to hold the position until after the first of the year. The reason Jarrod lost the election was because he was worthless as sheriff. Billy doubted being a lame duck would improve the man's law enforcement skills, and he said as much to Hugo.

"True," Hugo said, taking another sip. "Nor would the good-for-nothing lift a hand to stop Thatcher and his boys from ridin' out and killin' ever' last one of them Gypsies."

Hugo stuck the cork back in his bottle and his bottle back in his bag. "If Pov knows about the killin', I expect he's already got his people packin' up; but if he don't know—or even if he does—it couldn't hurt to ride out. Maybe we can get 'im movin' a little faster. The quicker they're gone from here, the better for ever'one."

A few minutes earlier, rushing out to Gypsy Rock and warning the Gypsies had made sense to Billy, too, but after giving it more consideration, he doubted it would do any good. "I don't know, Hugo," he said. "Even if Pov and his band headed out right this second, once Ben's body's found, Thatcher'll still chase them down. There's no way the Gypsies could be far enough away to keep from getting caught and slaughtered."

Hugo took off his hat and gave his head a good scratching. "Goddamn it," he said, and his curse was thick with frustration. He slapped his hat against his thigh hard enough to make his horse flinch and added, "We got us a mess."

"Maybe if we had a little more time," Billy said, "we could figure things out."

"Well," Hugo said, "when Ben doesn't turn up after quittin' time, Thatcher'll go lookin' for him, and the first place he'll look is the shack back yonder. We don't have a couple of days to figure things out. We got us four, maybe five hours at the most."

"There's one way," Billy said, "we could buy ourselves and the Gypsies more time."

Hugo said nothing but provided a questioning look.

"As long as folks don't know for sure Ben's dead, it wouldn't matter much if he disappeared for a while. Everyone would assume one night of celebrating not getting hanged wasn't enough for ol' Ben and he went off somewhere to frolic in earnest."

"What're you saying, boy?"

"We could take the body out of the shack and hide it somewhere." Merely saying the words caused his heartbeat to accelerate.

Hugo's leery expression told Billy the idea didn't sit well. "Seems to me," he said, "movin' a murdered man's body around would be contrary to both the law and common decency."

Billy knew of many times Hugo had been pretty flexible with both the law and decency, common or otherwise. Billy didn't point it out, though, and when he didn't say anything, Hugo asked, "How d'ya suppose we could get Ben outta there without gettin' caught, it bein' broad daylight and all?"

Billy had no answer, but one thing for sure was if they got caught hiding Ben O'Dell's body, it would make him and Hugo look guilty enough ol' Pov and the rest of the Gypsies would have nothing more to worry about.

On the short ride back to town, Billy and Hugo discussed how they might get Ben out of the cabin. It didn't require much discussion, though.

"The way I see 'er," offered Hugo, "the odds against success here range from real bad all the way up to damned poor."

Billy had to agree, but he was still turning it over in his mind when they came upon the sounds of a clanging bell, excited shouts, and general chaos. They exchanged looks, and without speaking, Billy spurred Badger into a full gallop. Hugo was right behind.

When they got to Second Street next to the White Star Livery, they saw what all the commotion was and reined in hard.

Ben O'Dell's shack was engulfed in orange flames that danced and rose twenty-five feet into the gray November sky. The air was filled with the acrid smoke of burning pine, and three or four men from the livery and perhaps a couple of passers-by had formed a bucket brigade that ran from a large watering trough inside one of the horse corrals over to the cabin. Billy and Hugo dismounted. Without taking the time to tie off their horses, they allowed their reins to fall, sprinted to the line, and joined in. With every passing second, more men arrived. Most carried buckets, and they formed their own lines.

Soon, another group of men pulled up to the shack with the John Rodgers Pumper the city had purchased used from Rawlins the previous spring.

All the men worked as a fine team, but it didn't matter. Billy knew there was no way in all this world they were ever going to save the shack.

The other firefighters must have come to the same conclusion; they stopped throwing water at the cabin and instead started dousing the work sheds, corrals, and the rear of the main White Star building. The shack was a total loss or soon would be. All they could do was keep the fire from spreading until it burned itself out.

Now that the Volunteer Pumper Brigade had arrived, most of the men who were tossing buckets of water at the blaze backed off and got out of the way. As Billy and Hugo watched the pumpers work, Billy felt himself smile. He figured both he and Hugo were thinking the same thing, but neither of them wanted to be the first to say it out loud, so without talking at all, they fetched their horses and walked over to Mrs. Oliver's Boarding House across the street from the livery. They tied the animals at the boarding house's rail and continued to watch the more or less controlled chaos of the fire and the pumpers who fought it.

"You know, boy," Hugo said, leaning toward Billy's ear, "this fire's a good thing."

And Billy knew it was, for the Gypsies anyway, and he was glad. He didn't want to think what would happen to Deya and the others if folks believed one of the Gypsies had killed a white man. Ben's body would be found, of course—what was left of it—but after a conflagration like the one before them now, there would be no way for anyone to determine Ben's throat had been cut, or even that he had been murdered. Everyone would assume Ben had gotten drunk, done something stupid, and set the place ablaze.

Because Billy knew that wasn't true, he had to wonder who had set the shack on fire. And since it happened so soon after he and Hugo left, he had to wonder if whoever did it had seen them leave.

The possibility of being seen was unpleasant. Maybe the fire solved some problems, but it also raised a lot of questions and bad possibilities.

After a while, the arm of the fire bell ringer must have gotten tired because, to the great relief of everyone within earshot, the clanging came to a stop. The crowd continued to grow, though. Fire was a big event in a young town constructed almost exclusively of wood.

"Well, well, what've you two been up to?"

The question came from behind them, and it startled Billy. It looked as though it took Hugo by surprise as well. At the very same instant, they both spun and found themselves looking into the smiling face of Enos Woodard.

Hugo did not return Enos's broad smile. "Comin' up on a man from behind like that is a good way to get yourself shot."

"If I was going to get shot coming up behind you two, it'd be Billy who did it, not you. I bet he could pull and fire twice as fast as you, you old codger."

Billy knew Enos had it wrong. Billy had once seen how quick Hugo was in a saloon in the town of Probity. He didn't correct Enos about Hugo's speed, though. Billy was smart enough to stay from between these two when one was gibing the other.

Hugo didn't rise to Enos's bait, which was a big surprise. He did offer his friend a sour look, however.

"How'd this fire get goin'?" Hugo asked.

"Couldn't say," answered Enos. "I was riding over from my house here in town, and I could hear the bell clanging from all the way over on South Center. Came by to see if I could give the volunteers a hand. I guess there's not much anyone can do at this point, though. The ol' shack looks to've gone up like kindling."

The onlookers continued to multiply on the street-side of the corrals, but Billy noticed there was another group of ten or fifteen people on the other side of the corrals about fifty or so feet away from O'Dell's burning shack. They were standing in a circle, looking down at the ground.

"What d'ya suppose is going on over there?" Billy asked,

pointing toward the group. Hugo and Enos turned their eyes to where Billy indicated.

"Couldn't say," said Hugo, "but they sure are interested in somethin', aren't they?"

Enos agreed. "Let's see what's going on."

The three crossed the street and walked around the corrals. As they approached, a few of the group noticed them coming and stepped aside. Even though he no longer wore a badge, Hugo still had a certain effect on people.

Once the circle broke, it was clear what held their interest. Lying on the ground, his dead eyes staring up at the gray midday sky, was the body of Ben O'Dell.

CHAPTER TEN:
LITTLE TIMMY

"My God," said Enos, "what do we have here?"

Everett Bonham, the White Star's man in charge of the feed lot, jerked his chin toward a boy who looked to be maybe eleven or twelve years old. "Little Timmy here's the one who discovered the shack was starting to burn. He run in and found O'Dell on the floor and dragged him out before the fire really took off."

Hugo, Billy, and Enos stared down at the body; no one spoke a word. After a bit, Hugo flashed Billy a look that said maybe things weren't working out as well as they had thought.

"Come over here, Timmy," said Hugo, motioning for the boy to step out of the circle. The kid did as he was told, but he appeared reluctant. Hugo didn't have the best reputation among the youth of Casper, and the expression on the boy's face suggested young Tim's fondness for Hugo might be even flimsier than most. Hugo eyeballed Timmy as he walked over. Once he got there, Hugo gave the boy a closer inspection. "I know you, don't I?" It wasn't a question.

"You know my pa."

"Why, sure I do. You're a Tyson, aincha? Irving's kid."

The boy nodded.

"How's ol' Irv doin' these days?"

"Walks with a limp."

"Well, a-course he does," said Hugo. "A forty-four-forty slug to the thigh's bound to hamper a fella's gait for a while, I reckon."

"The doc says he'll always walk like that. Says he's lucky to be walking at all. Ma figures you didn't need to shoot him the way you done."

Little Timmy impressed Billy. There weren't many twelve-year-olds around willing to say so many words to Hugo all at once.

Hugo scratched behind his ear with the edge of a thumb, shook his head, and said, "Well, ever'body gets an opinion, I s'pose. 'Course, I should think your ma'd be glad I did it. As I recall, Irv had already knocked out a couple of her teeth right there in McGregor's store and had grabbed up an ax handle off a display rack and was fixin' to lay 'er low. If I hadn't shot 'im when I did, you'd be a little orphan boy now what with your ma all dead and your pa hung for murder. What d'ya think about that?"

Timmy didn't respond.

"Hell, son," Hugo went on, "I figured I was doin' her a big favor. Your pa, too, for that matter. I made it a point not to shoot 'im in any of his vitals."

Enos smiled and said, "Some people are never satisfied, no matter how careful you are when you shoot them."

Hugo continued without acknowledging Enos's observation. "Me comin' into McGregor's when I did was your whole family's lucky day." A tone of conviction filled Hugo's voice, but Timmy Tyson gave no sign of being convinced. Even so, Hugo moved on to another topic. "What brought you over here to Ben O'Dell's shack, anyhow, boy?" he asked.

"Mr. Carlson, the city clerk, told me to come and tell Mr. O'Dell to sober up and get to work."

"Is that so?"

"He gave me a nickel outta the city's till to do it, too." Timmy dug in his pocket and produced a coin for all to see.

"So when you got here," Enos asked, "what happened?"

The kid turned toward the shack. "Smoke was coming from a couple of holes in the roof up yonder, and there was smoke leaking out through the walls where the chinking was missing. I pounded on the door and called Mr. O'Dell's name, but there was no answer, so I pushed my way in, and there he was. The cabin was smoky as could be, and I couldn't see much, but he was close enough to the door that he was easy to spot. By then it was pretty hot in there. The far wall was burning all the way to the ceiling. I figured it'd be wasting time trying to wake Mr. O'Dell up, so I grabbed his ankles and dragged him outside. Once we were here, I saw he wasn't sleeping at all." Timmy aimed an index finger at the big smile Ben was wearing—the long, wet, red one beneath his chin.

Enos placed his hand on Timmy's shoulder. "You did well, young man." He dug into his own pocket and brought out another coin for the boy. "Here, this is for your trouble and keeping a cool head. Go buy yourself some candy."

By the look on Timmy's face, it was obvious this was the first time he had held so much money.

"Say, thanks, Mr. Woodard, I will. Heck, I might even buy some for my baby sister." He glanced over his shoulder at the inferno. "First, though, I think I'll stay and watch the fire for a while."

Billy could see little Timmy wasn't the only one interested in watching the fire. Half the town now filled the street in front of the corrals, and the scene had turned into a kind of carnival. The crowd cheered the firefighters as they drenched the White Star, the corrals, and the outbuildings, and a fresh round of applause broke out every time the pumper fired a blast of water. At one point, with a great crash, the roof of the shack collapsed into the building, and the crowd went wild with yahoos and hoorahs. Had it not been for the firefighters and their pumper, what could have been a real calamity for the town had turned into an impromptu party, and everyone was having a grand old time.

Everyone except for Billy and Hugo.

Billy whispered into Hugo's ear the same thing he had been asking off-and-on all morning. "What now?"

Hugo didn't turn to face him when Billy asked the question, and the expression on Hugo's weathered features never changed. He stared straight ahead and watched the flickering flames dance shadows across Ben's cold, dead face.

With a shrug, Hugo finally answered. "Now we best get ourselves ready for the worst."

Once the surrounding structures were hosed down enough to ensure there was no threat of catching fire from the few sparks still popping, the firemen again turned their pumper toward the shack—or what was left of it. By now, it had been reduced to little more than a mass of smoldering black logs that, when hit with water, hissed and steamed like oozing pots in the Yellowstone.

Even though things were calming down, people continued to flow toward the livery from every direction. Among them were Avery Sloane and Sloane's brother-in-law, Scott Parrish, Enos Woodard's business partners.

Enos spotted them and went over to chat. When he was gone, Billy asked, "You suppose we started this fire, Hugo? You lit that lamp, and you had a smoke. You dropped the cigarette right onto the floor, as I recall."

"We didn't start the fire," Hugo said.

Billy suspected Hugo was right. He remembered Hugo had made a point of stepping on the cigarette butt, and he believed Hugo blew out the lamp, although he wasn't sure of that.

"We didn't start it, but somebody did," said Hugo.

Billy expected Hugo was right. The fire was no accident.

"Who'd do it, though? And why?" He wondered out loud.

Hugo, who couldn't seem to take his eyes off the smoke and steam billowing into the chilly air, said, "I reckon the why depends on the who."

"My first guess'd be the killer," said Billy. "But it doesn't make much sense. If the killer was going to light it up, he'd've done it before he left in the first place."

"Maybe he would; maybe he wouldn't. Could be he got to thinkin' 'bout it later and decided to return to the scene of the crime, as they say. Maybe he figured he left some clue that'd lead to him gettin' caught, so he came back to take care of it."

"Did you see any clues, Hugo? You checked the place pretty close."

Hugo shook his head. "Nope, can't say as I did, but, then again, I could-a missed somethin'."

Billy wasn't sure he had heard the last part right.

"But I doubt it," Hugo added. "So far as I know, I ain't never missed a clue yet at any murder scene. Never. Not once in twenty long years."

There we go, thought Billy, with relief. *That's more like it.* For a second, he feared ol' Hugo might have had a stroke, or something.

Hugo pulled his eyes away from the fire and the firemen and looked at Billy. "It could-a been the killer who came back for whatever reason. It could-a been someone else who set it afire for reasons of their own." When Billy nodded at those possibilities, Hugo returned his gaze to the fire. "There is one thing botherin' me for sure," he said.

"What?"

"Whoever did it, likely saw you and me leavin'. The fire was too far along when young Timmy arrived and pulled Ben out for there to've been more than a few minutes between the time we left and the time it was set. So the fire starter had to be nearby when you and me was in the shack."

Even though being seen coming out of the shack was a possibility Billy had already considered, he didn't like the sound of it; and he wished he could argue with Hugo's logic. The whole thing happened fast.

Billy had an idea. "I'll be right back, Hugo," he said, and he crossed to where Timmy Tyson stood watching the show. "Timmy," he said, "let me talk to you a second."

"Okay." Again the kid was reluctant. Billy expected the boy spent most of his day trying to avoid adults. Today, though, he was having to talk to way more grown-ups than he liked.

Billy put his arm around Timmy's shoulder and led him away from the others to a spot where they could visit without being overheard. "When you first showed up at the cabin, did you, by chance, happen to see anyone come out? Anyone at all?"

Timmy shook his head. "No, sir."

"Were there people in the area? Around the feed lot or the corrals?"

A quizzical and impatient expression spread across the boy's features. Billy could tell Timmy wanted to be done with these people, watch the fire awhile longer, and buy his candy. "No," he said, "not really."

"What do you mean, 'not really'?"

"Well, no one came out of the cabin, for sure. And I didn't see nobody from the livery around—no workers and such. I reckon if they was, they would've noticed the smoke same as me."

Billy nodded and agreed.

"So, no, sir, there wasn't nobody around at all except for those two at the far end of the corral yonder, down by where the alley starts." He pointed toward the west. "There was a couple of folks down there."

"What were they doing?"

"Standing there watching me pound on the cabin door. I figured it was strange they didn't come over, what with the fire and all. They didn't even come over when they saw me drag Mr. O'Dell out."

"That is strange."

As Billy and the boy visited, Timmy kept turning to watch the fire. As with Hugo, it was difficult for him to pull his eyes away from the few remaining flames.

"Did you happen to know who these men were?"

"No, I never seen 'em before, but it wasn't two men."

"Oh, it wasn't?"

"No, sir. It was a man and a woman."

"Really?" Billy was surprised. "A man and a woman, you say?"

"Yes, sir."

"What did they look like?"

"Ohhh," Timmy said, squinting skyward as he searched his memory, "I didn't pay a lot of attention. Mostly, I was hammering on the door trying to wake up Mr. O'Dell." He shrugged and added, "And once I drug him outside, it was kind-a hard to look at anything but that big ol' gash on his throat."

"I bet," said Billy.

"I did notice the man was a real big fella. Not so big as you, maybe—not so tall, anyhow. But big, you know?" Timmy puffed himself up from his cheeks to his belly. He lifted his arms and flexed his muscles to the extent his thin limbs would allow. "He had a big chest," the boy said. "Big shoulders and arms. He looked like he could maybe pick up an ox."

"What about the woman?" Billy asked. "Did you notice anything about her?"

"Oh, I noticed her, all right." Timmy's adolescent eyes flashed. "She was pretty. About the prettiest thing I ever saw."

Billy smiled. "She was, huh? Can you tell me anything else

about her—or the man, either one? Was there anything in particular about them that stood out? Anything at all. How they were dressed, for instance?"

"How they were dressed?" Timmy repeated. Now it was Timmy's turn to smile. "They weren't dressed like you nor me. That's for sure."

"Why? What do you mean?"

"Well, sir, those two folks was Gypsies, Mr. Young. So a-course, they was dressed like the way them Gypsies dress. All earrings and bangles and scarves and such. Them two was a couple of Gypsies, all right. No doubt about it."

It took a second for what Timmy said to break through Billy's suddenly fuzzy brain. When it did, he crouched down on one knee, took the boy by the shoulders, and looked straight into his eyes. "Have you told anybody else what you just told me?"

"Nah, sir."

"Timmy, I'm serious. Have you told anyone? Anyone at all?"

"No, you're the only one. I swear."

"You can't. Do you hear me? You cannot tell anyone else. Do you understand?" When Timmy didn't answer the question right away, Billy tightened his grip on the boy's shoulders and gave him a little shake to make sure he had his attention. "Do you understand me?" Billy repeated.

Timmy's head bobbed and his eyes grew wide. "Y-y-yes, sir." Billy knew he had frightened the boy, and he felt bad about it, but Billy had to make sure Timmy understood this was serious.

After a bit, Billy loosened his grip but still held his eyes fixed onto Timmy's. "If you tell," Billy said, "bad things will happen. Very bad things. Do you understand what I'm saying?"

Again the boy's head bobbed, and though Billy could tell Timmy understood what Billy said about not telling, Billy doubted Timmy understood the reason why.

"If you tell, Timmy, people are going to die. Innocent women and children are going to be murdered."

Billy was about to ask the boy once again if he understood, but before he could pose the question, he was stopped short by a scream. The scream came from a man, but it was high-pitched, shrill, and piercing. Billy stood and looked back across the yard toward the shack. Standing next to the circle of onlookers around Ben's dead body was his brother, Thatcher O'Dell.

CHAPTER ELEVEN:
A BROKEN NOSE

Thatcher stood over his brother, and he let out another scream. This one was not so shrieking and full of surprise and panic as the first. It came in a deeper register from some low place, and it was full of pain and grief.

Thatcher dropped to his knees, lifted his younger brother to his chest, and rocked back and forth. Everyone watched, stunned into silence. Those who knew Thatcher best appeared even more stunned than the others. Folks were aware the O'Dell brothers shared a fondness, but such a display of emotion coming from Thatcher seemed far beyond his nature.

The firefighters shut down their pump, and they, too, watched as Thatcher held his dead brother and wept.

The crowd stood with their mouths agape and their hands jammed into their pockets.

Lester Warbler and another of O'Dell's cronies went to Thatcher. Lester bent down and said something Billy couldn't hear. Lester and the other man tried to help Thatcher up, but Thatcher shrugged them away. After a few seconds, Lester said something else, and Thatcher gently laid his brother down. Using both of his thumbs, he closed Ben's clouded eyes. Exhaling a long, woeful sigh, Thatcher placed a hand on Ben's chest, above his silent heart. He held it there for a moment and stood without assistance.

Once he was on his feet, he scanned the dumbstruck crowd. When he found the face he looked for, his puffy eyes narrowed.

He lifted his right hand and aimed a finger at Hugo Dorling.

Billy, who was now standing next to Hugo, sensed Hugo stiffen.

Thatcher started in their direction, and when he had covered half the distance, Hugo extended his left hand, perpendicular to the ground, indicating Thatcher should stop where he was. But Thatcher broke into a run and slammed into Hugo at full speed. He drove his shoulder into Hugo's gut, and both men went sailing. When they hit the dirt street, Billy heard a *whoosh* of air explode from Hugo's lungs. As Hugo gasped, Thatcher, who had landed on top, slugged him twice—a right cross and a left cross. *Wham. Wham.* Blood shot from Hugo's nose and mouth.

Billy started in their direction with the intent to pull Thatcher off, but he felt a hand on his upper arm, and he turned and saw Enos.

"Let them go at it," Enos said. "Maybe it's for the better. As long as there aren't any guns pulled, let's count ourselves ahead."

Billy wasn't sure letting them go at it was such a good idea. In the few seconds it took Enos to say those words, Thatcher hammered his fist into Hugo's face a couple of more times. But despite a score of four punches to zero, Hugo wasn't out of the game.

The older man lay flat on his back with Thatcher astraddle his chest. Thatcher was in a position to pummel Hugo at will, but before Thatcher could hit him again, Hugo placed his hands on either side of Thatcher's waist and lifted him up. As he struggled, Thatcher's legs extended straight out behind him, and his arms flailed. For a moment, the two men were parallel to each other, Hugo on his back and Thatcher above.

Billy was amazed Hugo could lift him. Thatcher was not a small man. It was hard to say how much he might weigh, but, like his brother, he was heavy with muscle, and his weight had to be considerable. Also, the angle was awkward, but Hugo made it look easy. He held Thatcher that way for a moment and flung him into the dirt. Before Thatcher stopped rolling, Hugo was up and on his toes.

Thatcher bounced a couple of times before he came to a stop. When he did, his back was to Hugo. As Thatcher was bent over, pushing himself to a standing position, Hugo rushed up behind him and kicked him between his legs. Hugo maintained if you had the bad luck to be in a fistfight, you should kick the other fella in the balls as soon, as hard, and as often as opportunity allowed. According to Hugo, it was a basic rule.

This time, though, Hugo must have missed the mark. Thatcher was knocked forward and again hit the dirt, but unhurt he leapt to his feet and charged Hugo. This time Hugo was having none of it. He began his swing when Thatcher was three steps away, and Hugo's punch was timed just right. His fist made contact with Thatcher's jaw while Thatcher was still in a dead run. The punch landed with the crack of a whip. Thatcher was knocked back five or six feet, but, wind-milling his arms for balance, he maintained his footing. He was stunned, though.

Billy considered the fight to be over, but Thatcher shook his head and squared his shoulders. Thatcher might be mean and he might be crazy, but the man could take a punch.

The rowdy spectators had grown quiet when Thatcher was beside his brother, but they now regained their voice. They yelled out boisterous guffaws every time a fist was thrown. Except for Thatcher's pals who stood in the front of the group, none of the onlookers took sides. The crowd cheered both men with equal vigor. They were having a great time. Barely two o'clock, and already they'd seen a fine fire and now a rip-roaring brawl.

Enos stood beside Billy, and Billy could see from the corner of his eye that Enos's partners, Sloane and Parrish, had moved back with the crowd. They were more reserved than the rest of the bunch, but they watched with obvious interest.

Thatcher now faced Hugo dead-on, but this time he didn't repeat his charge.

Thatcher lifted his right hand and rubbed the back of it along the left side of his jaw where Hugo's fist had landed. He spit a gob of blood into the dirt and let the hand drop next to his holstered Smith and Wesson.

Jerking his head in the direction of Ben's body, Thatcher said, "You did that, Dorling." He made the comment through clenched and bloodied teeth.

Hugo responded in a soft yet strong tone. "If you think so, Thatch, you're wrong. I know you're upset and sad about your brother. I can understand it. Any man would be." Hugo paused. Billy guessed Hugo was considering what he wanted to say next, weighing it in his mind, but it was impossible to know what Hugo decided—if he tempered his words or spoke his first thought—but what he said was, "You should not start somethin' you're not willin' to die for. I'd prefer not to kill you, Thatcher."

Thatcher barked a quick laugh. "Not two hours ago, Mr. Ex-Deputy, you made a mortal threat against me and my kin. As I recall, you said killing a couple of O'Dells would give you lots of pleasure."

Hugo nodded. "I did say it, Thatch; you're right. A-course we both know it was little more than a couple of fellas tradin' huff-and-puffs in the street. I didn't kill Ben. You need to believe me. But," he added, "if you force it, I *will* kill you. So, real slow now, take your hand away from your self-cocker, there, tuck your thumbs into the front of your gun belt, turn and walk away. Let's be done with it. There's been enough death for one afternoon."

"Like hell," said O'Dell, and his right hand jerked. So did

Hugo's; but before either could clear their leather, Hank Green, who had pulled his own shooter while Thatcher and Hugo talked, stepped from the crowd, and in a wide sweeping arc, brought the barrel down hard on the back of Thatcher's skull. Thatcher's eyeballs rolled northward while the rest of him headed south.

When Thatcher got brained, Hugo took on the sort of surprised expression a man of his experience rarely wore. He lifted his gaze from the unconscious O'Dell at his feet to the man who had laid him low. "You move like a cat, mister," Hugo said. "I never saw you comin'."

The taciturn Green didn't respond. He gave his Colt Army a quick twirl as he dropped it into its holster. The twirl wasn't Wild-West-Show fancy, but, Billy thought it was eye-catching the way he did it. Hugo snorted to communicate he wasn't impressed with any of it—the twirl or the cat-like maneuvering, either one. Billy didn't believe it, though. He had seen the surprised look on Hugo's face when Thatcher took a big bite of street.

Green turned and walked off in the general direction of Center. Billy guessed he was headed to the Half-Moon. All the excitement must have given the fancy dresser an urge for a drink.

As Green passed the crowd, he motioned for Lester and a couple of the boys to go fetch Thatcher.

Billy had his own urge for a drink. "I'm going to dig into your saddlebag, Hugo," he said as he crossed to their horses. Billy unbuckled Hugo's right-side bag, and lifted out the bottle of Kentucky. He pulled the cork and took a gulp, grimacing as he swallowed. Once it was down, he inhaled a deep breath, raised the bottle, and took another pull.

"Go ahead, boy," said Hugo with sarcasm. "Help yourself,

why don't ya?" Hugo was pretty close with his whiskey. He was willing to offer a fella a drink from time to time, but Hugo liked to be in charge of the bottle.

"Glad to," Billy said, ignoring Hugo's sarcastic tone. "I believe I will." He kept the bottle and took another slug, or at least he pretended to. He was not a skilled whiskey drinker, and on the third pull he didn't get any more in his mouth than, maybe, a teaspoon's worth. He might've taken more if only because Hugo was being snotty about it, but the first two belts had scalded his insides. He swallowed the little he held in his mouth, corked the bottle, and handed it to Hugo.

To Billy's amazement, rather than having a drink, Hugo shoved it back into his bag.

Hugo's nose and lip had stopped bleeding, but coagulated blood covered his chin. He dug into a hip pocket, pulled out a kerchief, and wiped the blood away the best he could. "Thatcher caught me with a few good ones there at first," he allowed.

Billy made no comment. He wished the Kentucky would hurry and do its work. Maybe it would help him think of how to tell Hugo the things he had to say.

"You don't figure he broke my nose, do ya?" Hugo asked, as he turned his profile toward Billy. "I've been in untold numbers of fights and fracases, and I've made 'er forty years without a busted nose nor a scar on my handsome face, neither one." He patted his cheeks. "I'd hate to start collectin' 'em now at this stage of life."

Without giving the nature of Hugo's injuries more than a passing glance, Billy said, "Your nose looks fine," and he jerked a thumb toward the boarding house. "Let's go have a seat on Mrs. Oliver's porch. We need to talk."

Hugo gave him a curious look. "There ain't nothin' to sit on over there but a glider. Don't you think it might look a little odd for two grown men to be swingin' on a porch together in broad daylight?"

Billy wasn't sure what daylight had to do with it. If it did look odd, he doubted it would look any less odd to swing together at night, but he wasn't concerned with appearances, and he certainly didn't want to get into one of Hugo's sideways discussions. What he wanted was to sit, and Mrs. Oliver's appeared to be a convenient and likely spot. He climbed the porch's three steps and plopped down on the swing. Its chains gave a plaintive squeal.

Hugo followed him onto the porch, but he didn't appear thrilled about it. As he sat next to Billy, he said, "Don't you try to hold my hand, now, you hear?"

"Stop talking, Hugo, and start listening for once in your life."

"Well, if you're gonna be impolite, I might go do my porch swingin' with some other fella." Hugo started to laugh, but Billy turned and gave him a look that cut the laughter short.

"We got us a problem," Billy said.

"You mean a bigger problem than Ben O'Dell layin' over yonder with his throat gapin' open for all the world to see?"

"I'd say the problem I'm talking about goes hand-in-hand with that one." Billy rubbed his stomach. He could feel the whiskey sloshing around in an uncomfortable way, but at the same time he could also feel it wending its way through the wrinkles in his brain, which Billy counted a fair trade. "Little Timmy didn't see you and me coming out of the cabin, nor anyone else, for that matter."

"Well, hell," said Hugo, "sounds like good news to me. I don't see a problem there, Billy."

"Don't start celebrating yet. Timmy told me he did see someone standing back away from the cabin at a spot over by the corrals."

"He did? Who?" Billy had gotten Hugo's attention.

"He didn't know who they were, but he did know *what* they were."

"What're you drivin' at, boy?"

"They were Roms."

That morsel of information took Hugo up short. "Oh, Lord," he whispered. "What were they doin'?"

"Nothing but standing next to the corrals down by the alley watching Timmy when he was pounding at the door calling Ben's name. When he pulled the body out of the shack, they were still there."

"How long'd they been there?"

"Hard to say. They were there when Tim arrived. They stayed at least long enough to watch him tug Ben out. I suppose they skedaddled once the bell started clanging and folks showed up to fight the fire."

"Any idea which of the Roms it was?"

Billy shrugged. "It was a man and a woman."

"A *woman*?"

Billy nodded. "Of course, he didn't know who they were, but he said the man was real big and the woman was real pretty."

"That don't narrow it down much, does it? Who else has little Tim told this to?"

"No one, he says. I told him he couldn't. I made it clear if he did, bad things were bound to happen."

"Do you think he'll tell?"

"I don't think so, but he's a kid. Who's to say what a kid'll do?"

They sat for a while in silence. Hugo turned his gaze to the street. Staring out at nothing, he started to talk, but at least at first, it was little more than meandering mutterings as Hugo thought out loud. "Thatcher's first conclusion when he saw the body was I killed Ben. I'm guessing he came to that mostly because I happened to be standing there, but thinking I'm his brother's killer won't satisfy him long. His second thought'll be it was the Gypsies. Once he lands on that, it will be enough to send Thatcher and his pals out to Gypsy Rock with guns a-blazin'." Hugo looked back at Billy. "And if folks in town hear there was a couple of Roms hangin' 'round Ben's shack at the time of the fire, it'd be proof enough to send some of them out to the Rock, too."

Billy had to agree. As it was, things were bad; if it got out there were Roms anywhere near the shack, things would get worse fast.

And there was more. Billy could only guess what the two Gypsies were doing at the shack, but he couldn't even begin to guess what the next thing he had to tell Hugo might mean. It was way too peculiar. "Something else strange happened during all of this too, Hugo," he said.

Hugo looked tired. "I figure I've had 'bout enough strange happenings for one day, thanks."

"Sorry to hear it, 'cause here comes one for you, anyway."

Hugo let out a groan.

"Hank Green didn't decide on his own to step from the crowd and knock Thatcher out."

"What d'ya mean he didn't decide on his own? What're you talkin' about?"

Billy turned on the glider and faced Hugo dead-on. Hugo's lip was swelling, and so was his nose. It could be the nose was broken, after all.

To Billy, Hugo's concern about a busted nose was silly. Billy couldn't see it would do much to harm Hugo's appearance. No one would describe him as an ugly man, but he sure wasn't the handsome devil he considered himself to be.

Billy stared into Hugo's weary eyes. He had brought this matter up, and he knew he had to answer Hugo's question. Mostly he hadn't answered yet because he didn't know what to make of what he had to say, or even how to begin to say it.

But Hugo didn't take well to Billy's sitting there staring at him. He leaned forward and focused on Billy's eyes. "What the hell're you lookin' at, boy? Are you starin' at my nose?" He brought both hands to either side of his nose and winced with the touch. "It is broke, ain't it? Tell me the truth now, goddamn it."

Billy ignored this question, and instead he dove into answering Hugo's first question about Hank Green. "When it was clear yours and Thatcher's fight was about to turn to gunplay, a fella standing in the crowd next to Green nodded toward Thatcher, and whispered something into Green's ear. Right afterwards, Green clouted Thatcher on the head."

Hugo's hands dropped to his thighs. "Hmph," he grunted. "You don't say? That is strange, ain't it? I never knew Hank Green to take orders from no one, not even Thatcher. Who was this fella who was doin' the ear whisperin'?"

"Avery Sloane."

Hugo's forehead wrinkled and his bushy eyebrows knitted together. "Sloane? How in hell would Sloane know a sneaky, ne'er-do-well, bastard like Hank Green?"

Billy didn't answer that question, either, but he wasn't ignoring it. He just didn't have an answer. He had been asking himself the same question ever since Green stepped from the crowd and did what he did.

CHAPTER TWELVE:
LONG DAY

Billy headed home. He had chores to do, and he wanted to do them before dark. After four o'clock, the sun dropped fast, and so did the mercury in the thermometer nailed to the barn's outside wall.

Hugo said he wanted to go to his rooms in the back of the small office on Durbin Street the U.S. Marshal provided and paid for. Hugo no longer had the right to occupy either the rooms or the office—a minor detail Hugo brushed aside. He said he needed to go there to wash off the blood, but Billy knew what Hugo wanted most was to get to his shaving mirror and check the condition of his swelling nose.

They agreed Hugo would ride to the ranch later in the evening, and they'd decide if they were going to visit Gypsy Rock then or wait until first light. They hoped they had some time to figure out the best course of action regarding the threat to the Gypsies. With luck, whatever was going to happen wouldn't occur right away. It would depend on Thatcher's health. Hank Green had hit him hard. Maybe he had hit him so hard Thatcher's vengeance against the Gypsies, Hugo, or both, might be delayed for a while.

When Billy rode through the yard at his place, he noticed the corral held two unfamiliar horses and a pinto he knew well. She belonged to an old friend. He dismounted, walked Badger into the barn, and squinted through the gloom. A man raking out a stall raised his arm and waved.

"*Hola,* Billy." Orozco Valdez, family friend and ranch foreman, stood at the far end of the barn.

"I'll be," said Billy. He trotted down to the man and shoved out his hand. "Rosco, you made it home. Thank goodness." The two men shook. "Nice to see you. How was your ride to Coahuila and back?"

"It was long," Rosco said, rubbing his rear end. "Very long. Pinta's back grows harder the older I get."

"You should've taken me up on the offer of a train ticket."

"I think my *nalgas* agree with you."

Billy slapped Rosco on the shoulder, and they shared a laugh.

Orozco came to work for Joshua Young, Billy's father, before Billy and Frank were big enough to sit a horse. Until then, Rosco had traveled the West working many jobs, but he and Josh became fast friends, and the young Mexican decided he wanted to put down roots. He had been with the Youngs ever since.

"How're the relatives doing?" Billy asked.

"They are good. My sister's five daughters are all growing to be great beauties."

For a while after Rosco started working for them, the Youngs were worried he might one day decide to return to his home in Mexico. They wouldn't have blamed him if he had; still, they wanted him to stay. But the Youngs' Casper Mountain ranch became Rosco's new home, and as long as he could visit Coahuila every year or so, he had no wish to return there to live.

"It's good to see you, Rosco. I've been mulling over an idea I might want to talk to you about."

"What is that?"

"Well, sir, it's sort of a business arrangement between you and me, but I haven't made up my mind for sure if I'm up for doing it. Let me give it a little more thought, maybe put a pencil to the idea, and we can sit down and talk about it more. I think it might be a good thing for both of us."

Rosco shrugged. "You know where to find me," he said with a smile. Almost as an afterthought, Rosco asked, "Anything new happening around here since I have been gone?"

Billy gave another laugh, though it was not so jovial as the one he had shared with Rosco a moment before. "A lot," he said. "You remember, a while before you left, there was a Gypsy woman murdered along the trail to the big rock southeast of the ranch out there?"

Rosco nodded. "I remember, yes. A bad thing."

Billy nodded. "Well, Hugo Dorling arrested her killer."

"Did he? Good for ol' Hugo."

"Well, I'm sad to say that's not the end of the story." Billy related all the news, starting with Connie telling Hugo that Ben was the killer and ending with the afternoon's events at the livery.

When Billy was finished, Rosco shook his head and said, "There is even more to the story."

"What?" Billy didn't understand.

"Come with me."

Rosco led Billy out of the barn. As they passed the corral, Billy said, "Say, I was going to ask you where you picked up those new horses. They're a couple of beauties. Did you bring them all the way up from Mexico?"

Rosco's only answer was to repeat what he said when they left the barn. "Come with me," and he headed toward the bunkhouse. Once they were inside, they walked to the back, where some ten years earlier two large rooms had been added for Rosco's living quarters.

"What's going on here, Rosco?"

Rosco opened the door and stepped in. He held the door open for Billy to follow. Sitting in one of the two old wing chairs next to Rosco's Ben Franklin was a man—a huge man. Sitting next to the man in the second of Rosco's wing chairs—the good one, the one he saved for company—was a young woman.

Billy had to blink a couple of times to make sure his eyes were working. The man was Baul Emaus, the foreman of the coppersmiths at Gypsy Rock. The woman was Deya Andree.

Billy made no attempt to hide his surprise. "Deya, Mr. Emaus, what are you doing here?"

Rosco answered for them. "When I got home this afternoon, they were waiting. The young lady said she needed to see you. It was cold, so I brought them in here."

Billy's eyes moved from Deya to Emaus. Noticing how Emaus's enormous frame filled the chair, something in Billy's head clicked. The click was almost audible.

"My, God," he said. "You were the ones at the livery."

Billy invited everyone into the big house. Rosco declined. He said he would finish the chores and go to bed early. It had been a long day on the trail. Billy looked back to the beginning of his own day. It, too, had been long. He remembered Hugo riding in and relating his horse-apple story about the nail thief, and it felt as though it had happened weeks ago, not a mere few hours.

The events of yesterday—the jury's verdict, the Thanksgiving dinner, and Hugo losing his job—might well have taken place in a previous life.

They sat at the kitchen table. Billy and Deya had coffee. Baul Emaus had nothing.

"Would you like something stronger than coffee?" Billy asked. "I have some fine Scotland whisky in the cupboard."

The big Rom stared at Billy for a full five seconds before he answered with a curt shake of his head. When he did, the gold ring dangling from his right earlobe danced against the line of his jaw.

Baul was quite a sight. The top of his head was covered with a bright blue bandana. Before they came into the house, he had worn a black fedora over the bandana. He now held the hat in his lap. Beneath his dark broadcloth coat was a green vest festooned with large, shiny buttons. The vest extended below his waist, and the buttons began at the vest's collar and ran down its entire length. Beneath the vest, he wore a white shirt decorated with some yellow and green nondescript design— large flowers and vines, maybe; Billy couldn't tell for sure. Even in the kitchen's flickering lamplight, the designs stood bright against the shirt's white background. On his feet were black, heavy-soled boots with tall shafts. The legs of his canvas pants were tucked into the shafts and billowed over the tops like the crust of a cobbler.

Billy was glad the big Gypsy declined the Scotch. He feared the mere smell of it might cause him to toss up all the Kentucky he had foolishly poured down his throat before leaving Casper. With a grimace, he considered the possibility of the coffee doing the same.

Deya was dressed as she had been that morning, except her coat was heavier than the one she had worn earlier.

Noticing she still wore the coat made Billy realize the room had cooled. When they first came in from the bunkhouse, he'd lit the cook stove to make the coffee, but now the flames in the firebox had burned down, and he tossed in a few more sticks. It wouldn't take long for the big black-and-chrome Keeley to beat back the chill.

Once the fire was going, he returned to the table and cupped his hands around the warm mug of coffee. He watched the feathers of steam rise from the dark liquid and admitted to himself he'd been stalling since they left the bunkhouse. As with Hugo earlier, Billy did not know how to begin an uncomfortable conversation.

Deya, though, had no such qualms. "You said we were the

ones at the livery today. Did you see us there?" she asked. Despite speaking a language not her native tongue, she was seldom at a loss for words.

"No," he said. "The boy who pulled O'Dell from the burning cabin told me two Roms, a man and a woman, were there."

"How did you know it was us?"

"He described the man as large—very large. And the woman as—" He dropped his eyes to his coffee. "—pretty." He didn't dare look at her, but he sensed her smile at his discomfort.

"You're right. We were there. We came to see Mr. O'Dell."

Billy had to ask the obvious question. "Why?"

"Because ever since we found out it was Ben O'Dell who killed Gwenfrei, he had been locked away in jail. We had no way to get to him."

Get to him?

Billy didn't like the direction the conversation was headed. He turned to Baul. "Why did you want to get to him?" He asked it of the big Gypsy because he assumed it was Baul Emaus who wanted to get to O'Dell, or had been ordered to get to him by Pov Meche.

Baul didn't answer; Deya did. "Because," she said, "we wanted to ask him why he had murdered our *Puri Dai.*"

Now it was Deya who dropped her gaze to her coffee. From the corner of his eye, Billy could see Baul's thick jaw muscles tighten.

"In all of this," Deya added, "that is what I want the most—to understand why Gwenfrei had to die."

Billy didn't doubt she and the big Rom wanted to ask Ben the question. But he also had no trouble imagining the enormous Gypsy sitting across from him cutting Ben's throat.

"When were you there?"

"When?" she asked, looking up.

"Yes. Hugo and I found Ben's body before the fire began.

Were you there before we were?"

He heard himself and cringed. He sounded harsh and accusatory.

"We were not there before you, Billy Young," said Deya. Billy could tell by her tone she was also answering the hidden question he had asked: *Did you kill Ben O'Dell?* He could also tell she did not like the accusation.

"How did you know O'Dell was staying in the livery shack?"

"We didn't. We followed you and the deputy when you left the camp this morning. I knew you were going to town to find O'Dell."

Billy wondered how she could have known. He and Hugo hadn't decided to do it until their ride into Casper.

As was her way, Deya got into his head and heard what he was thinking. "Perhaps you were making a joke, but I knew what you would do because you said you should go to town and check O'Dell's health."

Deya leaned back in her chair and took a sip of coffee. "Following you down the mountain was easy enough," she said, "but once we were in town, it was more difficult. We wanted to stay out of sight. Since Ben O'Dell had been set free by the jury, we were afraid people might think we were in town to do him harm."

Billy didn't say anything.

"So," she continued, "we kept to the alleys and back streets. We almost lost you once. We were able to follow you to the saloon, but we could not ride our horses around the streets of Casper. While you were in the saloon, Baul took the horses to the river and tied them in some trees. "We lost you after you talked to the men. But Casper is small, and we were lucky. We saw your animals tied in front of the big building with the offices. We were waiting next to the building when you came out, and we heard the old gentleman tell you to look for O'Dell in the shack behind the livery. We came into the alley behind the stable as you and the deputy came out and rode away."

"So you and Mr. Emaus saw us leave?"

She nodded.

"If you saw us," he said, "and you were still there when Timmy arrived, you must have seen—" Billy allowed his voice to trail off.

Deya finished Billy's sentence for him. "—the person who started the fire. Yes," she said, "we did. It was a man, a *Gaje*."

"Did you know the man?" Billy asked.

Deya looked at him as though he were stupid. "The Gajes I know in Casper—" She lifted her right hand and raised its thumb and index finger. "—you—" She lowered her thumb. "—and Deputy Dorling." She lowered her index finger.

Hugo liked to call him a smart aleck. Billy wondered what Hugo would think of Deya. She had some smart aleck in her, too.

He hesitated to ask another question, but he took the risk and went ahead. "If you saw this man again, would you recognize him?"

After some consideration, Deya said, "I don't know." She turned to her large companion and asked, "Would you?"

Appearing to give the question no thought at all, Baul shook his head, indicating he would not. Billy could tell that even if Baul might recognize the man, he wouldn't admit it to Billy. For some reason, Baul didn't trust him. Billy had no idea why. He had done nothing to this man, or any of the Roms. He cared about them. He had shown them nothing but friendship.

Billy turned toward the Gypsy and said, "You don't talk much, do you." He didn't bother to make it a question because he knew Emaus wouldn't answer anyway. And he was right. The Gypsy's only response was to stare.

"Does this fella speak English?" Billy asked Deya.

"He speaks English and four or five other languages."

Billy felt his eyebrows lift. Try as he might, he didn't know how to respond. He did wonder, though, if Baul never talked, how it would be possible for anyone to know how many languages he spoke.

"The man who started the fire came out of the shack and left," said Deya. "At first, we didn't realize the place was afire, so we started to go in, but before we got to the door, we saw smoke coming from the roof. Then the boy arrived, and we returned to the corrals and waited to see what would happen. When the boy brought out Ben O'Dell's body, we left, and hurried to the river for our horses."

"Why did you come here?"

"First we went to our camp to warn the *Kapo*—to let him know Ben O'Dell was dead. He was angry with us for going to town without telling him, but he was glad to learn what had happened to O'Dell, not only because it's what O'Dell deserved, but hearing about it gave the *Kapo* an early start at preparing the camp for what we all fear will come. Pov sent us here to your place. He hoped Deputy Dorling would be with you when you returned. The deputy might have suggestions on what we should do to protect ourselves."

"Hugo's coming," said Billy. "He'll be here soon, I expect."

Billy was surprised to hear Pov Meche didn't know beforehand that Deya and Emaus were going into town, and he asked her about it.

"He didn't know because I didn't tell him," she said.

"Why not?"

"He would never have approved. He would have considered it foolish to try to talk to a man like O'Dell. He would have forbidden my going."

Billy looked across the table at Baul Emaus. "I see Baul had no problem with your going."

"He did," Deya said. "He thought it was as foolish and pointless as Pov would have."

"Then why did Baul let you go?" It felt strange to Billy talking about the man when he was sitting there next to them.

"Because he knew he couldn't stop me. Since he couldn't stop me, he came along to protect me."

Billy knew, or thought he did, that if a man told a Gypsy woman she couldn't do something, she wouldn't do it. Billy assumed even the headstrong Deya would have to obey a man telling her not to do something, especially if he was telling her not to confront a killer. "Why couldn't he have stopped you, Deya? What would make him think he couldn't stop you?"

"Because he knows me so well." She reached over and clutched Emaus's massive forearm. "He's known me all my life." With a smile she said, "Baul is my father." Her smile grew a little wider, and she added, "By the way, Billy Young, he told me he thinks your intentions toward me are less than honorable."

CHAPTER THIRTEEN: HOUSE AND HOME

"My intentions are not—I mean, I don't—" Billy stuttered and babbled, but he couldn't make the words come out. Baul Emaus's sharp, steely gaze caused Billy's brain to seize up.

Before he was forced to sputter out something even more foolish, there was a knock at the front door.

"I'll go and see . . ." As he rose, he started to explain but decided to let it drop. And with relief, he got the hell out of the kitchen.

When he opened the door, Hugo stood on the porch with a carpetbag in one hand and a leather satchel in the other. His saddlebags were thrown over his shoulder. His rifle was under one arm, and beneath the other arm was a rolled-up canvas that Billy assumed held Hugo's sawed-off. The man was a strange sight, but Billy was glad to see him. Hugo's well-timed arrival allowed Billy to put some distance between himself and Baul Emaus.

"Hugo, what're you doing?" Billy asked, opening the door wider so Hugo could fit through with his gear. "It looks like you're toting around all your worldly possessions." Billy took the satchel and carpetbag, carried them into the parlor, and dropped them in the corner.

Hugo followed and piled what he carried next to the two bags. "I *am* totin' all my possessions, ever'thin' I own, 'cept for my horse, which I put in the stall next to yours, if it's all right."

"It's fine, but what's this all about?"

"Well, sir, when I went back to my rooms, I found all my stuff packed and settin' out in the hallway. All the locks had been changed, too. Even the windows was bolted up." If Hugo knew the windows were bolted, Billy figured the old buzzard had made an effort to bust into the place.

"Looks like someone might be trying to send you a message, Hugo."

"Yes, sir, the someones bein' a bootlickin' marshal and a two-bit judge. Mind if I bunk here awhile?"

"Sure. You can stay as long as you like. I'll put you in Frank's old room."

Hugo took off his hat and scratched the scalp beneath his coarse hair. "I feel the urge for some coffee," he said. "Can you help me out there? I don't mind tellin' ya, kid, I'm beat. I am plumb wore out."

Billy believed it. Finding Ben's body, getting into a fistfight, almost getting into a gunfight, and being kicked out of his rooms looked to have taken a heavy toll.

"I got a fresh pot brewed," said Billy. "Come on in the kitchen." Since there was no way to avoid Deya and Emaus, Billy was pleased he didn't have to return to the kitchen alone.

When Hugo saw the Gypsies sitting at the table, he perked up. "Well, well," he said, "what've we got here?"

Deya smiled. "Hello, Deputy Dorling."

"Like I said before, girl, I ain't a deputy anymore, so call me Hugo." Hugo slapped Baul on the shoulder, pulled up a chair next to him, and took a seat. "Hey, there, Baul."

Billy knew Hugo had spent considerable time in the Gypsy camp over the course of his investigation into Gwenfrei Faw's death and had gotten to know a number of the Roms pretty well. One of them must have been Emaus.

"Sorry I didn't get to visit with you when I was at the Rock this mornin'. How've ya been, you scallywagglin' ol' giant?"

Baul eyed Hugo closely. "Better than you."

At last, Billy had proof the man could talk.

"Why do you say that, Baul?"

"Because my nose isn't broke."

Hugo smacked the table with the flat of his hand and shot to his feet. "My nose. By God, my damned nose." He headed to the mirror hanging in the hallway between the kitchen and the parlor—a mirror, which, to Billy's amazement, Hugo had neglected to look into when they'd passed through the hall a moment before. "What with bein' evicted from my house 'n' home, I done forgot about my poor nose."

Billy watched from the stove as he poured Hugo a cup of coffee. He had seen the vain Hugo look into mirrors before, and it was always an entertaining show. Hugo took great pride in the preening of what he called his "handsome moustachios." In Billy's opinion, what Hugo described as "handsome," most folks would describe as nothing more than big and bushy. The same went for the shaggy plumage of Hugo's eyebrows. This time, though, watching Hugo in front of the mirror provided no cheer.

"Ah, no," Hugo groaned when he got a look at himself. "You're right, Baul, she's busted for sure."

Billy knew it was true. The red, swollen nose exhibited a distinct list to starboard. The flesh beneath both of Hugo's eyes was a light purple, and caked blood still covered his whisker-stubbled chin. As Hugo stared at himself, his shoulders sank— drooped like a couple of windless sails—and he gave off another pitiable groan.

"Here," said Baul, standing, "let me look." The Gypsy crossed to the hall, and Hugo turned toward him. Looking down into Hugo's face, Baul put his left hand on the back of Hugo's neck, reached up with his right hand, and in a wink gave the nose a quick snap. It made a cracking noise loud enough for Billy to hear from across the room.

"*Jesus Christ,*" screamed Hugo. "Are you nuts?" Hugo's hands flew to his face. "You big blockhead. You could give a fella some warnin' before you start crankin' on his nose, goddam it."

"Watch your language, Hugo," Billy said. "There's a lady present, you know." Billy made this pronouncement even though the very lady whose sensibilities he was trying to protect was struggling to stifle her laughter.

Baul returned to his chair and sat down. For the first time ever, Billy saw the man smile. All the while, Hugo continued to cuss, stomp his foot, and hold his nose, which now leaked a trickle of blood that puddled in his handsome mustache.

Billy exhaled an exhausted breath, and as he rejoined the Gypsies at the table, he told himself, *Seems we all are having a very long day.*

Once Hugo's tantrum subsided, he made his way across the kitchen and pumped water into a pan. He washed his face, taking particular caution around his puffy nose, and returned to the table. Billy had set the coffee at Hugo's place next to Baul, and Hugo lifted the cup and took a sip. He cringed a bit when he did. Billy figured there was also a cut or two inside Hugo's mouth from the punches Thatcher O'Dell had meted out.

Hugo looked better now since he had cleaned up, and his nose, after Baul's ministrations, pointed more or less straight ahead.

"I'm gonna sit here next to you, Baul," Hugo warned, "but you keep your hands to yourself. If I need any doctorin', I'll let someone besides you know about it."

As Hugo drank his coffee, Billy told him Deya and Baul were the people Timmy had seen at the livery, and they had seen the man who set the place on fire.

Hugo showed his surprise. "When little Timmy said he'd

spotted a couple of Roms out there," Hugo said, "I figured *they* were the ones who put a match to the place." Neither Deya nor Baul responded. Eyeballing him over the rim of his cup, Hugo asked Baul straight out, "Did you kill Ben O'Dell?" He asked it in the same tone he might have used if he was inquiring whether Baul had eaten eggs for breakfast.

"I did not, but I would have, except for the harm it would have brought to the camp."

"Do you think someone else in your group mighta kilt 'im?"

"None of us killed him," answered Deya. "But people will believe we did." Frustration and fear settled into her voice. "I think we should leave this place. I think we should leave here tomorrow."

Billy said the group could not move fast enough if someone wanted to catch them.

"Plus," said Hugo, "where'd you go, anyhow? South Pass is your only route through the high country, and it's under God knows how many feet of snow right now."

"And," Billy added, "it will be for the next six, maybe seven months."

Hugo shook his head. "Nah, young lady, you ain't gonna be goin' over them mountains before May at the earliest. You could head to Lander or the Reservation, I suppose, and hide out."

"Not far enough," said Billy.

"No," Hugo agreed. "I reckon not."

"We should have kept going last summer," Deya said. But Billy knew the Roms had stopped at the Rock because they were short of both supplies and the funds necessary to buy them. They needed to sell their wares and make their trades with the Casper folks in order to continue their journey. When they'd been forced to stop, it hadn't appeared to bother the Gypsies, though—at least not at the time. Hurrying anywhere was not their way. Wherever they were headed would be there when they arrived.

Hugo rolled a cigarette and offered his makings to Baul, who rolled one for himself. "I'm thinkin' we're gonna have at least a couple of days before Thatcher's able to do anybody any harm. He was still out cold when I left to go to my rooms." Hugo fired up a match and lit both their smokes.

"Maybe he was dead," said Billy. "Anybody think to check his pulse?"

Hugo gave Billy the sort of look the comment deserved. "Folks was tendin' to 'im the best they could, but he wasn't comin' 'round. One of the firemen sent Timmy to fetch the doc. I left before the doc got there, so I couldn't say how it all turned out. But I gotta think takin' a whack with the barrel of a gun's gotta keep a fella's brains rattlin' for a while."

"Did Avery Sloane stick around?" Billy asked.

"No, I don't believe he did. He and Parrish corralled Enos, and the three of 'em went off together."

"I can't figure why Sloane would tell Green to stop Thatcher," Billy said. "Why would he care what Thatcher did? It is a puzzlement."

Hugo nodded in agreement but said nothing.

"Maybe he figured he was saving your life," Billy joked. He didn't think for a second Thatcher O'Dell could kill Hugo in a straight-on gunfight. Still, Billy couldn't resist rubbing it in. "Yes, sir, I betcha that was it. I hear ol' Thatch is mighty handy with his shooter."

Hugo refused to take the bait.

"There's lots-a questions here. I expect if we could figure out who the fella was Deya and Baul saw comin' outta the shack right before it burst into flames, that'd go a long ways toward answerin' some of 'em." He turned to Deya. "Did you notice anythin' about him that was unusual? Somethin' that might help identify the man?"

"No, it happened fast. The door opened, and he was out and gone. But from what we could see, there was nothing special about him, really. He was average size. He wore a dark hat and a long overcoat." She shrugged. "Sorry. I know it doesn't help."

"Whoever he was," said Hugo, "he's gotta be feelin' some disappointment."

"Why? What do you mean?" Billy asked.

"Well, sir, he set the fire for a reason, and the only reason I can figure is to keep the world from knowin' Ben had been murdered. Then little Timmy came along and foiled his plan."

"He set the fire to keep people from knowing O'Dell had been murdered, because he's the one who killed him," said Deya.

"You might be right," agreed Hugo, "but while Billy and me was watchin' the place burn, Billy wondered if the killer lit 'er up, why didn't he do it at the time he did the killin'? I've been thinkin' about it ever since he said it, and I've decided young Billy here's got it right. If the killer wanted to burn the place down, he would-a done it right after he cut Ben's throat. No, sir, our fire starter wasn't the killer, but for some reason, he wanted Ben's death to look like an accident."

"Got any ideas why that might be, Hugo?" Billy asked.

"Well, ever'body'll figure it was a Gypsy who killed 'im, so maybe he was tryin' to protect the Gypsies."

Deya gave a soft laugh of disbelief. "It was a *Gaje* who came out of the shack, and no *Gaje* would try to protect a Gypsy."

"You're a possible suspect too, Hugo, and so am I, maybe," Billy said. "Could be someone's trying to protect *us*."

"The only person who might think you or me killed Ben O'Dell'd be Thatcher O'Dell, and he doesn't believe it neither, not really. I expect he does blame us for some of what's happened since we was the fellas who caught Ben and brought 'im in, but Thatcher doesn't figure we did the throat cuttin'. No, once he comes out of his stupefaction, he'll be directin' his hate and anger to no one else but those poor souls at Gypsy Rock."

Chapter Fourteen:
It'd Be Nice to Know

Billy asked Hugo to go to the bunkhouse to see if Rosco wanted something to eat. "But he might be sleeping," Billy added. "If he is, don't wake him. He had a long ride today, and he might've already turned in."

While Hugo went to the bunkhouse, Billy went to the spring-house and came back with some paraffin-wrapped cheese and a small crock of butter. He placed the butter and cheese on the table and stepped into the pantry next to the kitchen and brought out a smoked ham. He took the ham to the counter and cut off a dozen or so slices. He tossed them onto a platter and put the platter on the table next to the cheese. On his return to the pantry to put the ham away, he said, "Deya, there's bread in the biscuit box yonder." He nodded in the direction of his mother's oak buffet set against the kitchen's far wall. "Would you grab a loaf and bring it over? There's a knife in the top drawer."

Billy came back into the kitchen wiping his hands on a large cotton cloth. "I baked the bread a couple of days ago," he said. "I hope it's still passable."

Deya, who was at the table cutting the loaf into three-quarter-inch slices, said, "It looks good. You are quite the hand around the kitchen."

Billy shrugged. "Our ma died at a young age. Pa, my brother, and I learned to make do."

The front door opened and closed, and Hugo came in, this

time stopping in the hallway to check himself in the mirror. He didn't appear pleased with what he saw. "I rapped on Rosco's door," he said, "but there wasn't any answer, so I figured he must be-a sleepin'."

Billy put four plates on the table and refilled everyone's coffee cups. As he returned the pot to the stove, he said, "Dig in, folks. It's not much, but it'll do, I guess." He brought over knives and forks and handed them out. He used the knife he kept for himself to cut into the paraffin-encased cheese. "A while back, my brother made a bunch of cheese and waxed it up. I tell you, I love this stuff." He peeled the paraffin away and sliced enough for everyone.

With a wince, Hugo rubbed the side of his face and said, "Thanks to Thatcher, I ain't sure my jaw hinges're workin' quite right." He jabbed his fork into a slice of ham, "But this all looks so good, I wouldn't dare pass 'er up."

After they'd settled into eating, Deya said, "Now, with O'Dell dead, I guess we'll never know the reason Gwenfrei died. It could be he did it for no reason other than who she was—*what* she was—but I don't think so."

Part of Billy had to agree. Ben was scum, for sure. He was a sot, a thief, a liar, and a bully. He had killed a fella in a barroom gunfight a couple of years before. Billy didn't know the man he killed. He was a saddle tramp who had the poor judgment and bad luck to get drunk at the Half-Moon and start something with Ben, who was equally drunk. All the witnesses, of course, agreed the stranger started it and made their war of words into something more serious. And Billy suspected he was not the first man Ben had killed. Still, even with his bad character, it was hard to picture Ben being upset enough with an old woman to shoot her down for no apparent reason. If Ben hadn't admitted doing it, Billy would've found it difficult to believe.

Deya looked at Hugo. "You say it was O'Dell's girlfriend who put you onto him in the first place?"

"That's right. Connie Baxter."

"How did you get her to do such a thing?"

"Didn't. She came to me."

"We suspect," offered Billy, "Ben made for a poor swain."

"What did she tell you about it?"

"That Ben'd bragged to her about doin' it."

"Did he tell her why he did it?"

"No, not really," Hugo said. " 'Bout what you'd expect, I reckon. You know, *The old woman was spendin' too much time 'round town. She didn't know her place. Sneaky ol' Gyp.* The sorta blatherskite you're apt to hear come out of a moron like Ben O'Dell."

Hugo broke off a piece of his cheese, lifted it toward his mouth, but stopped his hand halfway up and let it drop to the table. Staring at the cheese he held between his thumb and index finger, he said, "I never questioned her much. Lookin' back, I reckon it would've been a good idea to find out a little more about his reasons for doin' it." He lifted his eyes. "When she said he was holed up at the old stage station, I wanted to get there quick before he left. Plus, I didn't figure Connie'd be goin' anywhere. Turns out, I was wrong. She left my office and hightailed it direct to the train depot and was on the next train headed south. I'm thinkin' by the time Billy here had me talked into lettin' him come along and we had our gear 'n' such all collected, Connie Baxter was outta Casper before we were."

"Why *then*?" asked Deya. "When she told you, it had been over a month since Gwenfrei was murdered. Why would she tell you then, I wonder, after she'd already waited so long?"

"Maybe Ben didn't admit it until the day she looked Hugo up," Billy said.

Deya nodded. "Still, it's odd she'd tell you at all. It was a big risk for her to cross the O'Dells, especially for a *mere Gypsy*."

"People like the O'Dells are one thing," said Billy. "But it could be, Deya, most folks don't dislike the Romani as much as you figure they do."

Both Deya and Baul gave him a look of disbelief.

"It could be, Billy," Deya countered, "you are wrong. It could be they do dislike the Romani that much." She spoke in a flat, unemotional voice, which suggested Billy had no idea what he was talking about. She said it in a voice filled with resignation—the sort of resignation stemming from a lifetime—many lifetimes—of experience, and not merely here in the West, but beyond the West, beyond America, beyond oceans and continents. A resignation gained, not in years or decades, but generations. Millennia.

Billy sat straighter in his chair, cleared his throat, and said, "You're right. Could be I am wrong. Sorry."

The four of them sat for a few moments, eating without speaking.

Billy buttered a slice of bread and cut the slice in two. "It is true, though, Gwenfrei spent more time in town than any of the rest of you did, right?"

"Yes."

"Telling fortunes and such?"

Deya nodded and took a sip of coffee.

"At least some of those folks whose fortunes she was telling were women in the Lutheran Women's League?"

Again, Deya nodded.

"But you can't tell us who in particular?"

"Billy, we had this conversation by the creek this morning, remember?"

"I know, but some things've changed since then."

Deya seemed to consider that, and said, "I don't know any names. There was something about what she was doing in town, though, that bothered her."

One of Hugo's bushy eyebrows popped up. "What d'ya mean?" he asked.

"It's hard to describe, but the last couple of times she came back from Casper, she acted concerned. It wasn't something obvious, I guess. I never said anything to her about it. I'm still not sure it was anything more than my imagination. Still, since her death, I can't stop wondering."

"Do you know how many women she was seeing?" Billy asked.

"Not for sure. There were a couple she saw more often than the others, I think."

"You mean she was telling the same people their fortunes more than once?"

"Of course."

Billy was surprised. He couldn't understand why anyone would need to have his future read more than once. After you found out what lies ahead, what more is there to it?

He pointed out his thinking to Deya.

"Gwenfrei had skills. And not only as a *Chovihani.*"

"What do you mean?"

"Those who seek the help of a *Chovihani,* of course, want to hear what the *Chovihani* might tell them about their futures. But many times those people not only want someone who will talk to them; they also want someone who will listen. Gwenfrei Faw was very good at listening."

Hugo, despite saying how tasty the food looked, had eaten only a few bites. He pushed his plate away and leaned over the table toward Deya. "Are you thinkin' one of these folks who Gwenfrei Faw was seeing more often than she was seein' the others might-a been tellin' her things that got your ol' *Purree Die* upset?"

"I think so. She did tell me there was one who had many, many troubles. She felt bad for the woman."

"Well," said Billy, as though making a list, "we'd like to know who the man was who started the fire. There has to be some connection between the goings on around here and that fella. Also," he added, "I'd like to know who the folks were Gwenfrei Faw was seeing in town, especially the one or two you say she was seeing more than the others. There may not be any connection there to any of this, but it'd be nice to know."

Billy offered Deya and Baul a place to sleep for the night, but they declined. They wanted to get back to the camp before sunset.

As Billy and Hugo walked them out, Deya said, "We need to tell the *Kapo* there is a threat from Thatcher O'Dell for sure, but very little threat tonight, and perhaps we will have a day or so to prepare for when he comes."

They stopped in the entry before stepping outside.

"How're you folks at the Rock fixed for guns, Baul?" asked Hugo.

The big man shook his head. "Not much. A few rifles we use for hunting. Winchesters mostly. There's an old Henry I think still works. There are maybe a hundred, two-hundred rounds of ammunition. We have a couple of shotguns we use for birds. Not many shells, and whatever shells we have, they're bird shot."

"How many people're in your group out there?"

"Twenty-seven, counting the women and children. Fifteen males from thirteen up to early seventies."

"Tell Pov I'll be out to visit 'im 'round first light. We need a plan."

Baul nodded. His usual stoic demeanor now showed worry and concern. "Thank you. I will tell him."

Hugo, continuing to talk to Baul, turned toward Billy as he said, "If it's all right with Billy, I'll bring some of his weapons out to the camp when I come."

"Sure," Billy said. "Everything I have is in the cabinet over there." He jerked his head in the direction of the large gun case in the parlor. "You're welcome to take whatever you need. There are, I suppose, six or eight handguns, mostly Colt Armies. They're all shooting forty-four-forties, except for my short-barrel forty-five. Leave it. There are three or four boxes of shells in the cabinet, too. There are a couple of shotguns, twelve gauges, and shells, too. You probably ought to take them along.

"As for rifles, we've got mine and Frank's Marlin Eighty-Ones. Leave the one on the right; that one's mine. There are four Winchesters, all Seventy-Threes, I think. Could be one of them's a Sixty-Six. They vary in age, but they're in good shape. They're shooting forty-four-forties as well."

"Thank you, Billy," said Hugo. "That's mighty generous. And we'll take good care of 'em, too, you bet, and get 'em back to you safe 'n' sound."

Billy knew Hugo couldn't make that promise; it all depended on how bad things got and how they went once they did go bad. He felt a cringe at his bad-luck thought, and he shoved it from his mind as soon as he had it.

Baul, too, nodded a quick thank-you. It wasn't much, but it communicated Billy might have gone up half a notch or so on Baul's measuring stick. Certainly no more.

"If you don't mind, Billy. I'll haul them guns over in your buckboard when I head to the Rock in the morning."

"Sure."

They all stepped out to the porch, and Billy said to Deya, "I'll give you a hand saddling up." Deya and Baul had stored their tack in the barn, and Billy started in that direction.

"No, I can do it. Go back inside. It's cold out here." A chill had settled into the late-afternoon air. Deya pulled her coat around her shoulders and buttoned it to her throat.

The soft hoot of an owl drifted from the barn, and an instant later the large bird swooped cross the yard and out toward the field beyond the fence. When the owl passed, Deya and Baul exchanged a nervous look, and the big Gypsy said, "We must go."

Deya gave her father a quick nod of agreement, and as they stepped from the porch, she asked Billy, "Will you be coming tomorrow morning with Hugo?"

Baul stiffened, but Billy pretended not to notice.

"I'll come at some time. After chores, I'm going into town."

"Why?"

"I want to meet with Edith Baldwin."

"Edith Baldwin? Who is she?"

"Well, if you were to ask her, she might tell you she's the Queen of Casper. Really, though, she's President of the Lutheran Women's League, which around here I reckon is about the same as a queen."

CHAPTER FIFTEEN:
SQUATTERS. INTERLOPERS. FOREIGNERS.

Having Rosco home made things easier. In the winter the chores weren't as burdensome as every other season of the year, but, even so, having help was a luxury. After the morning chores were done, Billy and Rosco hitched a team to the buckboard and pulled it in front of the house.

"Come on in, Rosco. I'm going to wake that loafer, Hugo, and after I scrape some of this dirt off me, I'll fry some eggs and whip up some gravy."

Rosco liked the idea, and they both went inside. As Billy headed for the stairs, Rosco said, "I'll put on coffee."

"Make it strong," said Billy. "Hugo likes his coffee full-bodied." Taking the steps two at a time, he added, "We'll be down in a jiff."

Billy pounded on Hugo's door as he went by. "Wake up, old-timer. Rosco and I have already done a job-a-work while you dreamed of Denver dancing girls."

"I'm awake, goddamn it," Hugo called back. "Stop poundin'." He must have peeked out the window. "Hell, boy," he said. "It's still dark outside."

"You told Baul you'd be at the camp at first light, so get moving or I'll come in there and douse you with water. There are things to be done."

Billy heard Hugo mumble something. He couldn't make out what it was, but by its rhythm and tone, it sounded profane.

Billy hadn't bothered to heat any water. The water in the

145

basin in his room, though chilly, was clean and would do. He washed up and brushed his teeth. He even dragged a comb through his cowlick, which was not a thing he did every day. Once he had donned a clean shirt and a fresh pair of jeans, he went down the hall to his parents' old room. He dug in the chiffonier and found one of his pa's vests. Josh Young always wore a vest. He said he didn't feel all the way dressed without it. Billy, though, rarely wore one. A vest's extra pockets sometimes came in handy, but Billy figured a vest wasn't good for much else, except maybe decoration. Vests sure didn't do anything to ward off the cold on a windy Wyoming November morn. But today was special, and the vest he lifted from his father's still neatly folded clothes was made of a supple brown leather with tortoiseshell buttons. Pa had been fond of this one, and so had Billy.

Billy missed his father most at times like this, when things were dire or looking to become so.

He pulled the vest on and stepped back to see himself in the mirror above the chiffonier. The vest was fine, and no matter how hard he tried, Billy doubted he could make himself look any better. With a shrug and a smile, he told himself he had only so much to work with.

Still, he hoped this would do. A fella needed to look his best when he went before the queen.

By the time Billy, Hugo, and Rosco got everything cleaned up, and the buckboard loaded with Billy's small arsenal, it was a quarter of eight, a half-hour after sunrise.

"What're you plannin' to accomplish in town, Billy?" Hugo asked as he tied his bay to the back of the buckboard.

"Like I said yesterday afternoon, I want to find out who these women were Gwenfrei Faw was seeing."

"Well, go ahead, but I doubt you're gonna run across many

Lutherans willin' to admit to havin' their fortunes tol' by a Gypsy."

"Could be," agreed Billy. "It couldn't hurt to ask, though. Besides, maybe I can discover what's going on with Thatcher and what the mood of the town is."

"I expect the mood of the town is all *het* up," Hugo said. "That's what it is. It's one thing when a couple of cowpokes shoot each other on a drunk Saturday evenin'. It's altogether another kettle of fish when some citizen gets his throat sliced open in the dark-a night by some unknown attacker. It's enough to jangle any town's nerves, even if the citizen gettin' kilt is the likes of Ben O'Dell. The town's gonna want someone to pay, and I doubt they'll care who picks up the tab."

Billy hoped Hugo was wrong. Billy liked to look on the bright side. Finding a bright side was not always easy, but he hoped to avoid becoming a cynical, bitter old man like Ex-Deputy Dorling.

"*Oye*, Billy," Orozco called as he led Billy's gray out of the barn, "I threw your saddle on Badger. It's good to see the young rascal. It has been a while."

Billy took Badger's reins from Rosco and gave the horse's muzzle a rub. "Did he remember you, Rosco?"

"Sure, he did," Rosco said, and gave a gentle smack to the horse's rump. "We are best of friends."

Hugo walked to the front of the wagon, climbed aboard, unwrapped the reins from the brake lever, and asked, "When do you suppose you'll be out to the Rock?"

"Soon as I can," Billy answered. "I doubt it'll take too long, especially if you're right about no Lutherans wanting to fess up."

Billy mounted Badger. "I'll follow you out," he said.

Billy and Hugo bid farewell to Rosco and rode together

without talking until they were outside the gate where the trail split.

"I ain't sure I like you goin' into town alone like this," Hugo said.

"Ah, don't be a fretter, you ol' coot. It's you everybody hates, not me. Besides, I can take care of myself."

Hugo agreed. "I know you can, boy. I know." Hugo looked away from Billy and out toward the east and the dull yellow blot of sun hanging behind thick, gray clouds. He exhaled a long, steamy breath, shrugged, and said, "Still . . ." But he stopped there. Whatever he was thinking, he didn't put to words.

"I'll be fine, Hugo; don't you worry. You get over to Gypsy Rock and figure out how we can help those Roms."

Billy spun the gray and aimed the horse's nose toward the city of Casper.

Billy stopped at the Baldwin house outside of town, but no one was home. Owen Baldwin worked long hours as a train engineer, so Billy assumed the man was out on a run. He wasn't sure where he might locate Mrs. Baldwin. He decided the grocery or the bakery or Casper's one-and-only dress shop would be likely places to begin his search.

As he rode through town, Billy passed O'Dell's shack. It had stopped smoldering, but what little remained of its charred logs extended from the frozen earth at weird, grotesque angles, like the broken fingers of some buried-alive giant clawing his way out of a grave.

Seeing the place reminded Billy of the gaping gash across Ben O'Dell's throat. With that in mind, he tapped Badger with his right spur and picked up the pace.

As he rode deeper into town, he noticed how quiet things were—very quiet for a Saturday morning. There was scarcely anyone around.

He turned onto Center Street—a more respectable stretch of Center than the one Hugo liked to frequent—and spotted a fella stepping out of the Drug and Stationery Emporium.

" 'Scuse me, mister." Billy trotted his horse over to the sidewalk. Looking down at the man, he asked, "What's going on around here? Where is everybody?" He made a motion toward the empty street.

"Well, suh, I could not know fo-wah positive, but I suspect ev'ryone's ovuh to the Community Room."

Billy didn't know this fella, but it was clear that he was from well below the Mason-Dixon line.

"Why's that? Somebody having a party or something?"

"Sorry, all I know is when I arrived by ray-yul late yesterday afternoon some fellahs were going uppen down the streets on the back of a waggin shouting through a large megaphone, encouraging the citizenry to attend a meeting at the Community Room at nine-a-clock this mahnin'." He glanced around. "And it appears that's what folksuv done, du-zenit?"

Billy nodded. "Yes, sir, it sure does." He tapped the brim of his hat. "Thanks for the information."

The man provided a gracious smile. "At your suh-vis, suh."

A Southern gent through and through.

Billy couldn't imagine what kind of meeting the town might be having, but he had a bad feeling about it. He rode to the Community Room, and judging by the number of horses, wagons, and carriages out front, a good number of people were in attendance.

He tied the gray at a crowded hitching rail in front of the hardware store a couple of doors down from the CR. He checked his watch and saw it was a little short of a quarter past nine.

Inside, folding chairs were lined in rows rather than around tables as they had been on Thanksgiving. Not all of the chairs were occupied, but a fair number of folks were standing against the back wall. Those in attendance were mostly men, although there was a sprinkling of women and children, especially in chairs toward the back.

Down front was Lester Warbler and his friends. To Billy's dismay, sitting next to Warbler was Thatcher O'Dell. A strip of bandaging encircled his skull like an Arapaho headband, but instead of an eagle feather tucked in back, there was a huge, gauzy bandage.

Billy knew most everyone in the place to one degree or another. Some of those he made eye contact with nodded and smiled. Some shook his hand. Others were standoffish. Billy's and Hugo's fondness for the Roms was common knowledge, which did not endear them to some folks these days.

In one of the lower rows on the left sat Enos and his sister Stella. Neither of his business partners, Sloane or Parrish, were with them, which was odd. Enos usually sat with those two at events like this. As far as Billy could tell, Sloane and Parrish weren't here at all, which was odder still. Sloane liked to have his fingers on the pulse of the community.

A lectern had been placed at the front of the room, and behind the lectern were five straight-backed chairs holding the distinguished rumps of the town's clergy—ministers or priests from the major denominations: Catholic, Lutheran, Episcopal, Baptist, and Methodist. Billy knew at least a couple of dozen Latter-day Saints in town, but apparently the Mormon bigwig, whoever he might be, was not invited to attend this shindig.

The Right Honorable Theodore Hart stood at the lectern orating, as was his way. As Billy settled against the back wall, the mayor was in mid-sentence and full stride.

". . . such a grand turnout, too," he was saying. "It makes me proud. Very proud, indeed, to have been chosen as the representative of such a fine, *concerned* group of citizens. And today, my friends, our little community—" He shook an index finger at the ceiling, or, considering the lofty thoughts so common to Mayor Hart, he shook his finger at the skies above the ceiling, or the universe beyond those skies. "—does in fact have *much*—" He leaned across the lectern in what Billy assumed was an effort to get more intimate with his audience. "—for which to be concerned."

He stood there in silence, hunched over the lectern, for at least thirty seconds; then, with great dignity, he brought himself erect, and, with both hands, he grasped the lapels of his immaculate suit coat. "I shall not, however, burden you fine folk with *my* paltry words on the matter. Instead, allow me to introduce this morning's speaker, the man whose inspiration it was that we all gather together on this cold winter's day and discuss the grievous problems at hand." He turned and extended his arm in the direction of the group of men behind him. "Ladies and gentlemen, I give you the good Reverend C. Abner Sewell."

Hart began to applaud, and when he did, so did everyone else. Many of those who were sitting up front sprang to their feet. Thatcher did, too, although with less spring than the others.

Sewell approached the lectern and provided the mayor with a curt nod of thanks. The acknowledgment brought a wide smile to the mayor's face, and he applauded with even more vigor.

Without returning Hart's smile, the Reverend faced the crowd and lifted his right hand in a gesture that called for quiet. At once, the room went silent, and those who had stood resumed their seats. When they did, Billy noticed Mrs. Baldwin was sitting on the aisle in the next to last row.

Sewell, a sparse, bald, and lean-jawed man, had dark circles beneath his black eyes. This morning, the circles were even darker than usual, and from where Billy stood, the eye sockets appeared empty, giving the Reverend an eerie, skeletal expression.

Sewell surveyed his audience, taking everyone in. "I have been selected by my peers," he began, "to speak for all of the clergy this morning."

Billy noticed Sewell's comment caused a couple of the clergymen to sit up straighter and square their shoulders. It caused a couple of others to slump and stare at their hands.

"The message we bring to you is a message of great import. There is, my friends, a murderer in our midst; or, I should more accurately say, a *group* of murderers. A cowardly group of murderers who strike in darkness and by wily stealth. A group of heathens more vile than the most savage of red men who once prowled these rolling plains."

Billy recalled why he had stopped attending church. His absence was not from lack of faith so much as an inability to spend his Sundays listening to this long-winded blowhard. Even Billy's father, a devout Christian and good Lutheran, struggled with attending once Sewell came to town. He did, though, and he insisted his boys attend as well.

"Of course," Sewell continued, "you all know of whom I speak." He paused for emphasis, and then, in case they didn't know, through clenched teeth and in his strong, stentorian voice, he told them. "The squatters. The interlopers. The *foreigners*. Those aimless vagrants and thieves who have insinuated themselves into our lives and into our community. Of course, I speak of the foul *devil worshipers* camped at Gypsy Rock."

Applause filled the room. Some, both men and women, came to their feet. A few shook their fists and shouted their outraged agreement.

During the more demonstrative portion of the crowd's burst of fury, Mrs. Baldwin stood, but instead of joining in the shouts, she left her seat and made her way toward the door.

Billy watched her leave, and as she stepped outside, he pushed away from the wall and followed.

Chapter Sixteen:
Half-Again Better

Billy received scowls from some of the citizens for leaving before Sewell had finished rousing the rabble, and he suspected Mrs. Baldwin did as well. The hard looks didn't bother him, and from what he could tell, they didn't bother the imperious Edith Baldwin either.

Once they were on the boardwalk, Billy called out, "Mrs. Baldwin. Excuse me, Mrs. Baldwin."

The woman turned and with an arched eyebrow asked, "Yes?" When she realized who was calling her, she said, "Why, Billy Young, how are you? It's been ages."

"Yes," said Billy, removing his hat, "it has."

Mrs. Baldwin leaned toward him and said in a stage whisper, as though they were part of some grand conspiracy, "I see you've decided to leave early as well." At first, Billy was unsure what she meant, and the expression on his face must have told her so, because she glanced back toward the door leading into the CR and nodded.

"Oh, yes, ma'am. The truth is I never intended on going. I didn't even know about it until a little while ago. I came into town this morning to see you."

"Me? Whatever for?"

"I hoped we could visit about some of the bad things that have been happening around here the last few months."

"It has been a difficult time, hasn't it?"

"It has, ma'am, yes, and I fear it may get more difficult before things get better."

"If Reverend Sewell and some of the others have their way, I'm certain you're right." She motioned toward the hotel across the street. "Shall we step over to the Grand Central's dining room and get out of the cold? I feel like a cup of tea." With her regal but pretty smile, she added, "And, though I shouldn't, I might have a piece of pie as well."

Billy wasn't sure why she felt she shouldn't have pie. Her figure was trim.

"Yes, let's do that. That's a fine idea." As usual, Billy liked the idea of getting out of the cold. As they crossed to the hotel, he said, "I got chilled on the ride in from the ranch this morning, and I haven't warmed up yet. The CR was cold as could be, even though it was full of all those people."

"Well," Mrs. Baldwin observed in her wry and well-known fashion, "most of those who are there are cold by their very nature. They release a chill the way a skunk releases an odor."

Billy smiled.

Once inside the dining room, they were escorted to a table by a young waitress. Billy followed the two women. As she walked, Mrs. Baldwin's posture was stiff, but she moved with grace.

Billy didn't know Edith Baldwin well, but he did know she felt she was half again better than everyone else. And she might be right. She was bright, pretty, well-educated. And despite her arrogant demeanor and occasional sharp tongue, no one took much offense. Folks accepted her teasing ways and knew she bore no malice.

The dining room was comfortable. The large coal burners at either end kept the place toasty warm, a welcome relief to the thin-blooded Billy. He assisted Mrs. Baldwin in removing her coat, draped it over the seat of one of the table's four chairs, and held a chair for her as she sat. He took off his own heavy sheepskin, placed it next to Mrs. Baldwin's coat and took the seat across from her.

"Would you care for a menu?"

The young woman who had escorted them to their table could not have been more than fifteen. Billy had seen her around town. She was a plain, timid little thing who came from an impoverished family. In an effort to support their nine kids, the girl's father performed what work he could find, and her mother took in laundry. The children above the age of ten also worked to fill the family's scant coffers.

"No, thank you, Mildred," said Mrs. Baldwin. "I would like a cup of tea. And do you have your delicious lemon meringue pie today?" She placed a hand on the girl's forearm, gave it a squeeze, and offered an affectionate smile.

Haughty airs or not, Mrs. Baldwin was well-liked. She devoted both her energy and money to every worthwhile cause and charity in the county. Billy suspected it was through her acts of charity that Mrs. Baldwin became acquainted with young Mildred. The Baldwins had no children, and since Edith had recently crossed onto the far side of forty, it was doubtful they ever would. But she loved children and knew most of the kids in town, especially the poorer ones. Every December, she harnessed a horse to her old phaeton and delivered presents and food to the less fortunate. Edith Baldwin was a pillar of the community.

"Yes, ma'am," said the girl, "lemon pie, just like always. And I swear, the meringue this morning must be four inches high."

"Wonderful. Then I shall also have a piece of lemon meringue."

Billy said Mrs. Baldwin's order sounded good to him, too. "Only make mine coffee instead of tea."

"Yes, sir," said Mildred with an awkward little curtsy. "I'll be right back."

Once the girl left with their order, Mrs. Baldwin looked across the table at Billy, and again providing her pretty smile, she said, "My goodness, Billy, what a handsome vest you're wearing."

"Thanks, ma'am. It belonged to my pa." Billy felt himself blush at the queen's approval.

Edith Baldwin was a woman who liked to get to the point, and Billy was glad. "What is it you wished to discuss with me, Billy?"

"Well, ma'am, I was wondering if you had ever made the acquaintance of Gwenfrei Faw, the Gypsy woman who I believe Ben O'Dell murdered, even if the jury didn't agree."

There was a flash of surprise in the woman's eyes at his question, but her surprise was brief. "Why, yes," she said, "I did make her acquaintance. I found her to be a lovely woman. Very interesting, too. As you might imagine, I'd never had occasion to meet a Gypsy."

"None of us had except for Hugo. He's known a few over the years."

She smiled. "Hugo, yes. I suspect there's very little in life Deputy Dorling hasn't experienced."

"Yes, ma'am, I believe he's seen it all. He'd have us think so, anyhow."

"You and Hugo appear close," she said.

"Well, he was Pa's good friend, so I've known him pretty much my whole life, and he helped me out with another mess here a year or so ago."

"When your brother was killed on the train from Probity?"

"Yes, ma'am."

"Another bad piece of business," she said. "Of course, my husband and I knew those trainmen who were also murdered. Thank God Owen wasn't the engineer on that run. He might have been, you know, but as good fortune would have it, it was one of his few days off."

There was a brief lull in the conversation.

After a bit Mrs. Baldwin asked, "What would you like to know about my acquaintance with Madam Faw?"

"How did you come to know her?"

As he asked the question, the waitress brought their pie, tea, and coffee.

"Thank you, dear," Mrs. Baldwin said. She patted the girl's forearm again and added, "And please give my best to your mother."

"Yes, ma'am, I sure will."

Before Mrs. Baldwin answered Billy's question, she took a sip of tea and a bite of pie. Billy did the same.

She blotted her mouth with her napkin and said, "Madam Faw and some of the other Gypsies came into town several times after they set up camp at the Rock. The men would sell pots and pans, knives, a few leather goods, even a horse or two, I think. The women sold trinkets, jewelry, that sort of thing. Gwenfrei Faw was selling some of the most beautiful scarves I had ever seen. When I first saw them, I was so impressed, I asked if she would come back to town the next Friday. The Women's League meets at the CR every other Friday. We do our quilting, drink punch." She motioned toward the pie with her fork. "Eat pie, if we're lucky." She raised her left hand and held her thumb and index finger a half-inch apart. "Sometimes," she added, "we gossip the tiniest bit."

"So you invited her to this ladies' club meeting, and she came?"

"Yes, I was certain the girls would be interested in her scarves. And they were, too. Madam Faw did very well. She returned two or three times. At some point, and I'm not at all sure how it came about, she produced a deck of tarot cards and began telling everyone's fortunes. We took it as nothing more than a game, really. A sort of parlor trick. It was fun. I might be wrong, I suppose, but I doubt anyone took it seriously." She had another sip of tea. "Perhaps I should amend that. Abner Sewell dropped by the CR one afternoon, and he took it seriously, indeed."

"Oh, really?"

"Yes, very much so. He acted as though we were in league with the devil. He even said as much. He called us the Lutheran Women's League With the Devil." She laughed. "Which would have been funny and clever had he been making a joke. As it happened, though, Reverend Sewell was not making a joke. I'm sure he never realized what he'd said might be taken as a joke, because the man is devoid of any sense of humor." She took another bite of pie and again dabbed her napkin at the sides of her mouth. She swallowed and said, "He chased that poor old dear out of the building and forbade us to ever have her back." She added with a twinkle in her eye, "He took me aside and chastised me for allowing such a thing to happen."

"He did?" Billy couldn't resist asking. "What did you say?"

"I told him I not only allowed it, but I was the one who invited her, and if Madam Faw were willing to return after his embarrassing tirade, I would gladly invite her back. I pointed out that he had no authority over this situation. We were meeting in the Community Room, not the church, and if he ever again spoke to me in such a manner, I would remove the word 'Lutheran' from the title of our organization, and *he* could personally provide every Sunday's baked goods for the congregants after services, and he could *also* prepare our annual Thanksgiving dinner."

Billy liked her response to the reverend and told her so.

They shared a smile, but she looked away and said, "I fear, however, the whole situation only helped foster his hatred and prejudice for the Gypsies. I also fear where it will lead."

"Yes, he's over there right now whipping everybody into a frenzy." Billy ran his hand across his face and shook his head. "I knew when it came right down to it, the Gypsies would be the ones blamed for O'Dell's murder, but I figured it would come from Thatcher and his group, not from the townsfolk. I expected they'd need something more to hang their hats on before they looked to Gypsy Rock for a villain."

Something more to hang their hats on, Billy thought, *like two Gypsies being spotted outside O'Dell's shack at the time the place burst into flames.* He didn't put voice to that, however.

"When we leave here, I'm going out to the Rock to tell Hugo and the others things are moving way faster than we feared." He pushed his pie away and pulled his coffee closer. "Did you see Gwenfrei Faw after the day Sewell ran her off?"

"Yes, she was in town a few times selling her wares. I told her never mind what the reverend said, she was always welcome to attend our meetings. And she could bring her cards, tea leaves, whatever she wished."

"What did she say?"

"She said she would not go where she wasn't wanted. I assured her she *was* wanted, but still she declined. The Gypsies often set up their merchandise in front of the old stage depot. It's out of the way, but it gets a fair amount of traffic. It's a good place for them. When they did, I would walk by, purchase some little something, and visit with Madam Faw. I enjoyed her company. I mentioned one day the ladies missed her telling their 'fortunes,' and I asked if she still did that sort of thing."

"What was her answer?"

"She said she did."

"Where?"

She found Billy's eyes, and there was a long moment before she answered, "The Half-Moon Saloon."

"The Half-Moon?"

"Yes, not the saloon's clientele, of course. She read the fortunes of the girls. The working girls." Mrs. Baldwin hadn't needed to add the last part. There were never any girls at the Half-Moon but working girls.

Mrs. Baldwin went on to say, "I know many of those girls myself."

"You do?" Billy said with disbelief.

"Yes, sometimes they need help in their lives, and Owen and I are happy to assist, if we can. Theirs is a difficult and often dangerous profession."

Billy's first reaction was shock. Mrs. Baldwin being with the Half-Moon girls in any way was not an easy thing to imagine. But maybe not so surprising after all.

"Do you know which of the girls she saw?"

"All of them, I imagine, at one time or another." She paused, started to take the last bite of her pie, but stopped and placed her fork onto her plate. "There was one, however, whom she saw more than the others. Madam Faw seemed to have taken the poor child under her wing."

"Who was that?" Whoever this girl was, Billy wanted to talk to her.

Mrs. Baldwin hesitated.

"Is there a problem?" Billy asked.

"Well, there has been—" She searched for the proper words. "—some controversy."

"How do you mean?"

She shook her head. "I fear I've already said too much."

"Mrs. Baldwin, bad things are happening in the county, and Hugo and I are trying to understand why. Gwenfrei Faw was murdered. We can't allow it to be forgotten. She deserves better."

Mrs. Baldwin seemed to ponder what Billy said and relented. "The girl's name is Connie Baxter."

Billy wasn't sure he'd heard right. "Connie Baxter? Ben O'Dell's girlfriend?"

"She was. Now I'm certain all she feels for Ben O'Dell, or any O'Dell, is fear—terror, actually."

"Hugo's wanted to talk to Connie again ever since the beginning of all of this, but he's got no idea where she is. All he knows is she went off to the Cheyenne area somewhere. She has family in those parts."

"Yes, her parents have a small ranch down there."

"Do you know where?"

"Not for sure. It's between town and the state line, but she isn't there. She never went there. Her parents knew the sort of life Connie had chosen, and they disowned her some time ago. They'd never accept her back in their home. Never, and Connie was aware of that."

"Well, when she lit out, we know she bought a train ticket for Cheyenne."

Again, Mrs. Baldwin hesitated, but after a moment answered. "Yes," she said, "I gave her the money to purchase a ticket. There was no doubt Ben O'Dell or his brother would be looking for her once it was known she'd spoken to Deputy Dorling. I thought it would be a good idea to buy the ticket to throw them off." She shrugged. "And it worked."

"Throw them off? What do you mean?"

"She purchased the ticket, but she didn't get on the Cheyenne train."

"If she didn't go to Cheyenne, do you have any idea where she did go?"

"Nowhere," said Mrs. Baldwin after another pause. "She's still here. Owen and I have put her up at a small property we have. It's his family's old homestead on the North Platte three miles east of town."

CHAPTER SEVENTEEN:
YOU BET, SON OF A BITCH

Billy and Mrs. Baldwin stepped outside the Grand Central, and before they went their separate ways, Billy said, "Tell Connie when you see her that Hugo and I mean her no harm, and we'd like to visit with her, if we could."

"I will. I'm going out there in the morning before church. I'll tell her then."

"If it's okay, maybe Hugo and I could also come out in the morning."

Mrs. Baldwin nodded. "All right. She never sees anyone except Owen and me, but she can't continue living as she has. Where she is, it's nothing more than an old dugout cabin. There's a cot, a stove, and a well, but it's very rustic. We take her food every few days; still, it's no way for a young woman to exist, or anyone else for that matter. I'll let her know the two of you are coming over."

"It's a good thing she's laying low, ma'am. I'm convinced Thatcher O'Dell or one of his bunch'd gladly do her harm."

"I understand. You be cautious, too, Billy. As the good Reverend Sewell likes to say, 'There is evil afoot.' "

Billy suspected, even as she said it, Mrs. Baldwin was thinking the same thing he was: Part of the evil afoot right now was Reverend Sewell himself.

"I will, and thanks for your help."

She smiled, and as she turned to leave, she said, "Give my regards to that old rapscallion partner of yours."

Billy nodded. "Yes, ma'am."

Partner? He couldn't imagine people thought of Hugo and him as partners. As he crossed the street to fetch Badger, he gave the whole partner thing serious consideration and decided he needed to widen his scope of acquaintances.

"Look who's coming, boys. It's young Billy Young." Thatcher O'Dell, Lester Warbler, and Deke Norton, another of O'Dell's group, were on the far side of the street where Billy's horse was tied. Thatcher sat on a short bench pushed flush to the outer wall of the hardware store. Warbler leaned against one of the posts supporting the eave extending over the boardwalk. Norton was in the street, leaning against Badger. It surprised Billy that Norton managed to get away with it. The gray was not much better at suffering fools than Mrs. Baldwin.

O'Dell went on to say, "I was right, wasn't I, fellas? The big ol' gray there *does* belong to Billy. Sure 'nough."

Thatcher looked bad. His skin was as white as writing paper. Circles as dark as chimney soot drooped beneath his wild, glassy eyes, which bulged even more crazily than usual.

Billy approached Norton and said, "Your pal Thatcher's right, mister. The animal you're crowding belongs to me." Billy tapped himself on the chest with his thumb.

Norton, chewing a soggy toothpick, bit a piece off and spit it into the street, but he didn't move away. Billy held his gaze for a long moment, and Norton stepped aside.

Billy didn't know Deke Norton well, but he was aware that Norton was a first cousin to Dim Sam Marsh, the fella killed the night they captured Ben O'Dell. Rumor had it Norton was displeased about his cousin's demise.

Once Norton moved off, Billy turned toward O'Dell. "You don't look so good, Thatch. How's your noggin?"

"Well, Billy," Thatcher said, flashing a crooked grin. "I reckon I been better, but I reckon I been worse. Gracious me, though, it sure is Christian of you to inquire."

Thatcher's voice was rough, and his words came out in an odd little tremulous slur. Understanding what he said was not difficult, but the slur was bad enough Billy could tell one of Thatcher's talking gears had a bit of a wobble.

"I was worried about you," said Billy. "When I saw Hank Green knock you flat like he did, I figured you might be dead."

"I ain't dead."

"Not yet, anyhow."

"What's that supposed to mean?"

"Well, sir, I'm no doc, but I've heard when a fella takes a hard wallop to his brains the way you did, it can sometimes come back on him. You think you're doing fine, and the next thing you know, you got blood squirting outta your nose, your ear holes, hell, maybe even your eyeballs. It can be pretty horrible, from what I've been told."

Norton, who now leaned against the hitching rail to Billy's left, said, "I think Billy Young might be full of shit, Thatch."

"I expect he is," Thatcher agreed, although he didn't say it with much confidence. "What brings you to town, anyway, Billy? You come for the big meeting?"

Billy shook his head. "Nah, can't say as I did. But, speaking of being full of shit, I did step into the CR for a while and listened to some of what Abner Sewell had to say."

Thatcher gave a little snicker. "I bet it's a mortal sin to speak ill about a man of the cloth. You might-a just bought yourself a one-way ticket to hell, Billy Young."

"When it comes to Sewell, I'll take my chances. Tell me something. I can't help wondering why your good friend Hank Green clocked you like he did."

Ignoring Billy's question, Thatcher asked one of his own. "Where's *your* good friend, the always fun Hugo Dorling?"

When Billy ignored Thatcher's question, too, Thatcher cut

his eyes upward and began to tap his chin with an index finger as though he was giving something careful consideration. "You know, try as I might, I cannot recall the last time I seen one of you fellas when the other wasn't right there, too. I was starting to think you boys was a couple of Siamese twins."

Warbler and Norton chuckled.

Billy shrugged. "Ah, you know Hugo. He's off somewhere taking care of business, I expect."

"What sort of business? Could it be some kind of Gypsy-loving business?" Thatcher's crooked grin was gone. "You two's being a couple of Gypsy lovers ain't no secret. Ain't that right, boys?"

Warbler said, "From what I hear."

Norton grunted a noise that sounded like an affirmation of some sort, but it was hard to tell.

Thatcher asked, "Did you say you heard the Reverend's speech this morning?"

"I said I heard part of it. I left early."

"Too bad for you, Billy. It means you missed the best part."

"What part might that be?"

Thatcher looked at Lester and jerked his head toward the door of the hardware store. Lester shoved away from his post, stuck his head in the door, and said something Billy couldn't hear. It seemed they had someone tucked away, waiting for this very moment.

"The Reverend introduced a special guest to the townsfolk," Thatcher said.

As he made the comment, little Timmy stepped onto the boardwalk. Following right behind limped his gimped-up father, the wife-beater Irv Tyson.

Timmy looked worse than Thatcher. Huge red marks covered both sides of his face. A cut, which needed sewing, ran the length of his left eyebrow. His right ear bent forward at a strange, unnatural angle.

It looked like Irv spread his strict discipline equally among at least two of his family members. Billy wondered if the man had started beating Timmy's baby sister yet.

Billy looked from Timmy to his father and said, "I reckon the hard lesson of a forty-four-forty slug fired into your thigh bone didn't teach you much, did it, Tyson?"

Tyson didn't respond, but Thatcher, who must have known the story of Hugo shooting the man when he found him beating his wife, laughed and said, "You might be right, Billy. I expect ol' Irv here is a slow learner on most things, being as he's about as dumb as an anvil. But to his credit, he did learn something from little Timmy last night."

Billy didn't ask, but Thatcher told him anyway.

"Irv learned there was a couple of Gypsies who set fire to my brother's cabin. He also learned you told this little dickens here to keep such news about fire starting a secret."

Tyson held Timmy by the boy's upper arm. Timmy jerked away and with a quiver in his voice, he said to Billy, "I never said they was the ones who did it. I said I saw them there after it was ablaze." He looked toward his father and then to Thatcher. "These two's the ones who told the preacher fella I saw the Gypsies light it up. And the preacher told the whole town the same lie at the meeting. They made me come out and say it was true." Timmy started to cry. "I'm sorry, Mr. Young, but my pa—"

Before he could finish, Tyson backhanded him, knocking the boy against the wall of the hardware store and onto the boardwalk.

Billy started for the man, but when Norton and Warbler stepped between them, he pulled up.

With his eyes locked on Tyson, Billy said, "If I ever see you hit him again, or even hear about you hitting him or your wife or anyone else in your family, you're going to get another lesson, this time from a forty-five slug." He gave his holster a pat. "And I promise you, mister, it won't be into your thigh."

Tyson puffed up like a frog. "Are you threatening me, boy?"

Billy felt his jaw tighten, and he gave his head one quick nod. "You bet, son of a bitch, threatening you is *exactly* what I'm doing."

No one spoke a word.

Thatcher broke the silence with a laugh. "Killing talk kind of tenses things up some, don't it?" Warbler smiled and climbed the two steps from the street back onto the boardwalk where he resumed his position leaning against the post. Norton stepped away, too, but he didn't take his eyes off Billy.

Billy peeled his reins from around the hitch rail. As he did, Thatcher said, "Folks're coming out to the Rock tomorrow after services to have a little visit with your Gypsy friends."

Billy didn't respond.

Thatcher held his empty hands up in a gesture communicating no threat. "We only wanna talk. Ain't nobody gonna get hurt." He paused. "Not yet, anyhow. Mr. Woodard convinced everybody to give the Gypsies a chance to answer a few questions about the fire—" Thatcher's eyes narrowed. "—and the long, wide slash across my younger brother's neck." He cleared his throat and added, "Myself, I was against it, of course, and so was the Reverend, but Woodard muscled his way into the meeting, said his piece, and took a vote. In the end it was decided we'd give the Gyps a chance to explain. You tell 'em, Gypsy lover, we'll be out to the Rock in the early afternoon."

Billy still didn't respond

He looked toward Tyson, aimed an index finger at the man, and said, "Don't you forget. I am watching you." Tyson's face went a dark shade of red, which gave Billy enough pleasure that he sent the man a smile. The smile was hard, devoid of humor.

Or perhaps it was less a smile than a smirk. Billy couldn't know for sure, but whatever it was, it had a mind of its own, and Billy couldn't stop the thing from coming even if he wanted to. Which he did not.

Billy took hold of his saddle horn with his left hand and turned his back to the boardwalk as he moved to mount Badger.

As he did, Timmy shouted, "Mr. Young, *watch out.*"

Billy knew without looking what was happening behind him. He released his grip on the saddle, spun, and as he came around, he pulled his short-barreled, thumbing the hammer as he brought it up.

Tyson, whose shooter was out and aimed at Billy's center, was cocking his own hammer, but before he could get it done, Billy leveled and fired. The bullet caught the man high in the right chest, an inch or so below the collar bone. It knocked him against the wall behind him, and he fell screaming and spouting blood like a fountain.

At the same time, Deke Norton, who still stood only a few feet away, drew his piece. Before he could fire, Billy swung his Colt with everything he had. The gun barrel caught Norton with a solid hit to the man's left jaw. Billy felt Norton's face cave inward, and he heard a *crack* and a sharp *pop* as bone broke and the jaw snapped from its hinge. The force of the blow bounced Norton off the hitching rail, and with a heavy thud, he hit the ground where he lay unconscious.

Billy did a quick pivot in the direction of Thatcher and Warbler, and as he did, both men lifted their hands away from their bodies, high and wide. In unison they shouted, *"Don't shoot. Don't shoot."*

Barely catching himself in time, Billy took in a long, deep breath, lowered his hammer and snugged the Colt into his holster.

Chapter Eighteen:
Down to the Basics

Billy rode into the camp at Gypsy Rock well past six o'clock. Things looked different now from yesterday morning. Before, their caravans had been circled a hundred feet or so in front of the Rock. Now, they were arranged in a semicircle, and the last two on either end were butted against the Rock as close as they could get. This arrangement protected the camp from the rear and allowed them to set up a double row of caravans to better protect their front and flanks. In a way, it looked to be a fine idea. But Billy wasn't so sure. It also would make for a difficult retreat.

But it could be the Gypsies didn't plan to retreat.

Hugo must have seen Billy coming, because as he rode up, Hugo stepped from between a couple of wagons.

"Damn, boy, I'm glad to see you made 'er back. I was beginnin' to worry."

Billy dismounted, and they walked Badger through the camp to the rope corral.

"What took so long?" Hugo asked.

"I ran into trouble."

As he unsaddled and tended to the gray, Billy related the events of his busy day. Hugo sat on a stump, smoking and listening without comment.

Once Badger was brushed, watered, and fed, they crossed to the *Kapo*'s caravan, where Hugo reheated a jackrabbit goulash Tasar had cooked for supper. The food was filling, but tough and stringy. Next time they'd do better to kill a couple of cot-tontails instead of the jack.

"From what I heard," Billy said, as he shoveled in his last bite, "the doc stemmed the flood before Tyson bled to death, and the bullet put a hole in the wall behind him, so there was nothing to dig out. Doc figures Tyson'll end up with a floppy arm from me to go along with his gimpy leg from you, but it appears he'll survive."

"Lordy," said Hugo, "Ol' Irv needs to avoid gettin' shot so much. Pretty soon, he's gonna have so few workin' parts, he ain't gonna be nothin' but a lump. Somebody'll have to haul him from place to place in a wheelbarrow."

"For Timmy's sake," Billy said, "I'm glad he didn't die. Maybe no father at all would be better than a father like Tyson, but it'd be bad for a boy to see his pa killed right before his very eyes. I know I don't want to be the fella doing the killing in that situation."

"So was it your plan to shoot him in the shoulder?"

"No, hell, no. All I did was spin, fire, and hope for the best."

"Well," Hugo observed, "ever'thin' worked out fine. What happened once Tyson was down and Norton's jaw was hangin' sideways?"

"I told all the folks who had seen what happened to stay put, and I sent a fella up to the sheriff's office to fetch Dale Jarrod."

"I expect that was a big waste of time."

"Yep, pretty much. Jarrod came over, took a look at the mess, and said since it happened in town instead of out in the county, it was a job for the town marshal. So we had to wait for Marshal Conroy to get there. Once he did, he took each witness aside and asked what had happened. I guess they all told more or less the same story I did—except for Thatcher and Lester Warbler, of course."

"What did them two ne'er-do-wells have to say?"

"To be fair, I guess they said about what everyone else did, except they threw in that Tyson and Norton were merely responding to my vile threat to kill Irv Tyson, which was true, sort of."

"How did Conroy take it?"

"He figured making a threat was a bad thing, but since the fella who made the threat had turned and was about to climb aboard his horse and ride away, Conroy didn't see Tyson had much call to shoot the threat-maker in the back."

Hugo smiled. "Simon Conroy does have a knack for boilin' things down to the basics, don't he?"

"He figured I had the right to do whatever was necessary under the circumstances, and that Deke made a damned poor decision to try to kill a fella who was standing there ready with his shooter smoking."

"You know, by God, I admire ol' Si's powers of logic. I really do."

"The doc figures even though Tyson's arm probably won't work too good, in the long run, he might come out better than Norton."

"How's that?"

"I guess Norton lost three or four teeth outright, and a couple more, though still stuck in his gums, were busted into a whole bunch of little-bitty pieces."

Hugo winced and gave a shudder.

"But," Billy continued, "it was Norton's jawbone that caught the doc's eye. He said he'd never seen one dangle in quite that way in all his years of doctoring. He suspected Norton might be living on soup and pudding for the rest of his days."

"Soup or not, it turned out better for 'im than it might have."

"Must've been his lucky day," said Billy. "After the marshal let me go, I took little Timmy home to his ma, explained to her what had happened, and then I headed out here."

"I bet the poor woman was plumb sad, sad, sad," Hugo said.

"How so? I told her the same as I told you. Her husband would live."

"Yep."

Billy had tossed his bedroll in with the guns when he and Hugo loaded the buckboard that morning. He unrolled it now next to Pov Meche's fire and took a seat.

"Care for a snort?" Hugo asked, as he tugged the cork out of his bottle of Kentucky.

Billy pulled off his boots and folded his legs under him Indian-style. He answered Hugo's question with a shake of his head and lifted his cup to show he still had some of the coffee Hugo had brewed while Billy ate his goulash.

They sat there not talking. Hugo sipped his whiskey. Billy sipped his coffee and stared into the flames. As it happened, Billy did not kill Tyson and Norton, but it was close, and he knew he would have done so with pleasure had things gone a different way. That troubled him. Billy knew Hugo understood, which accounted for Hugo's silence. Usually, a campfire and a cup of whiskey brought out the man's jabber.

After a while, still watching the fire, Billy said, "I'm guessing Mrs. Baldwin'll take the supplies to Connie around nine-thirty or thereabouts tomorrow morning so she'll have time to get into town for church."

Hugo shook his head. "I can't get over Connie Baxter bein' holed up here in the county all this time. I'd sure like to talk to the girl, although at this late date I don't know what good it'll do us. We needed her around to testify at the trial."

"True," said Billy. "Still, she looks to have known Gwenfrei Faw better than any other of the townspeople. Out of curiosity, if nothing else, I'd like to visit with her."

"Let's go talk to her, then," Hugo said. "We'll give Edith

Baldwin a chance to let Connie know we'd like to see her. So let's plan to get to the old homestead around ten or so. That'll allow Edith time to deliver her supplies and visit with the girl before we get there. It'll also give us plenty of time to talk to Connie and still be back here for the big powwow tomorrow afternoon."

Billy agreed. "More than enough time, I'd say. Who knows if Connie'll even talk to us."

"I expect she's pretty scared."

"She has reason to be," Billy said. "But maybe we can put a stop to all this bad business tomorrow at the meeting."

"Could be, but I doubt it," said Hugo. "It's worth a try, though, I s'pose."

"There won't be much chance of putting it to rest if the only townsfolk doing any talking is Thatcher O'Dell, but maybe they'll bring along a few cooler heads."

Hugo didn't seem to have much faith in that possibility. "Thatcher and his boys aren't lookin' to put anythin' to rest. If they smell blood, they'll wanna see some, too. I'm sure Thatcher already has the blood scent in his nose. I expect in the end he'll wanna make somethin' of it."

Hugo poured another whiskey, and the boys sat through another round of silence. Billy felt his nerves start to jangle in anticipation of what tomorrow might bring. It wasn't the risk of death, although it was part of the mix, but Billy had faced down death more than once. What he felt now was something different.

Hugo, as usual, was eager. A kind of sparkle lit his old eyes. The sparkle was not the sort he got from strong drink. Hugo hadn't poured nearly enough whiskey into himself yet to set his eyes to sparkling. This sparkle was caused by something else, and Billy had seen it with Hugo before.

The old deputy was a strange one. The threat of impending

violence never fazed him. He appeared to welcome the excitement. Hugo had been in many dire spots over the years, so if the possibility of having to fight to the death was a thing a man could ever grow accustomed to, Billy figured that might explain Hugo's consistent lack of vexation.

Billy considered it admirable, but he doubted he could ever feel that way, no matter how many rough times he might have to fight his way through. And even if he did learn to accept the anxiety that came with risky situations—as he guessed he might someday, considering how things had gone for him over the last year or so—he knew he could never thrive on it as Hugo did.

If his jangly nerves did in time turn to tolerance or even excitement, Billy knew he could never feel that way toward the sort of thing they faced here. What they had at Gypsy Rock was something different.

He had no use for the O'Dells, their gang of thugs, or Abner Sewell, either, but it appeared it wouldn't stop with them. There were a lot of people in the meeting at the CR, and most of them Billy knew and liked. Most of them were good people. They may have developed a cloudy judgment, but they were good people. It appeared he and Hugo were headed toward a shooting war against at least a few of those good people, and not so long ago the people he and Hugo were now defending had been strangers.

As much as he liked the Roma, how he and Hugo came to be in a place where they were fighting neighbors on behalf of strangers was a perplexing turn of events.

Billy looked toward the crusty old scrapper on the far side of the fire, and in one long burst, Billy gave voice to his feelings.

Hugo listened without interrupting. When Billy finished, Hugo rolled a smoke. He pulled a stick from the fire, lit his cigarette, and tossed the stick back. All of this took long enough that Billy figured Hugo was taking some time to consider his answer. Which may have been the case, but probably not. Once Hugo began to speak, it didn't sound as though his response had required much thought at all.

"They may be our friends and neighbors," he said, "but it appears they're gonna let Thatcher O'Dell, Sewell, and a few other dimwits talk 'em into killin' a bunch of fine folk who've not done a single thing in all this world to deserve it. It ain't hard for me to choose which side I'm stickin' to with this one, Billy-boy." He jabbed all four fingers of his right hand at Billy. "And I betcha it won't be hard for you neither, once it comes down to it."

Billy listened to the old ex-deputy's short, simple response, shook his head and smiled. Hugo and Si Conroy had much in common.

Pov and two of his men rode into camp. Spotting Hugo and Billy, the three Roms veered in the boys' direction. When they pulled up at the campfire, Pov threw his right leg over his horse's neck and slid from the saddle. The horse was a huge vanner with long, flowing fetlocks the same golden color as its mane. Pov handed one of the men his reins, and the two men trotted off to the corral.

"So," Hugo asked as Pov dropped down between them, "didja get 'em all settled in?"

"I did, yes. You had a fine idea, Hugo." It had taken a while, but Pov had started calling him Hugo instead of Deputy Dorling. "I trust Billy has no objection."

"Objection to what?" Billy asked.

"Well, sir," Hugo said, "after I delivered the weapons here this mornin', Pov and me got to talkin', and the idea came up maybe we should find a safer spot than the Rock here for the women and kids. I figured your place'd be just the thing. Since you weren't around, I went back and visited with Rosco about it, and he figured you wouldn't mind. So we agreed to set 'em all up in your bunkhouse. Pov and a couple of the boys took 'em over there this evenin' after supper."

"Sure," said Billy. "Fine by me. Sounds like a good idea." He had noticed earlier that the camp was quieter than usual.

"We used the buckboard Hugo drove here this morning to haul some gear and food stores to the ranch for our people," Pov said. "We returned it to your helper after we unloaded everything."

"That's fine, too. Thanks."

Pov looked to have aged years in the thirty-six hours or so since Billy had last seen him.

The *Kapo* leaned toward the fire and poured himself a cup of coffee. Once he'd had a sip or two, Billy explained the townsfolk wanted a meeting tomorrow afternoon. Pov was agreeable enough to the idea.

"We can meet," he said, "but I think this will turn bad."

Billy wondered if Pov had come to his opinion using mysterious *Chovihano* powers, or if it was nothing more than a hunch. Maybe for a fella who could foretell the future, a hunch was all it took. Whatever Pov's source might have been, the Gypsy's prediction caused Billy to feel even more uneasy.

"I hate to hear you talk that way, Pov," Billy said, "but in case you're right, I'm sure pleased you got all the womenfolk and kids to a safer place."

Hugo's ears perked up. "Not all of 'em," he said, and it was clear the old mooncalf was trying to stifle a smile and making a damned poor job of it. "One of them women wouldn't budge. No, sir. She said if it came to gunplay, she could load 'n' shoot as good as any man among us. No matter how hard we tried to convince her otherwise, she flat out refused to leave with them others."

Billy felt his insides squeeze. He didn't need to ask who this stubborn woman was. Instead, he slipped back into the same rock-hard silence that had been overtaking him off and on ever since the unfortunate events in Casper. Turning his gaze away from Hugo and the Gypsy, Billy again stared into the fire's dancing flames.

CHAPTER NINETEEN:
MADAM FAW HAD A SKILL

Billy found Deya the next morning sitting at a table next to Baul Emaus's caravan. She was sorting and counting ammunition—what the Roms had before and what Billy had sent over the previous day.

Before Billy could say a word, Deya extended her left hand, palm forward, and said, "Stop." With her right hand, she penciled onto a piece of paper what Billy assumed was her count. When she finished, she laid the pencil down, turned to Billy and said, "Don't start. I'm here now, and you and everybody else need to accept it."

"It's crazy," said Billy.

"The whole thing is crazy." She crossed her right leg over her left, flashing above her shoe the briefest hint of creamy, smooth ankle.

Billy felt his breath catch with the sight of it, but he forced himself to make a fast recovery. "What can I do or say to change your mind?" he asked.

Without answering, she found his eyes and smiled.

"Come with me," she said, standing. She led the way past the cart and toward the trees. She walked far enough in Billy knew they were well out of sight. Even with the morning cold, knowing they could not be seen made him flush.

"All right," she said, spinning to face him. "Maybe you could change my mind with a kiss." She stepped into him, clutched the front of his jacket, and lifted her face to his.

He stared down at her, not believing what was happening. Once he had convinced himself it *was* happening, he knew it should not *be* happening. In an instant all the rules against their being together crashed through his head. Along with the rules were thoughts of her father, the enormous, ill-tempered Baul Emaus. There were many reasons this was a mistake, but instead of heeding the alarms, Billy pulled her closer and kissed her.

The kiss was long and deep. He felt himself fill up with the taste of her, the clean smell of her hair and skin. The feel of her fitted against him.

And to Billy's pleased amazement, she returned his kiss, pushing herself into him—her grip on him as tight as his on her.

The kiss had been months in the making. Maybe, he heard a tiny voice whisper, the making of it had taken a lifetime.

He had no idea how long the kiss lasted, but he was certain it was not long enough. When their lips parted, they both gasped for air, and steamy plumes of warm breath exploded around them. Deya placed her cheek against his chest and moved against him closer still.

After some effort, Billy found his words, and in a soft voice, he asked, "Did that change your mind?"

She lifted her eyes to his, and with another of her beautiful smiles, she answered, "No, but you're welcome to try again, if you'd like."

The dugout where the Baldwins were hiding Connie Baxter was easy enough to find. Billy and Hugo followed the river east and spotted it three miles out of town. Mrs. Baldwin's phaeton was parked out front.

Billy said, "I see Mrs. Baldwin hasn't left for church as yet."

Hugo, ignoring Billy pointing out the obvious, kicked his bay and loped into the sagebrush-infested front yard. "Hello inside the cabin," Hugo called as he pulled rein. "You got some company outside, ladies, and we are friends, not foes."

The door opened, and snuggling a shawl around her shoulders, Mrs. Baldwin stepped outside. Once she had made certain who had ridden up, her well-favored features blossomed into a smile.

"Why, Hugo Dorling, look at you."

Hugo stood in his stirrups and ran the edge of his index finger along the brim of his hat in a quick, jaunty greeting. "Hello, there, Edie. It's been awhile, but, my, oh my, ain't you lookin' pretty. I sure wish there was a band playin' music right now, 'cause, by golly, I'd ask you to dance."

She rolled her eyes and shook her head in a manner indicating she was a woman unimpressed by fiddle-faddle. But even so, her smile grew wider.

"Save the hokum, Hugo, and come on in. It's cold out here." She glanced at Billy for the first time and added, "You too, Billy. Connie's here, and we've been expecting you. The coffee's ready." She stepped back inside and closed the door without latching it.

Billy and Hugo dismounted, tied their animals, and started for the dugout.

The cabin, a primitive sort of place, had been dug straight into a hill overlooking the North Platte. Its only outside wall—the front wall—was constructed of pine logs and chinked with wood blocks and daubing mix. Since no pine trees grew here along the river, the logs must have been hauled down from the foothills along the base of Casper Mountain. At some point in the cabin's hard life, someone had attempted to spruce it up with whitewashed clapboards. But most of the clapboards over the years had fallen victim to the ever-blowing wind, and the sun had faded the whitewash into near nonexistence on the few that remained.

Boards to frame the doorway had been riven and hewed also from pine and pinned to the cut ends of the logs with wooden treenails driven into auger holes. The thick batten door, constructed of heavy planks and hung on large steel hinges, was built with enough solidity to deny entrance to any whooping Indian bent on a new scalp to adorn his teepee. The sturdy door, old as it was, could still serve such a purpose should there happen to be any Indians with bad intent around, a rarity these days, whooping or otherwise.

Hugo and Billy stepped inside, and Billy shut the heavy door behind them. The cabin measured fifteen feet wide by ten feet deep at its deepest. The low and gloomy place had no windows, and once Billy closed the door, the only light came from two kerosene lamps trying their meager best to push back the darkness. Connie, in her time here, had tried to make it homey, but she'd had poor luck. The bleak dwelling was designed for little beyond the basics of warding off villains and the hard-hitting fists of long Wyoming winters.

A steaming pot of coffee sat atop an old wood-burner. Next to the stove stood a rough, hammered-together table and four chairs. Connie Baxter sat in one of the chairs clutching a cup of coffee. She held it in both hands, pulled close against her breast.

Three more cups were on the table. One held Mrs. Baldwin's coffee, and she took the pot from the stove and filled the two empty ones. She replaced the pot on the wood-burner, returned to the table, and sat. "Connie and I have had a long, good visit this morning, and I decided to stay with her when you fellas came to call. It won't hurt me to miss one of Abner Sewell's sermons. I'm about done with him, anyway, I think."

"You goin' over to the Baptists, Edie?" Hugo asked.

"I will become a Hindu before I become a Baptist," she answered without a smile.

"You better think twice about bein' a Hindu."

"Why's that, Hugo?"

"From what I hear, to be a Hindu, you gotta wear a turban for a hat and learn how to blow a whistle good enough to make a venomous reptile poke his head out of a basket. Me, I might abide the turban, but I'd want no part of the rest of it. Never much cared for snakes."

"Well, I'd rather wear a turban and whistle a snake out of a basket," Mrs. Baldwin said, "than join the Baptists."

She nodded toward the full cups and empty chairs. "Have a seat and make yourselves comfortable."

The cabin was warm, and before sitting down, Hugo took off his coat and draped it on the back of one of the chairs. He pulled the chair out and plopped down. "Connie," he said, getting right to the point, "I been wonderin' 'bout you ever since you skedaddled outta my office and vanished like a dern ghost." A harsh timbre to his voice bespoke his frustration.

Billy removed his gloves and shoved them into his pocket but didn't take off his coat. The place was toasty, and the coat might prove too much, but Billy wasn't warm yet, so he kept it on. He hooked his boot around a leg on the fourth chair and scooted it back from the table. As he sat down, he said, "Take 'er easy, there, Hugo. You could at least say hello before you start scolding the poor girl."

"I ain't scoldin' her . . . not exactly," he said. Then in an awkward tone, he added, "Sorry, Connie. I'm glad to see you're all right."

Connie was just past twenty-two. Though pretty, she looked a decade older than her years. Billy had never seen her without the heavy makeup the girls at the Half-Moon always wore. He liked her better this way.

The girl set her coffee on the table. "What is it you want from me, Mr. Dorling?"

"Well, young lady, there ain't much I want from you now.

What I would've liked, and the reason I was lookin' for you when you left the way you did, was to have you testify at Ben O'Dell's trial. I reckon if you would-a done your duty and helped us out there, we might-a got the scoundrel hanged."

"I heard he's dead now, anyhow," she said in her own defense, "so what difference does it make?"

"You're right there. He is dead. Got his throat cut wide, and because of the way he died, there's gonna be a price to pay by someone who might not've had to pay it if the law could-a worked the way it should."

Connie leaned back in her chair and looked away.

Billy guessed Hugo couldn't stop himself.

"Whether you testified or didn't testify," Billy said, "doesn't matter now, Connie. Don't let this ol' chin-wagger here make you feel bad about things. None of it's your fault. We know you did what you did because you were scared, and we know you're scared still. It could be in the next day or so things'll come around and this will all be over, one way or another. Anyhow, we didn't come here to chasten you. I wanted to visit about the Gypsy Gwenfrei Faw. Mrs. Baldwin tells me you knew her."

Connie nodded. "Yes, she was nice to me. I reckon Madam Faw and Mrs. Baldwin here are 'bout the only folks in this whole world who've ever been nice to me."

"How did you get to know her?"

"She come into the Half-Moon one afternoon. Wasn't much going on that time of day. There were six of us girls sitting around doing nothing. When she come in, Charlie Martin tried to chase her off."

"Sounds like Charlie," Hugo observed.

"Us girls were able to talk him into letting her stay. We'd never been around anyone like her. She was old, but she still dressed young-like, you know? She was covered with bracelets and rings and bangles and such. She was quite a sight. She carried a big stack of cards the likes of which none of us'd ever seen. She said they were some sort of magical cards, and she could use them to know the future. She offered to tell our fortunes for five cents apiece. She said if we all six of us were up for it, she'd do the whole job for a quarter." Connie's eyes drifted toward Mrs. Baldwin, and she added, "I reckon there's never been a girl in our line of work who didn't ponder what was in store for them down the road, so we jumped at the chance to find out."

"Was that the only time you saw her?" Billy asked.

"Oh, no, she started coming 'round pretty regular. After a while, the other girls figured it was a bunch of poppycock and got bored with it, but not me. I liked her. She could tell you things about yourself. Sometimes they were private things, and I can't imagine how in all the world she could've known, but she did. It baffled me, for sure. Plus, the woman was nice, and she was easy to talk to. Madam Faw had a skill that made a body want to talk to her, and it made me feel better about things when I did. In a way, I believe she did have magic."

"Do you remember the last time you saw her?" Billy asked.

"Sure, I do."

"When was it?"

"It's easy to remember. The last day I saw her was the very day she was killed. She stopped by in the early afternoon, but we didn't visit very long."

"Why not?"

"I don't know. She was upset. I think the only reason she stopped at all was she'd promised me a couple of days before she would, and she had to pass right by the Moon on her way into town. But she couldn't stay. She had also promised to see someone else that day, and she was already late."

"What might she do on those times when she came to town? Do you know?"

"It depended. Sometimes she'd come in on a wagon with some of them other Gypsies. They'd sell their goods over at the old depot. Other times, she'd walk in by herself and come see us girls at the Half-Moon. For a while, she was going to visit the Lutheran ladies. I figured she was seeing the Lutherans right up 'til she died, but Mrs. Baldwin told me this morning that a while back, Reverend Sewell put a stop to it. Which surprised me some."

Mrs. Baldwin, who had been listening without comment, said, "Tell him why it surprised you, Connie."

"Well, I figured she *was* still seeing them Lutherans. She told me a few things about seeing one of them, at least, so I figured she was still going over to the CR. Most times she came to see me, she was either headed to see the Lutherans when she left or coming back from seeing them, and stopping off at the Moon on her way home. I'm positive the last time I saw her, it was one of them ladies she was off to see. She told me it was."

"Did she tell you the lady's name?"

"No, she said she doesn't tell names; but whoever it was, I know Madam Faw liked her, and the lady liked Madam Faw, too, from what I could tell. They was like me and Madam Faw was, I guess. They could sit and visit for hours. Maybe everybody was like that with Madam Faw, if they gave her a chance."

"When you saw her the last time, what made you think she was upset?"

"Cause she was. I could tell. She was all nervous and acting strange. She was in a big hurry to go."

"Did she tell you about it? Did she say anything about why she was so upset?"

"None of the details, no, but, earlier, some weeks before then, she'd heard bad things were happening around the area. I don't think she knew or understood much about it herself. She didn't know any facts—at least she didn't tell me any—only that some folks was losing valuable things, and it wasn't right. Of course, I didn't know what she was talking about, but it was part of what had her so distraught. It wasn't the biggest part, though. No, sir. There was something more. Something even worse."

"What?" Billy asked.

"I don't know exactly. But she was saying that sometime in the last few months there'd been a murder done. A murder done right around Casper somewhere."

Hugo looked perplexed. "I don't know about no murders around here in the last few months, or even the last year, for that matter, 'cept for Gwenfrei Faw herself and now Ben O'Dell. Who'd she say got hisself murdered?"

"She didn't say. All she said was there'd been a murder, and she didn't want nothing to do with murder. Nothing at all."

Mrs. Baldwin walked Billy and Hugo to their horses.

"So," said Billy, "Connie's saying one of the ladies here in town told Gwenfrei Faw about a murder."

"It's hard for me to believe," Hugo said, "there could-a been a murder I never was told about."

Mrs. Baldwin gave a shrug. "It *is* hard to believe, but that's what Connie's saying, all right. She told me the same story before you boys got here."

"Do you have a guess who Gwenfrei was talking to?" Billy asked.

"No idea," said Mrs. Baldwin. "And I believe Connie when she says she doesn't know, either."

"Well, it's a puzzler for sure, but the three of us aren't gonna make any sense of it standin' here in the cold," said Hugo. "It does warrant a closer look, though, if a man could ever find the dern time."

Billy untied the horses and handed Hugo the bay's reins.

Mrs. Baldwin said, "You fellas don't need to rush off. I'd be happy to fix some breakfast. I brought groceries with me. Bacon. Some eggs, too."

"Thanks, but no, thanks," Hugo said. "We got a big get-together with some of the citizenry and the Roms here this afternoon. I reckon we best be gettin' back."

"What kind of get-together?"

"After you and I split up yesterday," said Billy, "I was told there was a vote taken during the meeting they had at the Community Room, and it was decided to meet with the Roms and talk this situation over—try to settle things down some. They said they were all coming out to the Rock this afternoon."

Mrs. Baldwin's eyebrows rose a bit. "This afternoon, you say?"

"Right."

"That's odd."

"What is?" asked Hugo.

"As I was leaving to come out here this morning, I saw a group gathering at the edge of town. Quite a large group. There must have been ten or twelve men on horseback at the time I drove by. And I got the feeling they were waiting for more."

"Did you recognize any of them?" asked Billy.

"It was Thatcher O'Dell's crowd and a few others. Some of them I knew. Most of them, I didn't."

"Could be they were gettin' together," Hugo offered, "to figure out what they were gonna say to the Gypsies at the meetin'."

Billy considered Hugo's idea. "Maybe," he said, "but getting together four or five hours before they were due to be at the Rock is unlikely."

Hugo nodded in agreement. "It is, isn't it? If they're comin' early, we oughta be gettin' back out there. We wouldn't wanna miss the big powwow."

He started to lift a boot to his stirrup, but stopped himself, used his thumb to push his hat up a notch, and turned to face Edith Baldwin. With a slight, but what appeared to be a sincere, smile, he said, "Tell me somethin', Edie, before I go."

"What's that, Hugo?"

"Have you been happy these past years?"

The question appeared to take the woman aback, but only for the briefest second. She met Hugo's eyes and returned his slight smile with one of her own. "Yes," she said, with a single nod, "I have. Owen's a good man. He and I have made a fine life."

Their eyes held for a moment, and Hugo said, "Well, then, I'm glad for you, Edie." Mrs. Baldwin had her hands folded in front of her, and Hugo reached out with his left hand and took hold of her right. He gave it a gentle squeeze and said, "I truly am, you know."

She covered both of their hands with her left and said, "Thank you." She spoke so softly Billy almost couldn't hear the words.

Hugo and Mrs. Baldwin shared another smile, a larger one this time. After a moment, Hugo stepped away and mounted up.

"But Hugo—" Mrs. Baldwin said.

"Yep?"

"I'm sure over these many years I haven't laughed nearly so much as I might have."

When she said that, Hugo tossed back his head and bellowed out a laugh himself. "That could be true, Edie, girl. By golly, I'd bet it is."

Still laughing, Hugo nodded to Billy. Billy nodded back, and they gigged their mounts toward Gypsy Rock.

CHAPTER TWENTY:
Gaje

Billy and Hugo were in an easy lope when they first heard the gunfire. From this distance, the sound was faint, but the direction it came from was clear. Without a word, they kicked their horses into a gallop.

In front of the Gypsies' camp spread a broad, open area. Just to the west of this area rose a wide outcropping of rocks. Pine, spruce, and aspen lined the open space to the east where the trees grew thick on both sides of the creek. Billy and Hugo rode in from the northeast and slowed to a trot as they approached the spot where the trees petered out and the prairie grass began.

Dismounting and using this thinner copse of trees for cover, they walked to the edge of the open space. From here, they could see the entire area. Sporadic gunfire came from both the rocks and trees. Return fire came from the double half-circle of wagons.

"It appears Thatcher and the others have the Roms in a crossfire," Hugo said.

Billy lifted his hand and pointed. "And look." In the center of the clearing were two bodies. One man lay on his belly with his face in the dirt. Billy couldn't see him well enough to identify. The other lay on his back. This one he could see better. Pov Meche. Even from this far away, Billy could tell the *Kapo* was dead. Blood had soaked into the grass and dirt around his head.

First, Ben O'Dell. Now Pov Meche and the man on the ground next to him. Three deaths in three days. Those were the ones Billy knew about. He looked toward the Gypsy camp and was certain they'd find others there.

Now it had started, and there would be more death to come.

Billy couldn't tell how many men were firing into the line of wagons, but it had to be close to fifteen. Most of the shooting came from the rocks, where the cover was better.

"I'm guessin' there ain't no more than three or four men in the trees upstream," Hugo said. "Let's tie off our mounts down here and sneak up and kill them sons-a-bitches."

Hugo offered no fuller plan, but he didn't have to. At this stage, all they needed was stealth, a wary eye, and a willingness to pull a trigger.

Today, the willingness came easier to Billy. The blood-soaked sand around Pov made it obvious what needed to be done. Deya Andree and the others suffering the gunshots blasting into the curve of those wagons made it easier still.

Billy wrapped Badger's reins around a low branch and pulled his Marlin from its scabbard. Hugo did the same.

Jacking a round into his Winchester, Hugo said, "They'll be on the other side of the crick. Let's cross here. Yonder looks to be a likely spot." He nodded toward a natural bridge of four large, flat stones that traversed the narrow stream.

Once they were across, Hugo said, "Keep ten or fifteen feet between us. I'll go first." He bent into a half crouch and made his way from one tree to the next, avoiding the deer path that ran the length of the tree line from where the creek flowed onto the prairie all the way up to Gypsy Rock and beyond. They could move faster if they used it, but they would also make for a couple of fine targets sauntering up the path as though it were a boulevard.

The farther upstream they moved, the louder the gunfire. The shots came in volleys. First, a long period of silence, followed by a quick series of shots. Then another long silence, followed by another round of shots. The blasts came from every direction. The rocks, the trees, and from inside the camp. Billy couldn't know what might set off the shooting. Some abrupt movement, imagined or otherwise. A flash of sunlight. A sound. Anything might cause it, but when one shot was fired, it was followed by a dozen more.

It felt to Billy they'd been creeping upstream for hours, but he knew it was no more than ten minutes. They were close, though. Now, in addition to the sounds of gunfire, they could smell the gun smoke and hear the levering of rounds into chambers.

Still, Hugo led them on. They were well within a hundred yards of the first row of caravans when he raised his hand, signaling Billy to stop. Hugo crouched and motioned for Billy to come forward.

Billy made his way through the thick spruce to where Hugo, down on one knee, waited, his rifle at port arms. When Billy knelt beside him, Hugo lifted three fingers and jabbed them toward a spot thirty feet away, where three men were also crouched, looking out of the trees toward the Gypsy camp, their rifles leveled. The men were in a row a couple of feet inside the tree line. The distance between the two men on either end was twenty, twenty-five feet, with the third man halfway between them.

Hugo tapped his chest, pointed toward the man on the left and the man in the middle.

Billy nodded.

Hugo jerked his head at Billy and pointed to the man on the right.

Again, Billy nodded.

They both took in a breath, aimed, and fired. The heads of the two men on either end of the row exploded. Billy and Hugo jacked in a second round, and at the same instant, the whole place erupted into another deafening volley of gunfire. Billy wondered if the man in the middle heard it. Probably not. By then he sported two new holes—one hole from Hugo's forty-four-forty slug and a larger hole from Billy's forty-five-seventy.

Billy, who only the day before had almost been back-shot himself, didn't like the idea of shooting these three from behind, and with the roar of gunfire coming from the rocks and camp still hammering around them, he bent close to Hugo's ear and told him so.

"You think about things more than you need to, boy. Them three fellas got back-shot because they was unlucky enough to be lookin' away from us and instead was lookin' out toward our friends who they was tryin' their dead-level best to murder."

More boiling things down to the basics.

Despite the admonition against too much thinking, Billy also gave Hugo's rationale some thought. "All right," he said with a nod, "let's get to the camp and see what we can do up there."

"Fine," said Hugo. "But go easy. We don't want to walk into their camp and have them Roms killin' *us* by mistake."

Hugo stood and started down the deer path. Since the shooters in the trees had been dispatched, Hugo must have decided the path was safe enough, and Billy fell in behind.

They hadn't gone thirty yards, though, when Hugo pulled up short. Up ahead, leaning against the trunk of an aspen, sat Lester Warbler. He had a large, gaping bullet hole in his left thigh. The wound was bleeding bad, but Lester was still conscious and alert enough to have his rifle pointed at Hugo's chest.

"Well, well, if ain't Hugo Dorling," Warbler said, his voice hoarse and weak. "Right here at the end of my gun barrel. I wonder if I should kill you now or save you for Thatcher. He's been all pouty for the last couple of days 'cause he didn't get to kill you out by the livery fire."

"If I was you," suggested Hugo, "I'd kill me now, but a-course, Lester, you don't have to take my advice."

Lester cleared his throat and spat in the general direction of the creek. He didn't seem to have much spittle available, though. Billy figured about all of whatever wet Lester still had inside was draining out pretty fast through the big hole in his leg.

"Is that Billy Young behind you, there, Hugo?" Lester craned his neck so he could see better. "Why, sure it is. I should've known. I think I'll save you both for ol' Thatch. It'll be a feather in my cap to turn you boys over to him. Now, the first thing I want you to do is toss them long guns you're toting over into them bushes beside you there." He jerked his chin toward the shrubbery at Hugo and Billy's right.

Hugo, who again held his Winchester at port, didn't move.

Lester lifted his barrel higher. "I ain't joking." His eyes turned to slits, and the smile of a moment before folded down to a thin line.

"All right, Lester," Billy said. "Take it easy." And with that, he tossed the Marlin away.

When he did, Hugo, using both hands, sent the Winchester sailing out away from his chest, and it flew straight for Lester Warbler's face. While the rifle was still airborne, Hugo drew his side gun and fired. The Winchester smashed into Lester's forehead a half-second after the bullet smashed into the bridge of his nose.

Hugo crossed the distance between him and Lester and retrieved his rifle. "That oughta do it for the tree shooters," he said. "Now fetch your Marlin, and let's get into the Gypsies' camp."

Hugo sounded confident there were no others firing from the

cover of the trees, but Billy noticed this time when Hugo led the way, he decided against walking down the deer path.

As they came even with the first row of wagons, Hugo stopped and leaned his rifle against his leg. Cupping his hands around the sides of his mouth, he shouted, "Hey, inside the camp. It's Hugo Dorlin' and Billy Young. Don't shoot. We wanna come in."

Billy questioned the wisdom of shouting their names. Now Thatcher and the others would know they were here.

"Step from the trees where we can see you," called out a young voice.

They did as they were told, and a deeper, older voice said, "All right. Come in."

Keeping low, they entered through the creek-side of the first row of wagons and crossed into the camp's inner half-circle. Once inside, they were met by Baul Emaus and a young Gypsy of maybe fourteen or fifteen years, whose name Billy knew to be Stefan. All four stood behind one of the large caravans, where they were out of the line of sight of any potential shooter. Both Roms, young and old, bore a look of distress, even despair. Stefan held a rifle in the crook of his arm with the muzzle pointed more or less at the ground, but still in line with Billy and Hugo.

"You need to move your gun barrel one way or the other, son," said Hugo. "And you need to do 'er *pronto.*" Billy was not sure Stefan knew what *pronto* meant, but there was a threat in Hugo's tone that required no interpreter, and the young Rom did as he was told. Hugo had already drawn blood, and bullets were flying. Those two things got Hugo's fires stoked high.

Baul said something to Stefan in Romani, and the younger Gypsy returned to the line of defense set up between the two rows of wagons. Once Stefan was gone, Baul's look of distress deepened.

"They came early," he said. "They came unexpected. We were not yet ready."

Billy felt his anger rise, not only at Thatcher and the others, but toward himself as well.

"We didn't have to go see Connie," he said to Hugo. "It could've waited."

"We had no reason to think these bastards would show up here when they did," Hugo said. But he didn't say it with his usual self-assurance, and Billy imagined they'd both be questioning their leaving Gypsy Rock that morning.

"Is Deya all right?" he asked.

Baul held Billy's gaze for a moment and motioned his thumb toward the outer circle.

Billy nodded his thanks.

The moment Billy stepped into the open space between the two rows of wagons, a bullet slammed into the caravan to his left. An instant later came the report of the rifle that had fired the shot. The slug hit at the level of Billy's head, and a chunk of wood the size of a double eagle exploded into a hundred splinters. Slivers blasted into the side of Billy's face, barely missing his left eye and dropping him to one knee.

"God*damn*," he cursed as he lifted his gloved hand and cupped his cheek.

The curse had not left his throat before a dozen more shots cracked. Billy crouched lower and pulled off his glove. The tanned elk hide was already covered in blood. Letting out another curse, he used his fingertips to search the side of his face, plucking out slivers.

As the firing tapered off, Billy, still shaky from the close call, replaced his glove and scanned the row of wagons in front of him. A half-dozen Gypsies were spaced along the first row of caravans. They hunkered behind wheels and beneath the wagons. Some were focused on the rocks to the left, and others looked toward the line of trees to the right.

"Keep your eyes on the rocks," Billy shouted. "We killed the shooters in the trees."

One of the Gypsies who was stooped behind a large, solid cartwheel turned to face him. It was Deya.

At least he assumed it was Deya. At first, he wasn't sure. Her long, black hair was stuffed into a large, dark blue beret. She wore a heavy broadcloth coat and canvas pants. The coat extended to her knees. On her feet were thick-soled brogans at least a size too big. All of her get-up appeared a size too big, but Billy had never seen her look better. And seeing her, he took in a complete breath for the first time since he and Hugo had heard the distant gunfire.

He scuttled his way across the open space to where Deya crouched. He wanted to pull her to him, but he knew he could not.

Her perfunctory smile was empty of warmth or pleasure, but he could tell she was glad to see him. "They came this morning," she said. "Not long after you left." She tugged off her right glove and touched the side of his face. Gently, she picked what Billy hoped were the last two or three wood shards from his cheek and around his eye.

"How many are there?" he asked.

Putting her glove back on, she gave a little shrug and looked away as she remembered back. Her brow furrowed as though she were trying to recall something that had happened weeks before. "At first there must have been twenty of them," she said. "Maybe a few more. It's hard to say. All but the three men who rode in stayed far back and spread themselves out across the open space."

"Three of them rode into camp?" Billy asked.

"No, not into camp. They stopped out where—" Her voice broke. She swallowed away whatever had caught in her throat and continued. "—where the bodies are."

"What happened?" He could see the telling of it was difficult for her, and he reached into the narrow space between them and took her hand. She clutched him with the grip of a drowning person clenching the side of a boat.

"As they rode up, one of the men called out. He said they wanted to speak to the man in charge. The 'chief,' he said. He said, 'We want to speak to the *chief.*' " She frowned as though the word "chief" made no sense to her. "I didn't know what he meant, but," she added, "Pov did. He started to go out, and Papa—Baul—tried to stop him, but Pov said not to worry; it would be all right."

She stopped, and Billy allowed her to take her time.

"Pov went out there before we had even given out the weapons. The guns were loaded but stacked on a *taliga,* a small wagon inside the inner circle. I said to Papa we should arm everyone now. And he sent some of the younger men back to bring the weapons around. Before they could do it, though, Pov Meche was dead."

"How? What happened?"

"We couldn't hear what was being said, but as they were talking, one of the men pulled his pistol and shot. He shot the *Kapo* as he stood there, defenseless, looking up at them. He shot him in the head. He shot him for no reason."

Deya's eyes brimmed, but she refused to allow herself to cry.

"As soon as the shot was fired, one of the three men jumped from his horse and ran to Pov, but even from here, I knew nothing could be done, and I'm sure the man knew it, too."

The words came hard. She paused, took a breath and continued. "The man knelt beside Pov for a moment, and then he stood and said something to the two men who were still mounted. He was angry. Furious. He shook his fist at both men. I'm sure he raised his voice, but we still could not hear."

Another pause.

"Then the other man on horseback—not the one who killed Pov, the other one—pulled his gun and fired. When the man who had gone to help Pov dropped, they spun their horses and galloped back to the line of men behind them. There was much shouting, and many who had come out to the camp turned and left. They rode off in the direction of town. I suppose they wanted nothing to do with what had happened . . . or what was about to happen. The ones who remained, maybe twelve, fifteen men, split up. Some rode into the trees; most rode behind the rocks. Then they began firing into the camp."

"Can you tell me anything about the three men who rode into the clearing?"

"*Gaje.*" She spat out the word.

After a moment she added, "We couldn't see their faces. Of course, they all three wore heavy coats. The one who shot Pov wore a long black duster, split in the back. His hat was fancy. It had a thong kind of thing that hung down past his chin, and a shiny band. It was not the hat of a man who does work. The one who killed the man who dismounted and went to Pov wore no hat at all. He had a bandage on his head." She lifted her hand and touched her beret as she said it.

"Can you tell me anything about the man who went to help Pov?"

"Yes," Deya said. "He was the same man we saw at the livery. He was the man who set Ben O'Dell's shack on fire."

Chapter Twenty-One:
Got Any Ideas?

"Yep," said Hugo. "Baul recognized him, too."

"Who do you suppose it could be?" Billy wondered.

"Impossible to say. 'Course, if we can figure a way to either kill these bushwhackers or chase 'em off, we can go out there and take a look for our ownselves."

"I like the idea of killing them," said Billy. Seeing Deya hunkered behind the wheel with a gun in her hands did not appeal to him.

"Killin' would be a fine thing for 'em, all right," agreed Hugo. "But about all we got to offer to get the job done is you, me, and Baul. Come here. I wanna show you something."

Hugo led the way to a large caravan nestled in the shade against the Rock. There were two hinged doors at the rear of the wagon. Hugo flipped a latch and opened them and stepped back for Billy to look inside.

Billy stuck his head in, squinting into the dim light. Neatly placed and extending the length and width of the wagon were nine bodies, most of them men between the ages of late teens to mid-forties. Once Billy realized what he was looking at, he recoiled and said, "Sweet Jesus, Hugo, wouldn't it've been easier to just tell me what the hell was in there?"

"I suppose, but showin's always better'n tellin'. I figured doin' 'er this way'd make more of an impression on you."

"Well, for once in your life, you got something right. My *god.*"

"We got us some especially bad fellas up in them rocks, I'm thinkin'."

"No surprise there. It's Thatcher O'Dell and his band of bastards. We *know* how bad they are."

Billy dug in his pocket for his handkerchief, which he used in a futile effort to blow the stench from the wagon out of his nostrils.

"But maybe we don't know how *smart* they are."

"What are you getting at?"

"Baul tells me it was obvious from the first shot that they was singlin' out men of a fightin' age. If they had a shot at either a teen or a grown man, they'd take out the older fella every time. Up to a point, that is. After 'bout middle-age or so, they let them old fellas live as well."

From the number of youths Billy had seen defending the front line and the advanced years of at least a couple of the men laid out in the wagon, it looked as though they'd started shooting the elderly as well.

What Hugo said was far-fetched, but if it was true, that would explain why Stefan made it across the open space between the wagons without getting shot at, and a couple of minutes later, Billy had not.

"Maybe they were showing some mercy to these young fellas who're hardly more than kids," Billy suggested.

The comment was so dumb, Hugo didn't waste any time ignoring it. He said, "They're just makin' the best use of their ammo. I expect they'll start in on the young ones soon enough."

Another burst of gunfire caused them both to drop low.

"Somebody must-a blinked," said Hugo. "Folks're gettin' trigger happy on their side and ours, both. The problem is, once we run out of ammunition, we're done. Them fellas in the rocks can always send somebody back to town to fetch more."

Billy agreed. "We gotta end this," he said.

"We do, for sure."

"Got any ideas?"

"Not really, no," answered Hugo. "For whatever it's worth, I did get us another four rifles and a few more shells."

"How'd you do that?"

"Me and that Gypsy boy, the one who's lax about his gun safety, went downstream to fetch our horses. On the way back, we picked up Lester's and them other fellas' guns and ammunition. It isn't much, but it's somethin'."

"Good," Billy said, "especially getting the horses." He liked to be close to his ride.

More gunfire thundered through the camp, and in the midst of it all, Billy heard a scream. The moment he heard it, he knew it came from Deya.

Billy sprinted straight toward her. As he ran, a half-dozen bullets hit the ground around his feet, splashing dirt like water.

To his surprise, he made it across, and as he edged around the corner of a wagon, he saw what had caused Deya to scream. Two feet beyond the solid wheel Deya used for cover lay Baul Emaus. A hole in his chest spewed a tiny red geyser with his every labored breath.

To Billy's horror, he saw Deya drop her weapon and reach for her father.

"Deya, *no*," he screamed and dashed toward her. As he did, he heard the *fffp, fffp, fffp* of bullets zipping past his head. The gunmen could have easily shot Deya, but in her oversized man's togs, she appeared hardly more than a twelve-year-old boy. Billy not only looked the right age for killing, but thanks to Hugo calling out their names when they came into camp, Thatcher and the others probably knew who he was.

Billy ran with everything he had. Once he cleared the open space, he dropped and skidded into the solid cartwheel feet-first like a baseball player sliding into home. As he came to a stop, he reached out, grabbed Deya's coat, and jerked her back to the comparative safety of the wheel.

"Stay here," he said between clenched teeth. "I'll get him." Billy peeked around the cart and looked toward the rocks. Right above one of the rocks closest to the wagons, Billy could make out the rounded crown of a bowler. Billy guessed the hat to be atop the head of the man who had shot Baul.

Just in front of Billy, the big Gypsy lay on his back a few feet away, staring up at the scudding clouds. His eyes still held life, but they were vacant and unblinking.

If he stretched, Billy could reach Baul's left ankle and pull the man behind the cart. It was impossible to do, though, without exposing himself. Squeezing against the side of the cart as tight as he could, he extended his arm toward the wounded man. When he did, the ground next to his hand exploded. He yanked back, and three more bullets smashed into the spot where his hand had been. One missed Baul's leg by less than an inch.

Deya looked down the row of wagons at the few boys and young men who were left. She shouted something in Romani, and they all began to fire at the lowest stand of rocks. They fired even if they had no visible target. Deya grabbed her rifle and rolled beneath the cart, where she opened fire as well.

Even the lowest of the rocks the shooters used for cover were higher than the line of wagons, which made the angle ideal for Thatcher's boys and bad for the Gypsies. Still, the Gypsies' cover fire was enough. Billy reached out, took hold of the big man's leg, and dragged him in. Once he had him behind the cart, Billy dropped both hands over the bubbling hole in Baul's chest and pressed down with all his strength. The pressure allowed Baul to breathe easier, but, even so, Billy knew there was no hope.

"Papa," Deya screamed as she came from beneath the wagon.

"Papa, *Papa*," she repeated as she crawled toward them. Taking her father's head into her lap, she pushed back a lock of hair from his forehead. "Papa," she said once more. Billy could tell Deya recognized the sad truth. She pulled Baul close, and Billy took his hands away from the man's wound.

Making soft sounds, Deya rocked her father. Perhaps the sounds were words; Billy couldn't know, but whatever they were, they were soothing. Fear had cloaked Baul's face when Billy pulled him to safety, but now the fear was replaced with an expression of calm. Baul and his daughter's eyes were locked, and they shared a silent communication.

After a moment, Baul lifted his hand to Deya's cheek and tried to speak. It appeared to take most of what was left of him, but he forced out some sort of sound. His words were thick and wet, and even though he spoke Romani, Billy doubted even Deya could understand what the man tried to say. She lifted him higher and dropped her ear to his lips. The huge Gypsy spoke to her again, and this time Deya heard and understood. She nodded in response, and the nod brought an even more profound look of calm to Baul. Deya lifted her ear from her father's lips and again found his eyes. Again, Baul spoke in his rough voice, and again Deya nodded. She pulled him to her breast, and through her tears and sobs, she continued to nod over and over even after the big man's hand dropped from her cheek and fell to the frozen earth.

Billy pushed his way past Hugo, who stood between two wagons in the second row, reloading the rifle he'd used to provide Billy cover. Once Billy was behind a wagon and out of the line of fire, he headed for the corral.

"Whatcha up to, boy?" Hugo called out.

"I'm not sure, but I gotta do something. Help Deya with Baul. And shoot as many of those bastards as you can."

Billy worked his way around the camp's perimeter. When he got to Hugo's bay, he popped open the left saddlebag. He reached inside, pulled out the spyglass, and slid it into the right-side pocket of his sheepskin coat.

He crossed to Badger, opened one of his own bags, and took out a box of rifle shells, which he shoved into the left pocket of his coat. The box was not quite full, but he imagined it would do. He tugged loose the slipknot on his hornstring, and released his rope. Hanging onto one end, he dropped the coils to the ground. He hitched up his gunbelt an inch or so and dug into his left jeans pocket for his clasp knife. Using the knife, he cut about three feet off the rope and fashioned a rifle sling by tying one end onto his Marlin's octagonal barrel and the other end onto the stock. He slipped the whole rig over his head, snugging the rifle at an angle across his back. He retrieved the rope, and shoved his left arm through the circle of coils, sliding them up onto his shoulder.

Badger gave a snort, and Billy guessed the horse figured they were about to head out. As he stroked the horse's shoulder, Billy wished he had a lump of sugar. Or, better yet, two lumps. One for Badger and one for himself. The day had given him a sour taste.

"Be patient, there, fella," he said. "Be patient. I'll get you home real soon." Billy tried to make it sound convincing, but he expected Badger could hear the truth.

He gave the horse another pat and looked up at the Rock towering behind them. It rose more than eighty feet straight up from where Billy now stood. The Young brothers had spent much of their youth around this treacherous slab of granite. They had played here, and they had explored here. Back then, Billy felt he had come to know this monster fairly well. Now, craning his neck in an unsuccessful effort to see the top, he wasn't so sure.

CHAPTER TWENTY-TWO:
BILLY MADE THE CATCH

On its north side, Gypsy Rock was a sheer stone cliff. Billy had heard there were folks in this world who drew pleasure from climbing such things, but the Youngs were not among them. The south side, though, was more forgiving; at least it was the first two-thirds of the distance from its base to the top. The last third was as sheer as on the north.

Billy made his way to the Rock's far side and began his long ascent to the top. He was still well below the spot where the real work would begin, but even this first section was steep and unaccommodating. One misstep, and a fella would go tumbling nonstop onto the rocks below.

Billy looked down now and confirmed that unnerving truth. He was not fond of heights, and if it had been left to him, he and Frank would've never come near this place. But Frank was an adventurer. Not so much of an adventurer as to challenge the north side, but the south side suited Frank fine.

"You ain't scared, are you, Billy?" Frank would ask as he smiled his cocky smile.

And Billy would lie and say, "Of course I'm not." Frank would laugh and lead the way up.

Billy wished his brother were here to lead the way now.

Between the months of October and May, Billy spent most of every minute he was outdoors cussing the cold. Even though today was colder than any day so far this winter—and getting colder by the hour—now, as Billy climbed Gypsy Rock, the cold posed no problem.

He took off his hat and blotted sweat from his forehead with the sleeve of his jacket. He should have brought a canteen along, but it hadn't occurred to him until his parched throat sent him a reminder.

With luck, he told himself, he would not be up here long. He stole another glance at the rocks below. Maybe not long at all, if he broke his neck on the way.

He screwed down his hat and continued to climb. With every step, the going got steeper. After another fifty feet, he reached the five-foot-wide shelf where he and Frank would stop and rest before taking on the final leg of the climb. He hefted himself onto the flat spot and lifted his eyes to the precipitous wall above.

Once he caught his breath, he allowed the coiled rope to fall from his shoulder onto the outcropping's gravelly dirt, pulled the Marlin around so it draped across his chest, and leaned back. He took off his hat, and unbuttoned the sheepskin. He was hot and considered leaving it behind, but he knew once he was settled in at the top, the howling northwest wind would quickly blow his sweat away.

Twenty-five feet straight above his head extended another outcropping. The one above was a mere eight or ten inches wide and reached out like a skinny finger three feet from the cliff's edge. Frank and Billy never tried to free-climb this precipice.

Instead, they always brought a rope.

Frank was a much better hand at tossing a loop than Billy. Billy maintained the reason was simple. Frank got plenty of practice. If ever a calf was stuck in the mud, Frank would stay mounted and throw the rope. Billy's part of the chore was to slog through the mire and give the critter a shove. At brandings, it was Frank who did the roping and Billy who took the animal to the ground and held him while the iron burned the hair.

Eyeing the outcropping, he tossed his first throw. It took many tries and much profanity, but in time Billy made the catch. With a snap and a tug, he snugged the loop in.

He had taken off his jacket and gloves while he threw the rope. Now he pulled them on and was glad to do it. He was ready to have the sheepskin and elk hide between himself and the freezing air. The shelf where he stood was on the bright side of Gypsy Rock, but what little sunlight shone through the gray clouds made a poor effort at warming the day.

As he pulled the Marlin over his shoulder, he smiled and looked up at the chunk of granite holding his rope. By the time he had lifted his two-hundred-plus pounds hand-over-hand straight up twenty-five feet, whatever chill he felt now would be long gone.

Billy hefted a leaden arm over the outcropping and hoisted himself onto the mostly flat top of Gypsy Rock.

He'd been right—no more chill. The wind blew, of course, but less than he might have expected up here on a frigid day. Right now, it felt good. He suspected it would go from feeling good to feeling not-so-good soon enough, but for now the breeze was fine with Billy. He lay on his stomach and caught his breath.

The last time he had been here was almost three years ago. On that climb, Frank had brought along a hammer and chisel. Billy pushed himself to his knees and pulled off the Marlin. He turned and looked back at the granite outcropping. Neatly chiseled in the stone was "FY" and "BY." He removed his right glove and ran his fingers over the letters.

The chase, where he ran Ben O'Dell to ground, and these few days since the jury verdict kept bringing Frank to mind. Even now, going on two years later, he tried to fight off memories of his brother. But every time he would lose the battle. The memories would take on a will of their own, and lead to the same place: Frank's murder beside the tracks.

On the same day Billy had lost his brother to a killer, he had discovered his own capacity to kill. The discovery had caused Billy much turmoil. What he was discovering these last two days was the turmoil caused by killing grew less with the doing of it. Part of him considered that a blessing. Another part did not.

He heard a blast of rifle fire down below. Twice since he'd left Badger, he had heard shots, and both times his insides had clenched. He feared for his friends at the camp.

He recalled Deya saying many of the riders who arrived with Thatcher O'Dell had returned to town when they realized the true nature of their venture. Billy assumed the ones who left were regular townsfolk who hated the Gypsies and wanted them gone, but were not willing to be accomplices in a massacre.

Had they been of the same mind as Thatcher, they could have overrun the camp and killed everyone in sight. Even if Reverend Sewell had not specifically told the townspeople to kill the Gypsies, Billy knew Sewell would have been pleased if they had. As it happened, though, Thatcher was not left with enough men to overrun the camp. He and his gang were forced to resort to sniping from the trees and rocks.

Billy turned away from the carved initials.

Sniping, yes, he told himself as he retrieved his Marlin and pushed to his feet. *It has come to that.*

Billy chose for his spot a narrow berm of granite on the northernmost edge of the Rock. From here, the camp spread out in clear view—the open space in front, the trees to the right, and the stand of rocks forward and to the left.

Straight ahead, he could see the silver ribbon of the North Platte River; beyond the river, the prairie stretched all the way to the sky. To the northwest lay Casper, and between town and the horizon he could just make out the spout and handle of Teapot Rock.

The last time he was here, in addition to the hammer and chisel, Frank had brought along a pint bottle of rye. Since they still had to climb down from this towering bastard, Billy had questioned the wisdom in that; but as usual, he followed Frank's lead, and all had ended well.

Those, he mused, were less complicated days.

He dug into the pocket of his jacket and lifted out Hugo's spyglass. He shook the glass from its felt sack and placed the sack next to the Marlin lying at his side. After a moment, he returned the sack to his pocket. He wanted to avoid explaining to Hugo how the wind had blown away the sack for the telescope he had not asked to borrow.

Billy extended the glass and looked down into the camp. Deya sat next to her father. She stared at his lifeless body, but no longer cradled his head. Hugo sat beside her. They were not talking, but that was fine. Hugo was with her. What was there to say?

Ahead of the first arc of wagons lay the bodies of Pov Meche and the other fella—the fire starter. Even with the scope, Billy couldn't see the man's face.

He looked toward the line of trees and found the spot where they had killed the three shooters. The men's bodies weren't visible, but he could see gore on the grass outside the tree line.

He moved the glass to the other side of the open space and brought the two rows of rocks the shooters used for protection into focus. The first row was fifteen feet above the prairie floor. The second stood eight or ten feet behind and six feet above the first. Both ran parallel to the open area and perpendicular to the first row of wagons.

Four dead men the Gypsies must have killed were laid against an embankment.

Billy did a quick count of the shooters who were left: eight. Fewer than he had expected.

All were the derelicts who ran with Thatcher. Billy knew the names of half of them and recognized the others from seeing them around town.

Four shooters were behind the lower stand of rocks and four behind the upper. Two of those behind the upper were Thatcher O'Dell and Hank Green. Like a couple of generals, they stood together, overseeing the whole operation. Both held rifles, but using the cover of a large boulder, they had situated themselves in such a way that it was impossible for them to be seen by any of the Gypsies below.

Billy might have taken a shot at them, but even from his good vantage point, the angle was not ideal. With the other six, even for an average marksman, it would be difficult to miss.

Billy focused his glass on a man wearing a bowler—the man he knew had killed Baul. The hat was cocked at a jaunty angle, and the fella was laughing and apparently making jokes with the shooter who stood next to him. They both were having a fine time.

Billy shoved the telescope closed and dropped it into his pocket. He removed his right glove, lifted the Marlin, and rested his left hand and the rifle's forestock on the lip of the berm. Pushing himself up a few inches, he lowered the muzzle onto the chest of the derby wearer. He adjusted his angle until the man's black heart was in line with the Marlin's front sight and centered in the rifle's More-Light rear sight. The Buckhorn More-Light was a piece of custom work Billy's father had the Freund Brothers in Cheyenne install when he purchased the rifle for Billy's twelfth birthday. It had been a nice addition.

Now, with the Marlin aimed, Billy pulled the second and rearmost of his double-set triggers. This cocked a miniature action that transformed the first trigger from its normal pull into a hair trigger.

Billy took in a deep breath, filling his lungs. Steadying the Marlin, he let out half the breath and touched his finger lightly to the trigger in front.

The big rifle barked. Billy lifted his head and watched the man who wore the derby tumble.

The granite played tricks with sound, and Billy had taken down three more before the shooters realized where the shots were coming from. With methodical precision, Billy dropped those men one after the other. As he fired, Hugo, Deya, and the young Gypsies stepped from their cover and fired into the rocks as well.

When Billy stopped, six of the killers were down and dead. He came to one knee and watched the last two of the eight he had counted galloping off in the direction of Casper.

He didn't need Hugo's spyglass to know which ones they were.

CHAPTER TWENTY-THREE:
MENTION WHAT?

When Billy walked into camp, he stopped at the corral, tucked the Marlin into his scabbard, and returned the telescope to its place in Hugo's saddlebag. As he did, he spotted Deya and the half-dozen Gypsy males who survived sitting together at a caravan on the west side of the inner half-circle. They all sat dazed, and no one was talking. Billy started toward them but stopped when he heard Hugo call his name.

He looked to his right. Hugo was crouched next to a wagon on the far side of the half-circle, and when he saw Billy look his way, he waved him over. Billy wanted to talk to Deya, and he glanced again in her direction. Either she hadn't seen him or she was too lost in her grief to acknowledge him. Neither she nor any of the young Gypsies appeared interested in conversation. Billy decided whatever he might say to her—and he had no idea what it would be—could wait. He turned and started toward Hugo. As he approached, Hugo met him halfway.

"He's alive," Hugo said, "but I don't know for how long. He's been gut-shot, and the bullet must-a gone all the way through and tore into his spinal cord, 'cause his legs don't work, and he's got no feelin' from his chest down."

"What are you talking about, Hugo?" Billy asked. He looked to where Hugo had been sitting and saw there was someone lying next to the caravan. Billy could tell by his coat it was the man who had been shot just after Pov Meche. "He's still alive, really?" The man had been flat of his face on frigid ground for at least a couple of hours.

Billy stepped around Hugo and headed toward the wagon. Hugo fell in behind. The first thing Billy noticed was the man's coat had been unbuttoned and pulled open, exposing his shirt, which was white. At least the upper portion of the shirt was white. The lower portion was crimson.

"Good God," Billy whispered. To his amazement the fella still drew breath, but even if a doctor stood here in camp right now, no matter how fine his medical skills, there was no way a wound like this could be survived.

And the gunshot wound was not the man's only injury. When he fell, he must have struck his head. A long gash crossed his brow. The cut was not deep, and most of the bleeding had stopped; still, dark streaks of mostly coagulated gore traversed his face, distorting his features.

Not until he stood directly above the man could Billy recognize him to be his and Hugo's friend, Enos Woodard.

Hugo set a pail of water next to Enos's head and looked up at Billy. "There are clean rags inside Pov's caravan. Go fetch 'em and see if you can find some blankets."

Billy did. When he returned, Hugo had torn open Enos's shirt, revealing the wound. Enos had been gut-shot at close range, and the high-caliber bullet had blown a gaping hole in his abdomen. A portion of his torn-up intestines was visible. Bile rose into Billy's throat, and he struggled to swallow it away. He got it down, but he wasn't sure how long it would last.

Hugo dipped one of the rags in the water and with a surprising gentleness cleaned Enos's face and stomach, taking special care around the wound. The gesture was futile, but Billy recognized the impossibility of Hugo sitting idle when his friend lay before him like this.

"I sent Stefan into town for the doc," Hugo said. He must

have said it to Enos, because he turned to Billy and added, "There's a couple of them young Roms who're hurt some, too. I also told Stefan to bring Teasdale as well."

"Teasdale? Barnett Teasdale, the undertaker?"

"He's the one," said Hugo. "If you ain't noticed, boy, we got us a whole passel-a dead bodies around here."

Billy *had* noticed, and any other time Hugo's insulting tone might have raised Billy's hackles. Now, though, he was too tired. All he said was, "I figured you and I could use one of these wagons to haul in Thatcher's people. And the Roma will want to take care of their own."

"Them Roms don't take care of their own."

Billy wasn't sure what Hugo meant, but before he could ask the crusty old bastard to explain himself, Hugo said, "I'm gonna use this water here to clean Enos up some. Go get another pailful so we can give him a drink." In what was an obvious afterthought, Hugo added, "If you would, please, Billy."

When Billy came back with the water, he looked across the camp at Deya. She still had a dazed expression, but she was up and tending to some of the injured Gypsies. None of the young men's wounds appeared mortal.

As Billy approached Hugo and Enos, Enos was speaking, or trying to. His voice was soft and rough, and Billy couldn't make out what he said. Billy handed Hugo the bucket. He'd found a ladle in the caravan where he had located the bucket, and Hugo dipped some water. With the same gentleness he had shown earlier, he helped Enos take a drink.

"So thirsty," Enos said. "Thank you." His voice worked better now, but not much. He squinted and focused onto Hugo. "How's it look, Hugo?" he asked.

"Well, sir," Hugo answered, "not so bad."

"Not so bad, huh? Have you ever seen a wound like this?"

"Sure I have, a couple-a times at least."

"How'd it turn out for those fellas?" Enos asked. When Hugo didn't answer, Enos gave a weak chuckle. "That's what I thought."

Enos's face was about as white as the clean part of his shirt. He was growing weaker fast, but he didn't show much sign of pain. Billy wondered if the bullet hitting his spine might be a blessing. He had heard getting gut-shot was a painful way to go.

"I tried to make up for things," Enos said. "And I tried to stop this." He waved his hand in a feeble gesture, taking in the camp and all that had happened. "When Ben O'Dell was killed, I knew the Gypsies'd be blamed. That's why I set the fire, but—" He shook his head. The gesture was quick and communicated dismay, or frustration, or sadness.

"Don't talk, Enos," said Hugo. "Save your strength."

"Save my strength for what? Are we going to a square dance later?"

Hugo blinked a couple of times in disbelief at the sassy remark. "I wonder how many bullet holes you'd have to have before you stop bein' a smart aleck."

"Hard to say, but I expect this is my first and last bullet hole, unless one of you boys'd care to put me out of my misery."

"Ain't hardly an option there," said Hugo, "but I have considered puttin' you outta *my* misery from time to time."

Enos swallowed, but his difficulty doing it was obvious. "It all got out of hand, Hugo."

"What did?"

"What Sloane and Parrish were doing with the small land holders. What I helped them do." His already-red eyes welled with tears. "I helped them do it. God forgive me, but I did." He gave his head another weak shake and grasped at Hugo's sleeve. "But I didn't think it would make any difference to anyone, Hugo. Not really." He paused and added in his raspy voice, "At least not for a generation or two."

"I don't know what you're talkin' about, Enos, but it don't matter. Hush up now and take 'er easy."

Ignoring his friend, Enos continued. Even as he faded, he spoke with determination. "Sloane forced me to do it. That's no excuse. But I didn't think I had a choice. So much debt." He struggled to swallow again. "We always have choices, though, don't we? I was a fool. I didn't know how far he'd go. I didn't know—" He stopped whatever he was about to say and veered into something new. "I told Stella, and I wrote those folks in Cheyenne. I told them about what was happening, too." He turned from Hugo and focused his rheumy eyes on Billy. The grief and regret Billy saw made his chest constrict, and he dropped to a knee next to Hugo. "But not everything," Enos said. "I couldn't tell them everything. I should have, but I couldn't."

The more Enos talked, the more worked up he became.

"Eventually, I admitted to Sloane I'd told Stella some of it, but that was before—" His words drifted off, and he turned from Hugo and Billy and looked toward the sky. "We did bad things, Hugo," he said. "We did bad things."

It then seemed Enos wanted to shut out everything, even the distant sky. He clenched his eyes. The way his features contorted, it appeared the bullet bashing into his spinal cord might not be stopping his pain after all; he sure looked to be in pain now. Billy couldn't know if it was pain from his bullet wound, his head wound, or if it was a pain coming from some other place.

Despite his agitation, Enos nodded off, or perhaps slipped into unconsciousness. When he did, Billy and Hugo left the caravan where Enos lay and stepped into the center of the camp.

"So," Billy asked, "what was he saying? I didn't understand a bit of it."

"Me neither, but whatever it is, it has the man burdened."

Billy had to agree.

"I ain't never seen him like this. The more he talked, the worse it got."

"He said he told Stella something. What d'ya think he meant?"

"I reckon whatever them bad things him and Sloane and Parrish was doin'."

"I suppose, sure. Something they were doing to the local landowners. Maybe it's what Gwenfrei Faw said about folks losing something valuable."

Hugo nodded.

"Hell." Billy slapped his leg. "The other woman Gwenfrei Faw told Connie she was going to see could've been Stella Woodard."

"Makes sense, I guess," agreed Hugo. "Fits with what Connie said the Gypsy told her."

"If that's true," Billy said, "then it must've been Stella who told Gwenfrei about some murder."

Hugo didn't respond. He only turned and stared at his friend lying next to the Gypsy caravan.

Billy understood how close Hugo was to Enos and Stella, but if the track this conversation had taken was too uncomfortable for Hugo, too bad. Billy had a lot of questions.

"What do you figure Enos meant when he said he wrote those folks in Cheyenne?"

Hugo released a tired breath, but this time he responded. "Impossible to know. But whatever Enos, Sloane, and Parrish did together, the way Enos is talkin', it must-a been a crime of some sort."

A sadness now settled into Hugo.

"I always figured Sloane and Parrish were a little shady—Sloane for sure," said Billy, shoving his hands into the sheepskin's pockets. "He likes to have his own way, but it's hard to believe he would commit crimes." Billy then said what he figured both of them were thinking. "Especially murder. Do you think murder's what Enos is talking about? Is he saying they committed a murder?"

Hugo seemed lost in his own contemplations, but when Billy said that, Hugo snapped, "Whatever bad thing Enos was a part of, we don't know if it had a damned thing to do with this *supposed* murder. We don't know it, so don't say it." He looked away. "Even if the one is true, it don't mean the other is. Could be two different things altogether." He paused for a beat and repeated, "Two different things."

After at least a full minute of stony silence, Hugo shook his head. "There's bunches we don't know, boy." Again, he looked toward Enos. "But I don't wanna ask him any more questions. Not right now, anyhow. The poor man is dyin'."

"He is," Billy said. "His dying is why we should ask him some questions, Hugo."

Hugo didn't comment, which told Billy he agreed. Anytime Hugo didn't agree, he was quick to let Billy know.

"We don't have to push him hard on anything," Billy said in an effort to temper his suggestion they pump a dying man for information.

"All right," said Hugo. "But let's let him rest for a few more minutes. It looks like talkin' tuckers 'im out."

If they were going to visit again with Enos Woodard, Billy doubted there was much time to spare, but he let it drop.

Hugo lifted his head toward Gypsy Rock. "Clever thinkin' gettin' on top-a that big bastard. I reckon you could see things pretty good from up there."

Billy nodded. "It worked out. I couldn't figure any other way, but I wish I could've done it before we lost so many." Billy had not yet counted the number of dead. He would save that chore for someone else. "What were you saying about the Roma don't take care of their own?"

"Them Romanis have some different beliefs about the dead. Baul explained some of 'em to me when we was haulin' the bodies and stackin' 'em in the wagon over yonder."

"What beliefs?"

"At first Baul didn't even wanna touch them dead men. He said if you touch a dead body, you run the chance of gettin' contaminated. I guess he finally did it because he figured I couldn't do the job by myself, but he didn't like it. He made it a point not to look any of them dead ones in the face."

"These folks are an unusual race, aren't they?" observed Billy. As appealing as she was, Billy figured Deya was about as unusual as any woman he had ever run across.

"Hell," Hugo said, "it gets even more unusual."

"How do you mean?"

"Like I said, they won't tend to dead bodies, so some outsider has to do it. That's why I told Stefan to bring along Teasdale. Another thing is they don't eat or wash themselves until after the funeral and the burial's all done."

"My god."

"They'll drink things, I guess. Coffee. Brandy. Water, too, I suppose, but no food. Nothin'. Not a bite. Baul and me had quite the conversation. All this killin' got ol' Baul pretty het up. Which a-course you can't blame 'im for, but, I swear, I never heard the man talk so much. He said the Roms figure death is a mindless, crazy thing. Outside the normal, you might say. Baul figures it's likely when someone dies, he's gonna be mad about the whole situation and might start takin' revenge on whoever happens to be standin' around. Gettin' revenged on by a dead man is somethin' the Roms'd like to avoid."

"You're making this up, aren't you?" Billy recalled back to Hugo's long-winded embellishments to the nail thief story.

"No, I swear, Billy. This is what the man said. He told me all about it right over there by the wagon." He jerked his head in the direction of the caravan holding the dead Gypsies., "They got certain things they *gotta* do when someone passes."

"Like what?"

"Have a big funeral. Lots of mourning. Weepin' 'n' wailin'. Then after the dead's buried, they all have a huge meal, which I reckon they're ready for because, by then, most times they ain't had anythin' to eat for at least a couple-a days."

Despite his denials, Billy suspected Hugo, the tall-tale teller, was laying all this on extra thick, and he said as much.

"I can see how you might think so," Hugo said, "but this time you got 'er wrong."

"None of it makes any sense."

Hugo shrugged. "It does to them. They wanna let the dead folks know they were too sad to eat. That way, if the dead is of a mind to do any hauntin', there's a better chance they'll haunt somebody besides them."

"I can't imagine Deya believes such things."

"Maybe she does; maybe she doesn't. Deya's some different than the rest of 'em. I'll give you that. Still, the girl grew up the way she grew up. And she's just lost her pa. At times like this, folks of every sort like to grab hold-a their old ways." Hugo turned and squinted off toward the river. Taking a deep breath, he added, "Their way of thinkin' gets even stranger yet."

Billy's eyebrows popped up a ways. He was unable to imagine how it could get much stranger. "Why? What do you mean?"

"Once someone dies, them Gypsies burn all the dead person's belongin's. Everythin'. Clothes. Personal goods." Hugo swooped his arm around, taking in both rows of caravans. "Wagons and all."

"No."

"They even kill his animals. Maybe not the horses, but everythin' else. Kill 'em all."

"I don't believe it."

Hugo placed his right hand over his heart and raised his left hand to the sky. "I'm tellin' you what they do, Billy-boy. I swear."

As Billy and Hugo crossed the camp to check on Enos, they spotted a couple of wagons, a buggy, and a small group of riders in the far distance. They were headed toward the Rock from the direction of town.

"That'll be Stefan with the doc and undertaker," said Hugo.

"Who're those other fellas?" Billy wondered. He wished he had waited before returning the spyglass.

"If there was any law enforcement around this place," said Hugo, "it'd be the county sheriff and a posse."

"Not likely before January when Jarrod's term ends." Folks around Casper were marking the days on their calendars when they could be rid of their worthless sheriff.

"If we had a pretender like Dale Jarrod around when I started out," said Hugo, "there'd be a big portion of the population pluckin' geese and boilin' up a pot of tar."

"Things're more civilized now, Hugo." Considering the events on this cold day, Billy cringed at the absurdity of his own comment and wished he could take it back.

Hugo must have also found the comment absurd. He voiced an expletive that communicated civilization was an overrated concept.

As they neared the caravan, they saw Enos was still as they had left him a few minutes before.

They also saw—or at least Billy did, and he assumed Hugo did, too—that Enos Woodard was dead.

Hugo dropped and took hold of Enos's hand. He knelt there awhile before pulling one of the blankets over Enos's face.

"I wonder," Hugo said, "which-a them sons-a-bitches is the

one who murdered my good friend Enos." He spoke in a soft, distant voice. It didn't sound as though he was addressing the comment to Billy, but more to the universe in general, or whoever the hell was in charge.

"I know who it was," said Billy.

Hugo stood. "You do? How?"

"Deya told me who shot Enos and Pov Meche, too."

"She knew the bastards?"

"No, but she described them to me. The one who killed Pov was dressed all in black and wore a fancy hat with a stampede string and a shiny band."

"I'd wager what made his band shiny was a whole bunch-a Liberty Quarters all strung together."

"I expect you're right," Billy agreed. "Hank Green."

"What did she say about the one who shot Enos?"

"She said it was a man who had a large bandage on his head."

Hugo sighed. "Thatcher O'Dell."

Billy nodded.

Hugo turned away and looked out to the group riding toward the camp. "Well, Billy-boy, it's good you climbed the Rock. You had a fine idea there. But I gotta say, it would've provided me some great pleasure to be the lucky man who got to put a bloody end to the last O'Dell—a lot of pleasure for sure. In a way, I'm kind-a sorry you already kilt 'em all."

For a second, Billy didn't understand what Hugo meant. "Killed them all? What're you saying?" And in an instant his mind raced through all that had occurred since he climbed down from the Rock, and he understood. "Wait," he said, "I didn't tell you, did I? With everything going on here with Enos, I guess it never crossed my mind to even mention it."

Hugo turned from watching the distant riders and looked toward Billy. "Mention it?" he asked. "Mention what?"

Chapter Twenty-Four:
The Romani Must Stay Pure

Billy left Hugo with Enos's body and crossed to where the Gypsies were gathered. Deya saw him coming and stood. She looked as if she had contracted the influenza or some other bilious malady. Her eyes were swollen, and her nose was red. As Billy approached, she dabbed at her face with a heavy shawl she wore over her coat.

"Thank you for what you did, Billy," she said, lifting her eyes toward the top of Gypsy Rock.

He acknowledged her thanks with a nod. "I'm sorry about all this, Deya," he said, and added, "I'm sorry about your father." Though it was obvious she had been crying and was still upset, she now had a handle on her composure. At least she did until Billy mentioned Baul. At that moment, all Deya's features came unscrewed and fell apart.

"Oh, Billy," she said. She dropped her head to his chest and deep, horrible gusts of sound erupted from her. It no longer mattered that they were not allowed to touch. In a short few hours on a cold Wyoming day, the world had changed forever.

Billy folded his arms around her and pulled her into him. He laid his cheek on the crown of her head, held her close, and allowed her to cry. Even if all Hugo said earlier about the Roma's ritualistic mourning to appease angry spirits was true, her tears were genuine. They came from a well of pain. They came from a young woman who had witnessed the murder of her father and most of the men she had ever known.

After holding each other for a long moment, Deya took Billy's hand and led the way to a fire pit away from the others. The fire had burned down, and Deya took a couple of pine logs from the stack next to the pit and tossed them onto the coals.

She dropped to one of the blankets spread around the fire and patted the space next to her. "Sit," she said. When Billy did, she took his hand again and held it in both of hers.

They sat without speaking. After a while, Deya broke the silence. "I knew bad would come to us."

"We all feared it," Billy said. "Thatcher wasn't going to let it rest, and some folks in town did their best to stir things up."

"Yes, but I *knew* it. Papa knew it, too."

"How could you know it for sure?" he asked.

"The omen."

"Omen? What do you mean?"

"The owl."

"What owl?"

"The other day when we were on your porch an owl flew from your barn."

"Oh, that ol' thing. Heck, Deya, I doubt he's much of an omen. The fella's been around so long, I think Rosco's given him a name."

"It was late afternoon," she said, "but the sun had not yet set. We heard his hoot. If an owl hoots in the daylight," she added, "it is an omen of evil. Of death."

Billy couldn't believe she felt that way.

He shrugged and conceded, "Could be, I guess." Of course, he didn't believe an owl could be an omen of death, no matter when he chose to hoot, but now was a poor time for debate.

More silence, but Billy didn't mind. Though the events of these last days ate into him as well, sitting here with Deya was the first time he had felt at all settled since before Ben O'Dell's trial. He could offer no explanation why he should feel this brief moment of peace, but he did.

"Ours has always been a small group," Deya said for no apparent reason. "We liked it that way, but we were too small."

Billy searched for something to say.

"We knew we were too small, and the *Kapo* decided we must go to California and join other bands—other families. It made sense, but many of the older ones were against it. I never was, though. None of the young ones were." She looked toward the Gypsy boys and young men huddled together. The oldest of them was at least three or four years younger than Deya. "Those who are left are only the youngest among us, the old women, and me."

She pulled her hand from Billy's and drew her shawl tighter around her shoulders. The clouds were thicker now than earlier, and the temperature had dropped.

"When Pov was killed, the leadership fell to my father." She took in a long breath of cold air. "But he was the last." She looked toward the wagon that held the bodies and back to the caravan where the young men sat. "There is no one to take his place. They," she said, nodding toward the boys, "are too young, and the rest of us are women."

Since the fighting had stopped, except for tending to the young men who had injuries, Deya had shuttered herself in her own thoughts. He hoped allowing her to put things in words now might help, but he wasn't sure it would. She appeared lost.

The riders approaching the camp were still a mile or so away. Deya turned, and as she looked through the space between the line of wagons, she saw them for the first time. "More men are coming from town," she said.

"Those fellas don't mean us any harm," said Billy. "Hugo sent for the doc and a man named Teasdale."

"There are more than two men coming."

"Yes, but they're not Thatcher or any of his people. I promise."

Again, Deya looked toward the young Gypsies. "No one's injury is very serious," she said, "but it'll be good if they can see your doctor. We should get to the ranch as soon as we can so they can also see our own *Patrinyengri*."

Her eyes welled again probably at the thought of the heavy task ahead—telling more than a dozen women their sons and husbands were dead.

"You mentioned someone named Teasdale. Who is he?" she asked.

"The local undertaker—the mortician who tends to bodies. He also does the funerals and the burying."

She sat up straighter. "I see."

"Hugo tells me you have certain customs."

She smiled, but it held no mirth. "We have many customs," she said.

"I mean customs about death. Hugo felt it was a good idea to send for Mr. Teasdale. I hope he did right."

"Yes," she said, "it's good a body tender is here. The Romani must stay pure. We cannot risk *marimé*."

Billy tried to parse out the sarcasm in her comment, but he couldn't find any. Deya had proven many times she was not above sarcasm. Now, though, all he heard was . . . exhaustion. Deya sounded very tired.

"There will need to be funerals," she said. Her brow furrowed with an idea. "Perhaps we can have one large funeral for everyone." She shrugged. "I'm not sure. It may not be allowed. I'll have to speak to the others." She considered it for a moment more and added, "It could be *no one* knows if it's allowed. Such a thing as this has never happened. But it would be best to have only one funeral, if we can."

Billy agreed. For lots of reasons, the quicker this was done, the better it would be. "I have a cemetery," he said.

"A what?"

"I have a family cemetery on the ranch. It's on the northern slopes of the mountain, a mile or so from the house. My mother and father and brother are there. It's a good place, Deya. It overlooks the river and the town. There are trees."

She smiled and nodded. She took his hand again and held it even tighter than before.

"We can get through this," he said. "I'll help."

She smiled her smile again, but it faded. "Papa said things to me before he passed."

"I know. I saw he did, but I couldn't hear."

"He knew he was dying. It made him angry." She spoke in a matter-of-fact tone. "It made him angry for himself and for the others who were killed. Dying," she said, "is an unnatural thing."

Billy didn't understand what she meant. Death was sad, mysterious, even fearsome. It had been brought to him at times when he was least prepared for it. And, even though he had also brought it to others, death was a thing he wanted to rage against. But everything the world had taught him in his short twenty years said that death, though a curse placed upon us all, was not unnatural.

"Papa said those of us who survive today must leave this place. We must leave it now and go to California to be with the others." She shook her head. "I don't know how we can, though. The winter is here, and even if it weren't . . ."

Her voice trailed off, but Billy knew what she was thinking. The Gypsies' dilemma was obvious. There was no way those few who were left could trek across twelve hundred miles of wilderness.

★ ★ ★ ★ ★

Billy joined Hugo where he leaned against one of the caravans on the outside arc, and they watched as the men from town drew near.

"Do you recognize any of those fellas?" Billy asked, but he already knew the answer to that loaded question. The group was still a few hundred yards out, and there was no way Hugo's mediocre eyesight could see so far with any accuracy. Barnett Teasdale's black hearse was easy enough to spot, as was his large buckboard, which was probably driven by Teasdale's helper, Freddy Alvins. A buggy was also with the group. It no doubt belonged to Doctor Ezekiel Waters. From this distance, though, even Billy, who prided himself on his fine vision, couldn't tell much about the five men on horseback who rode along with them. He did suspect the smallest man on the biggest horse was Stefan, but that too was little more than a guess.

"How's Deya?" Hugo asked.

"Heartbroke, mostly."

Hugo nodded. "She has plenty-a reasons to be. It's been a bad day."

"She says one of the last things her pa told her before he died was they needed to get outta here and head to California as quick as they can."

"Though there's no threat to 'em now," said Hugo, "I can see how they'd feel that way. I don't blame 'em. Not a bit."

"Are we sure there's no more threat?"

Still watching the approaching men, Hugo said, "I'd say so. Once the first shots were fired, the few townsfolk who'd got riled enough to ride out here decided they wanted no part of what was happenin'. And thanks to the Gypsies' hard fightin' and your fine marksmanship, the real troublemakers've been depleted down to a scant two. It's my plan to kill them two at my earliest opportunity." He turned to Billy. "If you're of a mind, you're welcome to lend a hand."

Billy didn't say anything. He knew the statement was one of those people make without expecting a response because they already knew what the response would be.

They continued watching the riders. After a while, Hugo asked, "Are them fellas close enough for you to make anythin' out about 'em?"

"The one to the right of doc's buggy is for sure Stefan," Billy said.

"I figured so, since he's atop a vanner."

"The others I've never seen before, but . . . now, wait a second." Taking a closer look, Billy squinted at the other men on mounts. They rode four abreast next to the hearse. "Can you see the one with the gray hat?"

Hugo pushed himself away from the caravan, stood up straight, and jutted his head forward in order to get his eyeballs a couple of inches closer to what he was trying to see. "Which one?"

"The man with the gray hat. He's the second rider from the left."

"All right. What about 'im?"

"I have seen him before. I even talked with him some."

"Zat so? When did you do that?"

"A couple of days ago, out in front of the drug emporium on Center. He's the fella who told me about the big meeting at the CR, the one where Sewell tried to light everyone up against the Roma. He was nice enough, I suppose. A real Southern gentleman sort of fella."

CHAPTER TWENTY-FIVE:
FORWARD THINKERS

Billy knew the gore where Enos and Pov fell was frozen into the dirt and grass, and it must have caught the attention of the incoming riders. They stopped there, and when they did, Hugo and Billy walked out to meet them.

"Gents," Hugo said. He tapped the brim of his hat. "It's good to see you. We've had us a sad and unfortunate day."

"So we hear, Hugo," said Barnett Teasdale in his well-practiced somber tones. "Stefan told us about it." Stefan looked at Billy and Hugo, but he made no comment. He glanced at Dr. Waters and turned toward the double row of caravans.

"Go on and lead the way in, son," said the doc. "I'm right behind you."

Stefan nudged the heel of his brogan against the side of the big horse and started for the camp. The doctor snapped his reins, and followed, acknowledging Billy and Hugo as he passed.

"We got lots of work for you here, Barney," Hugo said.

"Yes," said Teasdale, "I understand that to be the case."

"You're gonna be plenty busy, I'm sorry to say. *Mostly* sorry, anyhow. Many of the dead got less than they deserved."

Teasdale took off his hat and used his coat sleeve to blot away a line of perspiration from his brow. Barnett Teasdale weighed at least three hundred pounds, and despite the chill, he found the capacity to sweat.

Hugo pointed to the trees. "You got four customers over yonder. We'll show you where they are here directly." He turned to Billy. "How many's up in them rocks, Billy?"

Billy had to give it some thought. There were the six he got and the ones the Gypsies had killed before he made his climb. "Ten, I think. Nine or ten."

"And there's twelve total in the camp," said Hugo.

Teasdale, who had seen more death than Billy cared to imagine, cleared his throat and said, "My word." He turned toward his assistant, Freddy, and they exchanged a quick look. To both their credit, it was not a look of avarice, more a look of dismay.

"I want you to know, Mr. Teasdale," said Billy, "eleven of that number are Roma. If you'll send me the bill for your efforts on their part, I'll see you're paid. It could be, too," he added, "their services will be held at my ranch with burial in our family plot. I'll know more about those plans later."

"Thank you, Billy," said the large mortician. "We can discuss the particulars at another time."

Billy looked toward the rocks. "I don't know what to tell you about the fellas up there. Fees for tending to them might be scarce."

"It's not a problem," said Teasdale. "I'm not worried about it."

Billy was unsure why he felt so much concern that Mr. Teasdale be compensated for his services. Billy was more concerned than Teasdale appeared to be, which lifted the man another rung or two in Billy's estimation.

"Hell, Barney," Hugo said, "I figure these murderers have all got their horses tied over somewhere behind them rocks. I'll make sure their animals get sold along with the saddles 'n' tack and whatever else there is out there, and I'll see you're paid out of the proceeds. Plus, we know them sons-a-bitches all had workin' rifles and sidearms. We'll sell them along with every-thin' else. By the time we're done, I expect we can see your bill and still have enough left over to donate to one of Edie Baldwin's charities."

Billy supposed both his and Hugo's feelings stemmed from shame and embarrassment at the sheer scope of the carnage. Though it was Thatcher O'Dell who should have those feelings, Billy and Hugo were left to suffer the burden. A little consideration for the poor soul charged with the unpleasant chore of cleanup was the least they could offer.

A lengthy silence fell over the group, which in spite of its duration felt natural rather than awkward. After a bit, Teasdale said, "Pardon me, fellas, damn, but I almost forgot my manners." He raised his gloved hand in Billy and Hugo's direction. "These boys here are Hugo Dorling and Billy Young. I'll gladly vouch for their character." He nodded toward Hugo. "Though I gotta say the older one is a rascal who has a weakness for drink, cards, and, I suspect, other vices as well."

Everyone chuckled politely and then laughed outright when Hugo added, "I'll admit to a weakness for other vices of all sorts and varieties. It's a failing in which I take considerable pride."

The man Billy had met in front of the drug store leaned down and shook Hugo's and Billy's hands. "Y'all's' reputations precede ya, gentlemen," he said. "It's an on-nah for me that we finally meet." He turned to Billy and added, "Mr. Young, we've spoken briefly once befo-wah, I do believe."

"Yes, sir, we have."

"It is a pleasure, young suh. My name is Beauregard Burns. Mah friends call me Beau. And I would invite y'all to do so as well."

"Beau here," said Barnett, "is the United States Marshal for the District of Colorado."

"He's right, boys," confirmed Beau Burns. "Let's us locate a fie-ah somewhere to huddle 'round. It's cold out hee-ah and we have much to discuss."

As everyone filed into camp, the morticians headed toward the large caravan at the base of the Rock to begin their dark labor, and Marshal Burns introduced his three companions to Billy and Hugo.

Now, as he made the introductions, less molasses dripped from his drawl than earlier. Not that Billy considered the marshal's cornpone Southern accent was an affectation—not entirely, anyway, but perhaps there were times when Burns spread it on a little thicker to portray himself as an affable rustic. But Billy felt certain those who counted Marshal Burns a rube did so at their peril.

Their first introduction was to the well-dressed Euless Lonegan, Beau Burns's chief deputy. Lonegan wore a dark gray woolen frock coat. His hat was of a light cream color and bore a wide, finished brim. Though his duds were dapper, the hard look in Lonegan's eyes and the big forty-four strapped around the outside of his coat suggested he was neither a dude nor a dandy.

"Deputy Lonegan has been in town here for a while now," said the marshal, "though I doubt you boys've ever run across him. He's been laying pretty low." *Purdee lowah* was how it came out.

The marshal jerked a thumb toward the other men. "These two young fellas are with the State of Wyoming, the Offices of the State Geologist and the Attorney General. The little one is a lawyer with the AG, and he goes by the name of Featheringill Moody. I suspect that is, however, some sort of questionable alias. What mother in all of creation would name an innocent child Featheringill?"

The young man gave an embarrassed smile, and, as an

explanation for his mother's poor judgment, provided that Featheringill was a family name of long standing. "Everyone calls me Gil," he said, then added with another smile, "Everyone except my mother, that is."

The marshal returned the young man's smile and gave him a gentle chuck to the shoulder.

Turning to the third man, Burns said, "This large fella standing next to me is Dexter Stoll. He's a geologist, and he has a peculiar fondness for rocks and dirt that hardly seems natural."

The big man wore a heavy canvas jacket, and jeans tucked into laced boots that rose almost to his knees. Beneath the jacket, his white tow-cloth shirt was buttoned all the way to his enormous Adam's apple. On his head was a narrow-brimmed town hat. The hat showed signs of having spent much more time among the rocks and dirt than it had in town.

They all shook hands and settled in at the same fire pit Deya had stoked a little while before. Hugo filled a coffee pot and set it on the fire's grate. Everyone made small talk until the coffee was ready. Then, Hugo poured cups all around, and soon the chill from the ride from town had eased enough that the small talk ended and conversation began.

"I'm saddened to hear of Enos Woodard's passing," said the marshal. "Fact is, this whole mess out here is a hard thing to get a hold of. Those O'Dells must've been quite a family of miscreants."

Billy expected a comment like that to send Hugo into one of his rants about how the O'Dells were a bunch of skunks and scoundrels, but for once, Hugo chose to sit and listen.

"I had the chance to meet Mr. Woodard yesterday," the marshal continued. "I found him to be a fine fella, all in all. What's transpired is a shame. A real shame."

The marshal nodded toward the smaller of his two companions. "Young Gil got the chance to spend considerable time with Mr. Woodard here of late. And Dex did, too." He looked across the fire at Billy. "As you know, Mr. Young, I did not arrive in town until a couple of days ago."

Billy had to ask, "I'm curious, Marshal. What brings two Colorado lawmen all the way up here?"

"A simple question, Billy, with a complex answer."

"You're investigatin' someone," said Hugo. "Someone who the local law either can't be trusted to investigate or might have a conflict of interest somehow. One or the other."

The marshal nodded. "Or both."

"And since you're with the federals, I'm guessin' one of the folks you're investigatin' is our very own United States Marshal, the shiny-haired Webster Pierce."

Again, the marshal nodded. "I was told you are a smart fella, Hugo."

"Smarter," offered Billy, "than he looks is the way most folks put it."

"The State Attorney General," the marshal said, "received a letter a while back from Enos Woodard. In that letter, Mr. Woodard admitted to certain illegal acts and implicated others. He also wrote the United States Attorney for the District of Wyoming. Both the U.S. Attorney and the AG decided Mr. Woodard's letters warranted looking into. The AG contacted the State Geologist and the U.S. Attorney contacted me—or, rather, he contacted the judge for the District Court of Colorado. The judge looked me up." Beau nodded toward the two young men he had ridden in with. "I'm going to let these fellas tell y'all what they've been doing and what they've found. Once they're finished, Deputy Lonegan and I will fill in the part we've been asked to play."

Burns glanced at Gil Moody, who took a sip of coffee and set the cup on the ground next to his leg.

"Mr. Woodard," Moody began, "was educated as a geologist

and worked as one when he first arrived in Wyoming from the East back in territorial days. He practiced his profession for a few years, but in time he started investing in various businesses around Central Wyoming and was doing less and less work as a geologist."

Gil Moody was relating facts already known by all. Apparently, young lawyers were as long-winded as old ones.

As Moody continued speaking, Billy pulled his watch and popped it open. He was curious as to what these fellas had to say, but he hoped it wouldn't take long. He glanced across the camp to where Deya assisted the doctor in ministering to the wounded Gypsies. Billy and Hugo had things to do, and Billy was eager to get at them.

"At first," continued Moody, "Mr. Woodard was doing quite well with his investments, but from what he told me and from what I've verified through my examination of his bank records and other documents, he grew too big too fast, and when his loan payments became delinquent, the local bankers got nervous and let Mr. Woodard know it."

Now the lawyer was saying something Billy hadn't known. And what he said was surprising. Billy had always counted Enos a fine businessman.

"Mr. Woodard's cash flow was not what he'd anticipated it would be, and he needed an infusion of capital to meet his loans."

"That," added Beau Burns, "was when he brought in Avery Sloane and his man Parrish as partners."

"Well, sir," corrected Gil, "maybe not so much partners, but investors—or at least Sloane was—and an investor who, as it turned out, wanted more than a piece of Mr. Woodard's businesses."

"What d'ya mean by that?" Hugo asked.

Dexter Stoll answered Hugo's question. "Sloane and Parrish," he said, as he tamped tobacco into the bowl of a short-stemmed pipe, "are what you might call forward thinkers."

"Forward thinkers?" asked Billy.

"Yes, sir, I'd have to say that's what they are—" He gave the two lawmen across the fire a sideways look and added, "—or were, I suppose." He struck a match on the sole of his boot and lit his pipe. "They had a fondness for minerals."

"For the last year, Sloane and Parrish," said Gil Moody, "have been approaching some of the landowners in your county here and offering them cash for their mineral rights."

"They were doing that," Dexter agreed, "and with some success, too. Most of the folks they had their sights on were small farmers and ranchers, which means they were more concerned with what was on top of the ground—water, grass, cattle—than what was underneath it. Even before these recent dealings, Sloane had acquired some pieces of the Salt Creek area north of town from a fella out of Laramie by the name of Stephen Downey, who is a great man, but, regarding his mineral rights around this area, he was not so much a forward thinker."

There was that term again. "You keep saying 'forward thinker,' " said Billy. "What're you talking about?"

"Petroleum, my friend. I am talking about petroleum."

Chapter Twenty-Six:
Certain Inconsistencies

Billy must have revealed a quizzical expression. The young geologist huffed out a blue smoke ring that floated between them until it was caught by the heat of the fire and carried skyward. Dex smiled, waved the stem of his pipe a couple of times in Billy's direction for emphasis, and repeated, "Petroleum. There are some forward thinkers who feel petroleum, or rather the many things that can come from it when refined, might someday be a valuable commodity. A fella from Pennsylvania named Shannon drilled a well in the northern part of the Salt Creek Basin here a while back, and he's pumping seven or eight barrels a day. The problem is, there's no market for it in Wyoming, or anywhere else for that matter. But those forward thinkers seeking petroleum figure that'll change. It might take a while, but maybe not so very long. Me, I suspect fellas our age'll see plenty of big changes long before we knock on the pearlies."

"So you're a forward thinker, too," said Billy.

"I believe I am, yes."

"Well, the stuff's sure good for lighting lamps," Billy said. "And since there are fewer and fewer whalers around, I can see how in time it could be worth quite a lot."

Deputy Lonegan, who until now had been listening without comment, added, "It turns out some of them landowners up north of Casper needed some convincing before they were willing to sell Sloane their mineral rights."

"Very true," agreed Lawyer Moody. "And that's where Enos Woodard comes in."

"What are you sayin'?" Hugo asked. Billy wondered if either of them really wanted to hear this part. As Enos lay dying, it was clear whatever he had done with Sloane and Parrish had brought him considerable shame.

"Of course, all of the ranchers up there, to one extent or another, are aware of petroleum," Moody said. "And Sloane and Parrish didn't even approach the ones closest to Shannon's field in the northernmost part of the Salt Creek. But there are those to the south and east whom they did approach. Most landowners in that area are not what Dex here calls forward thinkers. First, there's not been much talk of petroleum around there. For years, those folks have considered the few tar pits they've seen on their neighbors' places to the north as more of a curiosity, or even a nuisance, than a potential asset. When they think of valuable minerals, they think of gold and silver, of course. And some believe there's copper in the area."

"Not much," offered the geologist.

Gil smiled. "Maybe, but probably more copper than gold or silver."

"I'll give you that," agreed Dex.

"What Sloane and Parrish were doing with these small operators was telling them they doubted there was any gold or silver or copper, or really any other valuable mineral, but they suggested there was salt. Whether there was enough to warrant mining, who knew? It could go either way. Tests were required, probably even drilling—all at a lot of expense and a lot of risk. A risk, however, Sloane and Parrish were willing to assume. Also, many of these places out there—most of them, I should think—have areas of limestone and—" Searching for a word, Moody rubbed his chin and looked to Dexter. "I'm thinking gravel here, Dex."

"Basalt."

"Right. Limestone and basalt, which might allow for the quarrying and crushing of gravel, a profitable enterprise, indeed, in the rapidly growing Casper area, if you could keep your costs down, and knew what you were doing."

"Something," said Marshal Burns, "the farmers and ranchers did not know."

"So," asked Billy, "are you saying Sloane and Parrish were interested in gravel?"

"No," said Dex, "not at all. Only petroleum. They didn't believe the petroleum deposits were limited to the northern Salt Creek area."

"But they told people in the south part that they were?" Hugo asked.

"That's right."

"Why did *they* believe there was petroleum there?" asked Billy.

Gil Moody answered. "Because Enos Woodard told them there was."

Dex nodded. "There's an obvious anticlinal dome on the surface there in the Basin. That bodes well for there being oil, and, of course, Mr. Shannon's well has proven there is. Woodard, at the behest of Sloane and Parrish, took a closer look at the geology of the area on the Basin's fringes, and he felt certain there were pools in other areas as well. The clues weren't so obvious as in the north, but, at least to Enos's thinking, those clues exist. I've been out there myself, and I agree."

"So," said Moody, "what Sloane and Parrish did was draft an agreement where they purchased all of the landowner's mineral rights—everything—for a one-time fee of five hundred dollars. In addition, they put in their agreement that they would pay for all costs to determine the viability of the mining of gold, silver, copper, salt, and the quarrying of gravel. If it was determined any of those specific minerals could be extracted at a profit, the landowners would be paid royalties at one-half of one percent above the going market rate in the area, a rate that would be reassessed at the beginning of every calendar year until such time as it was determined that a sufficiently profitable extraction of those minerals was no longer viable. Of course, the viability was something to be determined by Sloane and Parrish or their representatives."

Beau Burns said, "It sounds pretty reasonable, doesn't it?" *Purdee reezunnubbul.*

"Maybe," said Hugo. "I'd like to read one-a them agreements before I said for sure, but it does sound pretty fair to me, I suppose."

"You're welcome to read it," said Gil. "I have one right here."

He lifted the flap on a small satchel he had brought with him, but stopped when Billy said, "It doesn't sound very reasonable to me."

"Why's that, Billy?" Beau Burns asked.

"Well, it sounds like they got the landowners to sell them the rights to all of their minerals, but Sloane and Parrish only agreed to pay royalties on certain listed minerals. And," Billy added, "petroleum wasn't one of them."

Marshal Burns and his three men all looked at one another and smiled.

Hugo lifted the coffee pot from the grate and refilled everyone's cup. "You still ain't told us how Enos fits into all this," he pointed out, as he poured the pot's last few drops into his own cup. "So what if he used his geology skills to predict there might be more oil in the Salt Creek than some folks figured? That don't sound like a crime to me."

Gil smiled. "I'm a lawyer, Mr. Dorling. I like to present all the facts in a certain order, and it takes time."

Time and lots of it, Billy thought, but he didn't take another look at his watch.

"After a while," said Moody, "one of the landowners pointed out what Billy had mentioned, and people started asking more questions about what really was out there. It was then that Sloane had Woodard—coerced Woodard, the way Mr. Woodard told it—to put together a formal mineral assessment of the area. After all, Woodard was a trained geologist and a respected man in the community. All of the landowners who were still considering selling their rights agreed to accept Mr. Woodard's assessment, and he prepared his report."

"Which," Dexter said, "oddly enough, tracked right along with what Sloane and Parrish had been telling the landowners all along: a remote possibility of gold and silver, a distinct possibility of copper, an excellent possibility of limestone and basalt. No possibility of other minerals in sufficient quantities to make extraction profitable."

"Woodard's report was enough to make those who were holding out willing to sell," said Moody.

"So Enos wrote up a false report?" Hugo asked.

"Well, yes, as it turns out," Dex said. "Mr. Woodard admitted, both in his letters to Cheyenne and to Gil and me when we talked to him, that he had lied in his report to the landowners. He *was* of the opinion the areas in the southeastern portion of the Basin he described in his assessment were capable of producing oil, and, as I said, I agree. I'd be willing to wager there is a veritable ocean of oil under the ground up there, and I expect it goes from the southern area of the Salt Creek Basin up to the north at least as far as the Teapot, and probably farther."

"And," added Gil Moody, "Enos admitted to preparing his false report in order to induce the landowners to sign Sloane's agreement."

"Why," Billy wondered, "if Enos was helping Sloane bilk these people out of their mineral rights, would he write those letters to the AG and U.S. Attorney?"

Marshal Burns answered the question. "It turns out he had something that proves to be a hindrance when you engage in criminal behavior."

"What's that?" Billy asked.

"A conscience," answered Hugo. "Enos had a conscience."

Both the conversation and the campfire died down once Lawyer Moody and Geologist Stoll finished. Deputy Lonegan crossed to the woodpile, brought back three logs, and placed them in a neat stack over the glowing coals.

Once Lonegan sat back down next to Marshal Burns, Hugo said, "So, Marshal, now that we know what Dex and Gil've been doin', what brings you and your deputy all the way up here from Denver?"

"A few reasons, I suppose, though they've changed a bit since Euless first arrived. Early on, we figured someone with a badge oughta be looking into this, too."

"Yes, sir," agreed Hugo, "but what I'm hearin' is a few farmers and ranchers've been cheated outta some mineral rights. That doesn't sound like a federal offense."

"No, but bribing a United States District Judge is."

"*Whoa*," said Billy, "are you saying Sloane, Parrish, and Enos bribed Thomas Reed?"

Burns shook his head. "No sir, not all three of them, but in his letter to the U.S. Attorney, Enos Woodward accused Avery Sloane of that. Euless has made arrangements for us to meet with Mr. Sloane at his house this afternoon at five o'clock. It is my intention to inform him of Mr. Woodard's accusation. I expect he will deny it."

"I wouldn't mind bein' around for that," Hugo said. "What

does Reed have to say about it?"

"Right before I left Cheyenne to come up here, three of us, Judge Carson, who's the U.S. District Judge for Colorado, the U.S. Attorney for Wyoming, and I all paid a visit to Judge Reed, and we informed him of Woodard's accusations."

"Let me guess," Hugo said, "Reed denied 'em too."

"He did so emphatically."

"Big surprise."

"There was more discussion, though, in this get-together with Judge Reed," said Burns. "Mr. Woodard's letter convinced the U.S. Attorney's office to investigate the judge's financial dealings, and it turns out he was involved in numerous business ventures with a lot of folks, including Avery Sloane."

"Might one of those ventures be the acquisition of mineral rights in Natrona County?" Billy asked.

"No," said Burns, "to everyone's surprise, there wasn't. All the financial stuff so far appears to be on the up and up—mostly, anyhow."

"Then what was Sloane bribing Reed for?"

"What Enos said in his letters was Sloane wanted to be sure that Ben O'Dell was acquitted of the murder of some Gypsy woman. He wanted Reed to do whatever it took to make that happen."

Hugo slapped his thigh. "I knew it, goddamn it. I *knew* it."

"Why would Sloane care if Ben O'Dell was acquitted of murder?" asked Billy.

"Euless and I posed the same question to Woodard more than once. He said he didn't know, but I wonder. I think Enos *did* know, but for some reason he wouldn't tell that part of it."

"It's clear you didn't arrest Enos when you had the chance," said Hugo. "And it's too late to do it now. Have you arrested Sloane or Parrish?"

"No, as for the mineral rights bunco, like you said, Hugo,

that's not what we do, but I'm confident something can be made of it. Gil thinks so too." He turned to the young lawyer. "Don't you?"

"I do, yes. Or at least I did. I believe Mr. Woodard's testimony would have convicted Sloane for sure and possibly Parrish as well. But now that he's passed away and can't testify, it would be more difficult to get a conviction."

"Well, sure, Enos can't testify," Billy pointed out, "but you have the letters he wrote explaining the whole flimflam they pulled on those farmers and ranchers. Couldn't you show the jury those letters? Plus, Enos told you and Dex all about it. Couldn't you two testify about what he said to you?"

Gil shook his head. "We wouldn't be able to get any of it into evidence. It'd be hearsay. There needs to be a further investigation to try to find something more to be used in the criminal case. It's possible they covered their tracks well enough there's nothing else out there to find. But, of course, we'll never know without more investigation."

"The problem is," said the marshal, "Euless has been trying to work with your local sheriff, but the fella isn't cooperative."

Billy and Hugo shared a look.

"As for the bribery allegation," continued Burns, "Enos said it was all Sloane. He wasn't involved, and he didn't figure Parrish was either. As I mentioned before, Reed denied it, so unless Sloane happens to confess, which isn't likely, all we have there is what Enos told us about it."

"And again," said Gil, "no way to use it in the bribery case either."

Billy didn't know whether to laugh or cuss. He had always imagined the law was set up to get to the truth of things, but it looked to him like all these rules were designed to make the truth harder to find, not easier. It was crazy.

The marshal continued. "Enos knew about bribing Reed

because Sloane told him. As far as Enos knew, he was the only one Sloane told, but Enos was vague about why Sloane chose him to tell and no one else. I'm sure Enos was holding back on something, but I can't figure what or why." Burns turned to Hugo and added, "This whole thing with Enos is a puzzlement at every turn." He shook his head. "I'm thinking Enos Woodward was a good man, who did something bad. A thing true of all good men from time to time, in my opinion."

He gazed into the fire, which was going strong again. "I suppose bad men do something good every once in a while as well. Good and bad. We are all of us capable of both behaviors."

Burns lifted his cup and took a sip, but the expression on his face showed the coffee had gone cold. He tossed the remains onto the hot rocks surrounding the pit, and as they all sat thinking of good men and bad men, they watched the coffee hiss into steam and vanish.

Still staring toward the fire, the marshal said, "I agree with you, Hugo. Enos had a conscience." He lifted his eyes to Hugo and added, "But he was hiding something. I don't know what it could be, but he was. If your sheriff would get busy, maybe something could be made of the mineral rights con, but the bribery accusation isn't going anywhere. I wish it could, but it can't. Although, in the end some good has come of it."

Billy sat up straighter. "What do you mean?"

Burns's sad, puzzled expression eased a bit, and he said with a smile, "Let me tell you something, boys: Your federal prosecutor down in Cheyenne is a crafty little dickens. In the meeting we had, he let Reed know because of Enos's letter, he'd opened an investigation into Reed's business dealings, and even though, so far, nothing illegal showed up with Sloane or anyone else, there were a few inconsistencies that caused the prosecutor concern. That's the way he put 'er, too. 'Judge,' he said, 'I've run across *a few inconsistencies* in certain of your dealings that cause me real concern.' And when he said it, everyone in the room could see ol' Judge Reed started feeling some real concern himself."

"Well, sir," said Hugo, "listenin' to all this about my friend Enos has been painful, but I gotta say I like the direction this conversation's startin' to take."

"Once the comment about *real concern* was made and Judge Carson saw Reed's reaction, Carson asked the prosecutor and me to step out so he and Judge Reed could have a visit. We left, and not ten minutes later, Carson called us back in and said Judge Reed, due to the many stresses of the bench, had decided to tender his resignation."

"*Yahoo*," shouted Hugo, smacking his gloved hands together with a loud pop. "Then this horrible day has brought at least some good news."

"A little while ago, Marshal," Billy said, "Hugo asked what brought you here from Denver. I guess I'm wondering, why you came here today?"

"One reason we came out is there was talk around town this morning that something bad had happened at Gypsy Rock. We also heard you and Hugo were here and Mr. Woodard had been wounded."

"This is federal land," added Deputy Lonegan, "and the marshal and me wanted to find out what was going on."

"True," agreed the marshal, looking around, "but it appears all the wrong-doers in today's sad events have already been dealt with by the Gypsies and you two boys."

"Most of 'em have been," said Hugo, "but not all." He told Burns of O'Dell and Green's escape.

"That makes my answer to Billy's question about why I came here today even more important, and why, once I heard you were out here, Hugo, I asked Gil and Dex to come, too, so they could explain all they'd discovered as they've been looking into this mess."

"I appreciate it. The part about Enos is disheartenin', but I appreciate you tellin' me."

"Even though there's nothing, really, to be done, you needed to know what has happened for more reasons than because Enos was your friend. You were right when you mentioned that my deputy and I were asked to come up from Colorado because it wasn't possible for local law enforcement to lead the investigation. As it turns out, the inconsistencies the prosecutor noticed with the Judge's business dealings happened to also involve Marshal Webster Pierce. The prosecutor has not, as yet, followed the leads on those inconsistencies, but I guess the mere mention of them made the marshal decide it was best if he tendered his resignation as well."

As Hugo shouted another cheer, Burns dug into his pocket and pulled something out. "After some brief discussion, a decision was made," the marshal said. "And as a result, the real purpose of me coming here to Casper was to make a delivery."

"A delivery. What kind-a delivery?" Hugo asked.

With his thumb and index finger, Burns lifted a badge high enough so they all could get a good look at it. Once everyone at the fire had seen what he held, he tossed the star to Hugo.

CHAPTER TWENTY-SEVEN:
ONE THING MORE

As Billy and Hugo led their horses out of the camp's corral, Hugo said, "Let's hurry into town. I don't wanna miss Beau Burns confront Sloane about bribin' the Dishonorable Judge Thomas Reed."

The boys had discussed what Thatcher O'Dell and Hank Green might do next and decided the killers would want to get out of the Casper area fast, but it was doubtful they would be willing to leave in the cold and dark. They'd want to hole up at least until morning. Maybe there had been a number of townspeople who disliked the Gypsies enough to show up at Sewell's meeting at the CR, and a few of those were even willing to ride with Thatcher to Gypsy Rock—at least they were until the shooting started—but the citizens of Casper would not stand for a massacre, and there would be few places for O'Dell and Green to hide. So the question was, where would they go?

Before they reached the first arc of wagons, Billy stopped and lifted his stirrup. "Yes, sir," he said. "I'm looking forward to watching the show at Sloane's house myself." He tightened his cinch. "I hope it doesn't take too long, though. We have work to do."

"Once we see Sloane squirm some, we'll sniff out them sons-a-bitches, O'Dell and Green," said Hugo. "If possible, I'd like to have them two fellas kilt by bedtime."

Billy didn't expect Hugo was serious. He assumed if O'Dell and Green were willing to surrender peaceably, Hugo would take them in for trial. But Enos's murder had hit Hugo hard, and nothing Hugo did would be a surprise.

Billy finished with the cinch and dropped the stirrup. He gave Badger's neck a pat and handed his reins to Hugo. "Here," he said, "you walk the horses out of the camp. I need a word with Deya before we go. I'll be quick."

The Gypsies were hunkered at their fire. Each sat silent, staring with glazed and vacant eyes toward their own particular visions. The doc had finished and was helping Barnett Teasdale with his grim duties. Deya sat with the boys, but she stood and came to Billy as he approached.

"Deya," Billy said. "Hugo and I are leaving. I'll have Stefan hook a team to one of these caravans here so you can get your people to the ranch. You'll be safe and comfortable there."

"All right," she said. Her voice was raspy, but she was no longer crying.

"Stefan'll have to trail over the rest of the horses and what few cows you have, but that shouldn't be a problem. It's not far. As for the goats and hogs . . ." He stopped, not knowing if it was even possible to trail goats and hogs. He had never tried. As far as he knew, it might be like trying to trail cats and chickens.

Deya's left eyebrow lifted a notch. "Thank you, Billy," she said. "We are travelers. We can get ourselves and our animals to your ranch."

"Sure you can, Deya. Of course. Sorry."

"Where are you and Hugo going?"

"First, to the house of a fella named Sloane. We want to be there when the two lawmen who were in camp earlier deliver Mr. Sloane some disturbing news." He checked his watch. "After we leave there, we're going after the remaining two who did this to you." He glanced around the camp. When his eyes landed on Mr. Teasdale, the doc, and Freddy, who were still loading the dead, he said, "Those fellas there are taking the bodies of your men into town."

Deya's eyes did not follow his toward the undertaker and the others.

"I've been considering what to do," she said, "and I've decided we will have only one funeral."

"I thought you had to discuss it with the other women."

"Yes, but I've decided one funeral is what we will do. We can't do it any other way. So many separate funerals would—" The edges of her eyes crinkled as she searched for a word. Billy didn't know if she was searching for a word in English or if whatever word she sought was elusive in any language. After a moment, she took in a deep breath and said, "So many funerals would ruin us."

Billy expected "ruin" was the perfect word for what she wanted to say.

"I told Mr. Teasdale we might have services at the ranch."

"Yes, you're kind, Billy. I would like to do it there. And the burials—"

"The offer still stands to have the burials at the ranch as well."

"Thank you," she said. "We will."

"I wonder, though, if these are things you *should* talk to the other women about before you make a final decision."

"No, when there is a death, it is our tradition to have the service and burial as soon as possible. So that's what we'll do."

"All right, I'll tell Mr. Teasdale before I leave. Is there anything else you need?"

"After the funeral, it is also tradition to have a large meal. We've already taken food to your place. We'll take the rest of what we have today."

"Okay, I suspect Rosco's already shown the women our cook-shack and springhouse. When the time comes, you'll be able to cook up as much food as you'll need. It won't be a problem."

"Also," Deya said, "it's tradition that the property of the one—or ones—who have died must be burned and their animals killed."

"Right," Billy said, "so I've heard." He gave an embarrassed shrug. "I don't understand it, but I've heard it."

"It *is* tradition to do those things," she said, "but under some circumstances it's permissible to sell the items instead."

"It is?"

She nodded. "Even the strictest among us know that sometimes traditions have to be broken. I want to sell everything you see here and what's already at your ranch. The items cannot be sold to another Rom." After a beat, she added, "There are no other Roma around to buy them, anyway, but even if there were, they would never buy the goods of the dead. It could bring the worst kind of bad luck. No, these things must be sold to outsiders."

"Well, Deya," said Billy, looking around at the fine wagons and strong, healthy livestock, "I don't think it'll be a problem, not at all. We can have an auction. You'll make a tidy sum. I'm sure you will."

"Good," she said. "We need money."

Billy nodded. "Money's one of those things folks always need."

"We need it now, though, and we need lots of it."

"What are you saying?"

"We need it for our travel. I've decided we'll continue to California by train."

"Train? Really?" At first, her plan to travel by train surprised him, but he soon decided it was a fine idea. Ingenious, really. It solved a lot of problems. "A train," repeated Billy. "Why, sure. It makes sense." He pulled a hand from his pocket and rubbed the back of his neck. "But, again, Deya, I don't know. You're making a whole bunch-a pretty big decisions here all at once."

He shoved his hand back into his pocket and added, "Don't get me wrong. They sound like good decisions for sure. They do. But won't the others want to have a say in some of these things? They might want to take a vote or something."

A sudden frigid wind sent icy arrows through the camp. Deya turned her back to the gust. When she did, the gray, November light struck her face at an unflattering angle. It caused her cheeks to hollow, her jawline to take on a harsh set, and her dimples to narrow into deep lines around her mouth. It gave Billy a prophetic look at another Deya—the Deya of thirty or forty years from now. One who, perhaps, was not so quick to joke or flirt or smile.

After the gust, the wind eased, and she took in another of those long breaths that signaled she had something to say. "I told you earlier Papa talked to me before he passed."

"Yes."

She didn't face Billy as she spoke but instead stared out across the camp. The bright colors of the caravans, like Deya's beauty, were diminished by the cold day's unforgiving gray light. "Papa said we need to get to California as soon as we can."

"Yes, and I can see why he'd feel that way." Billy looked down at his boots. "I expect he was right about it, too." And Billy believed what he said. He knew it was best for the group to get away as soon as they could. But whether they were here or in California or anyplace in between, Billy feared for them.

And even though going was the right thing to do, Billy hated to think of Deya leaving. He had always known she would have to go. Still, the idea of it made him ache.

"Also," said Deya in a near whisper, "Papa said one thing more."

Billy had been so locked into his own musings, he only half heard what she said. "One thing more?" he asked in a dull voice.

"Yes."

"What?"

"That I must become our *Kapo.*"

He wasn't sure he had heard her right, and in an even duller voice, he asked her to repeat herself.

"Papa said I must become the *Kapo.*"

Billy placed his hand on Deya's shoulder and turned her toward him. He lifted her chin with his gloved index finger and looked into her eyes. An uncertain wariness floated there. It lay like low clouds. But her uncertainty wasn't all Billy saw. A light shone through those clouds. The light was small but growing brighter, and seeing it made him feel better. It told him in the end, he needn't worry; these Gypsy travelers would be all right.

Billy felt the corners of his mouth lift in the tiniest of smiles. The dead were still in camp. More dead lay fallen in the trees and behind the rocks. The injured young men huddled around their fire, and tragedy hung over all of it. Billy knew that now was neither the time nor the place for smiles, but his smile came nonetheless. And to his surprise, a smile tugged at Deya's lips as well.

As they mounted up and rode out of camp, Billy noticed Hugo wasn't wearing his new star.

"Where's your badge, Hugo? Have you lost it already?"

"It ain't lost. It's in my pocket."

"Why haven't you pinned the thing on?"

"I ain't so sure I want the job."

"What?"

"It ain't a deputy's star he gave me. It's a marshal's star. When them fellas was getting ready to go, Burns pulled me aside and asked if I'd noticed the word 'deputy' did not appear on the badge."

"Had you?"

"Sure, I had, but I figured it was some mistake or somethin'. Maybe it was the only badge the Colorado Marshal could get his hands on, since he wasn't in his own office. I didn't figure it to be a problem, 'cause Burns also gave me a key to the new lock Pierce put on my office door in Casper, and I got a couple of deputy badges stored in my desk."

"Did you tell Burns that?"

"I did, but he said the marshal's badge wasn't a mistake. He said they weren't offerin' me my old deputy job; they were offerin' me Pierce's job."

Billy let out a laugh. "Well, I'll be switched. Good for you, Hugo. Congratulations. That's fine news."

"You think so?"

"Sure, I do."

"I don't know. I'd rather be a deputy. Less paperwork. More time outdoors. Lots-a good reasons to be a deputy. Not so many to bein' a marshal. I told Burns that, too, and he said he reckoned I could be a deputy, if I wanted. He said for me to consider myself a deputy for now, but the folks down in Cheyenne would like to see me in the marshal's slot. He says for me to take a couple-a days to think on it.

"Anyway," Hugo added, "at least now I'm back to bein' a deputy, so when we kill Thatcher and Hank Green it'll be pure legal."

"About that, Hugo. I think if there's any way we can take 'em alive, that oughta be the way to go."

Hugo provided Billy a hard look and said, "We'll see."

The boys rode into town a few minutes before five and headed straight for Avery Sloane's place a little ways past the Episcopal Church on Wolcott. They were still a couple of blocks away when they saw Marshal Burns and Deputy Lonegan walking down the middle of the street toward Sloane's house, which was located at the end of the next block. Billy and Hugo put their horses into a trot, and once they caught up, they dismounted and all walked together.

"Thanks for coming along, boys," said Burns, checking his watch. "Looks like we'll be right on time."

"That's good," Hugo said. "We wouldn't wanna keep Mr. Sloane a-waitin'."

"Mr. Parrish'll be there too. When Sloane agreed to meet, Euless asked if his brother-in-law could join us, and Sloane said he'd make sure he was there."

"Sloane at least *pretends* to be cooperative," said Lonegan.

"And he'll keep pretending," Burns added, "at least until we start asking the hard questions."

"Once them hard questions start flyin'," said Hugo, "I'm guessin' Sloane'll tell us to get the hell off his property, unless we have an arrest warrant."

"Which, of course," Lonegan pointed out, "we do not."

"You're probably right, Hugo, about him giving us the toss," agreed the marshal, "but we might get to see him squirm before he does. If we can, it'll be worth the discomfort of mine and Euless's cold walk from the hotel."

Billy didn't know how long Marshal Burns had lived in Colorado, but he suspected this tall Southerner was no fonder of the frigid climate in the high elevations of the Northern Prairies than he was.

Billy was eager to finish with Sloane and Parrish and begin the search for the two remaining Gypsy Rock killers. He didn't mention his feelings to anyone, though. He doubted their visit would take long, and it was good they came. Hugo's dislike for Judge Reed was bone-deep, and he would not want to miss a confrontation with the man who bribed Reed to manipulate Ben O'Dell's trial into an acquittal.

"Sloane's place is up ahead there on the left," said Lonegan, pointing toward a brick two-story. Lamps burned in the downstairs windows, and a row of lamps hung from the ceiling of the wide front porch. The place was handsome, one of the most impressive in Casper, and bigger than Billy's house on the ranch by at least a couple of thousand square feet.

"They'll be expecting us," said Marshal Burns, "and I bet they're plenty nervous about why we asked to have this chat. So if we want to get anything out of them, we need to make them feel comfortable. When they answer the door, I want you boys to be wearing big ol' smiles and exuding lots of charm." Burns glanced at Hugo.

Hugo lifted both hands, palms skyward, and gave the marshal a why-are-you-looking-at-me expression.

Once they arrived at the house, Billy and Hugo tied off their horses at the rail and followed Burns and Lonegan up the three stone steps and across the porch to the massive front door. A decorative ceramic handle protruded from the wall next to the door, and the marshal gave it a yank.

Chimes could be heard inside the house, but no one responded. The marshal gave the handle another tug, and again the bells rang. Billy stepped over and peeked through one of the front windows, but he couldn't make anything out, so he returned to his place next to Hugo and behind the marshal and Lonegan.

When no one came to the door, Marshal Burns glanced toward his deputy, and they shared a frown; but before either of them could say anything, the sound of footsteps could be heard crossing the big house's foyer. As the door knob turned, the marshal bobbed his eyebrows a couple of times and gave Lonegan a wink.

The door swung open, and on the other side of the threshold stood Thatcher O'Dell and Hank Green. Their six-guns were leveled, and they both opened fire.

Chapter Twenty-Eight:
It Hurts, Don't It?

Billy watched Thatcher's lips peel back in a feral grin as his first bullet caught the marshal in the side. The smile widened as a second bullet tore through the marshal's hip.

Green's first bullet sent Lonegan's big hat sailing over Billy's shoulder. For the briefest instant, Billy figured Green's aim had been too high, and it was Euless Lonegan's luckiest day ever. That idea vanished when Lonegan crashed to the porch with a sizable chunk of skull absent from the top of his head.

Thatcher and Green both stepped through the broad doorway with their guns still leveled and firing. Green's second bullet blasted past Billy's left ear. Before Green could get off a third, Billy lifted his short-barreled and delivered a shot to Green's right side. The force of it caused Green to twist a quarter turn. Before the killer could come back around, Billy fanned the palm of his left hand over the Colt's hammer and sent another bullet into the center-left of Green's chest.

Billy guessed Hank Green was dead before he fell. No man could last long once a forty-five slug tracked a path through the middle of his heart.

Billy was too busy to see what happened with Hugo and Thatcher. All he knew was that Thatcher O'Dell was on the porch floor screaming a high, piercing banshee screech.

Traversing the writhing man's lower abdomen was a straight horizontal line of three reddening holes.

Billy turned his gaze to Hugo. The craggy features of the

deputy's weathered face were as immobile as stone. Hugo stared down and took in a deep breath. Jabbing his smoking forty-four for emphasis, he asked, "How does that feel, you gut-shootin', murderin' son of a bitch? It hurts, don't it?"

CHAPTER TWENTY-NINE: GOOD FOR THE SOUL

Once the shooting stopped, a small group of neighbors congregated at the front of the house. Billy figured Dr. Waters was still assisting Mr. Teasdale at Gypsy Rock, so he sent one of the onlookers to fetch the doctor's wife, who was an accomplished nurse.

Deputy Lonegan and Green were dead. The marshal, though alive, was severely wounded and bleeding bad. Thatcher O'Dell was also alive and still screaming, but his screams diminished in both volume and intensity with every passing minute.

Though she was skilled, Billy wasn't sure how much the doc's wife could do. Both men were in bad shape.

Billy tore the coat from Green's body and cinched it around Burns's wounds as tight as he could. It didn't stop the bleeding, but it did slow it down. The marshal was conscious, but he wasn't talking. He lay on his back and stared at one of the flickering lamps hanging from the porch's ceiling.

"We got a nurse on the way, Marshal," Billy said in an effort to reassure the man. "She'll be able to help you." Billy knew he didn't sound very convincing. Even so, without taking his eyes from the light, the marshal gave a nod of thanks.

A Southern gentleman. Polite even in dire situations.

"I don't reckon Nurse Waters'll be able to help this worthless bastard," said Hugo pointing to the still-writhing Thatcher. "I hope not, anyhow. I kind-a like watchin' 'im wiggle."

"Watching him wiggle?" Billy repeated. "You're a strange

one, Hugo." Looking around at the bloody scene, Billy could barely contain his gorge. Thatcher O'Dell's screams and thrashing about were not helping.

Billy stepped to the edge of the porch and took in a couple of breaths of cold air. "We need to look in the house," he said after his insides had settled. He faced Hugo and jerked his thumb toward the open door.

Hugo called to a couple of men he knew who stood out front. "You boys come up here and keep an eye on things while me and Billy look around." The men did not appear eager, but they did as Hugo said.

Before he and Billy went in, Hugo glanced again at Thatcher, and for a quick moment their eyes met and held. When they did, Hugo smiled a gleeful smile. "I'm gonna step away for a while, Thatch. While I'm gone, you keep right on a-dyin', ya hear? Don't you let me down now. I'm countin' on ya."

Billy shared a look with the two men who were now on the porch. The disbelief on their faces matched the disbelief Billy felt. "Strange," Billy said again, shaking his head at Hugo's cold ability to taunt a dying man. He turned, and as he led the way through the front door and into the foyer, he added, "Real, *real* strange."

Hugo followed him in. "Think what you will, Billy Young," he said, "but I'll be showin' no mercy to the scum who killed my friend."

Inside, a large staircase led up from the foyer. To the left of the staircase were a couple of French doors opened onto a parlor. Billy and Hugo headed in that direction.

The second they walked in, they pulled up short. Lashed to two straight-backed chairs in the center of the room were Avery Sloane and Scott Parrish. Sloane's head was bowed, and he appeared to be in prayer. But even from where he and Hugo stood,

Billy could see Avery Sloane had prayed his last. The front of the man's suit, his lap, and the floral carpet on which the chair sat were drenched in blood.

Parrish, tied and gagged in the chair next to Sloane's, stared across at Billy and Hugo with wide, bulging, terrified eyes.

"I watched them beat Avery to death," said Parrish in a quivering voice. He swallowed and looked up from the sofa where he now sat. "They were about to start on me when you men arrived."

After making certain Sloane was dead, Billy and Hugo had untied Parrish and helped him onto the sofa. They left Sloane where he was for the time being. Once Parrish's breathing settled into something closer to normal, Hugo crossed the room to a liquor cabinet and poured the man a snifter of brandy.

When the parsimonious Hugo Dorling wanted information or someone to do his bidding, he dug deep and paid for the drinks. Here in Sloane's parlor, Hugo was lucky enough to be generous and provide the treats without it costing him a cent.

He also poured himself one.

"No thanks, Hugo," said Billy as Hugo handed a snifter to Parrish. "No brandy for me." Hugo didn't need anything from Billy right now, so offering him a drink must have slipped his mind.

"Sorry, boy, would you—"

Billy shook his head.

"Suit yourself." Hugo tipped his glass toward Parrish. "To your health," he said.

Parrish took a hefty slug of the brandy without responding or even looking in Hugo's direction.

"Why were O'Dell and Green here?" asked Billy. "What did they want?"

Parrish looked frightened and wary. He also looked very tired in a way no amount of sleep could fix.

"Money. They said they had to leave the country and they wanted their money now."

"What money would that be?" Hugo asked.

"The money they were owed for going after the Gypsies."

"Going after the *Gypsies*?" Billy shouted the question. "What the hell are you talking about?"

Parrish appeared even more frightened and wary. He looked away from Billy and dipped his eyes toward the amber liquid in his glass. "Earlier today we heard what had happened out at the Rock. Avery was furious. When O'Dell and Green showed up demanding their money, Avery told them to get the hell out. He said he'd sent them to the Rock to run the Gypsies off, not to massacre them, and he wasn't paying them a dime."

"Why did he want them run off?" Billy asked. "Why would Avery Sloane care about the Gypsies?"

Parrish answered in such a soft, low voice, Billy had to ask him to repeat it.

"He was afraid of what they knew."

"Knew about what?" asked Hugo. "How you and Sloane and Enos was stealin' mineral rights out from under a whole buncha Natrona County landowners?"

Parrish's eyes popped up. "How did—" He stopped himself and again lowered his gaze. Parrish had been sitting upright, his shoulders tense, his spine stiff. Now he expelled a long whoosh of air and deflated into the sofa.

"Yes," Parrish said. "The mineral rights were part of it."

Billy and Hugo stood on the far side of a cocktail table. "What do you mean '*part* of it'?" Billy asked as he walked around the table and sat on the opposite end of the sofa.

Parrish turned his head toward Billy, and when he did, Billy recognized not fear and wariness in Parrish's face, but something different. It was surrender. And acceptance. And maybe relief.

Billy repeated his question. "What do you mean, Mr. Parrish, when you say the mineral rights were only part of it? What else was Sloane afraid the Gypsies knew?"

Parrish's already wet, red eyes filled. He blinked once, and two tears leaked onto his cheeks. "The murder," he said in a near whisper. "The murder of Phil Pritchard."

Billy heard voices on the porch and went to see what it was.

The two men Hugo had told to keep an eye on things had Burns by the legs and shoulders and were hefting him into the back of Mrs. Waters's buggy, which was parked in the street.

"Go gentle there, boys," called the woman from the porch. She was a tiny thing with a big voice. When Billy stepped outside, she said, "Why, Billy Young, what're you doing here, and what in the world is going on?"

"Bad things, for sure," said Billy.

Looking at the men still prone on the porch floor, she said, "My word," and stepped into the house. "And you were a part this mess, Billy?"

"Yes, ma'am, I was."

"Barney Teasdale," she said, "came to the clinic a few hours ago. He grabbed Zeke and took him out to Gypsy Rock. Barney said there looked to be a big mess out there, too."

"Yes, ma'am." Billy chose not to mention he was a part of that mess as well.

The nurse crossed into the parlor and stopped in front of Avery Sloane. Without saying anything, she touched two fingers to Sloane's neck. She didn't leave them there long. She gave her head a quick shake and made a noise as though sucking liquid through the space between her two front teeth. "He's gone," she said.

She pulled a white cloth from a large pocket on the side of

her coat and gave the fingers she'd used to touch Sloane's neck a thorough wiping.

"So Thatcher O'Dell and Hank Green are the ones who did this?" She nodded toward the body lashed to the chair.

"Yes, ma'am. They also killed the deputy and shot the marshal."

"How's the marshal doin'?" asked Hugo.

"If I don't get him to the clinic and stop the bleeding, he won't live long enough to likely die when Zeke digs out the bullets."

"But he's alive yet?" Hugo asked.

"He is. He appears to be a strong one. Maybe he can make it."

She pulled on her gloves, turned, and as she started for the front door, she said, "You boys get Avery out of that chair. Lay him out decent and cover him up." She nodded toward the porch. "And get something to cover up these other fellas, too. I expect to see Barney shortly. When I do, I'll tell him his workday's far from over. He has four more dead ones over here."

Billy escorted the woman from the house to her buggy. "Would you have someone tell Mrs. Parrish about her brother," he asked, "and let her know her husband's all right?"

"I will."

"Also, you may not know this, but Enos Woodard was killed at Gypsy Rock today."

The woman's gloved hand darted to her mouth. "Oh, my god," she whispered. "What is *happening* here?"

"It's been a hard, cold day, ma'am. I'm sure when Enos didn't return home this afternoon, Stella Woodard has been worrying. She also needs to be told."

"All right."

"I fear what it might do to her," Billy said.

The woman nodded. "She is a fragile little thing."

"Stella's close to Edith Baldwin. Perhaps we could have Mrs. Baldwin tell Stella about her brother."

"It's a lot to ask of poor Edith, but you're right. I doubt there's anyone better suited for the task. I'll let her know, and Reverend Sewell also. He can go along with Edith to the Woodard house."

"That's fine," said Billy, although considering Mrs. Baldwin's feelings about Abner Sewell, he wasn't sure it was. Still, not having to perform the sad chore alone was a good idea. "I expect she'd appreciate his help."

Again, the woman nodded. "I'll make sure it's all done as soon as I plug the leaks in this poor soul." She motioned toward the marshal, and without saying more, she climbed into her buggy, cracked a whip, and sped off down Wolcott.

When Billy returned to the Sloane parlor, Hugo asked, "I might-a misheard. Did Nurse Waters say there was *four* more dead ones?"

"She did. Thatcher O'Dell died while we've been in here talking to Scott Parrish."

"He did, eh? Well, by golly," said Hugo, heading toward the liquor cabinet and wearing a broad smile, "such happy news calls for another drink."

"Tell us everything, Mr. Parrish," said Billy as he sat on the couch. Hugo grabbed the back of the chair Parrish had been tied to, dragged it over to the table, and straddled it.

They had done as Nurse Waters said and taken Sloane out of the chair and placed him on a rug in the foyer. Billy then went upstairs, found a linen closet, and brought down enough sheets to cover all the dead.

"I don't know where to start," said Parrish.

"We know what you fellas done with them false mineral assessments," said Hugo. "Tell us about Phil Pritchard."

Billy was curious about Pritchard, too. Everyone had assumed his death was an accident.

"He found out about the assessments," said Parrish, "after he'd already signed away his rights."

"I reckon he wasn't too pleased about that," Hugo said.

"He was not. He threatened to go to the law and have us arrested. He threatened to sue us for everything we had. He said he was going to make certain everyone in the state knew what we'd done. Avery tried for days to reason with him, but Phil wouldn't have it. Once Avery realized there was nothing he could do to keep Phil from following through on his threats, Avery—" He stopped himself.

Billy waited for the man to start again. "Say it. Avery what?"

"He told the O'Dells and Hank Green to take care of it, and to make it look like an accident. And they did. They took Phil by surprise out north of town and clouted him with a rock. They even broke the leg of Phil's horse, scuffed up the ground, and made it look like Phil had taken a fall."

Hugo, who had placed the bottle of brandy on the table, added another couple of sloshes to Parrish's snifter. Parrish took a long drink and said, "I didn't know anything about it until after it happened." He looked up at Billy and across to Hugo. "I swear I didn't. I knew about cheating folks out of their mineral rights. I admit I was a part of it, but I didn't know anything about any of the other things until afterwards. You have to believe me." Parrish started to cry again. "I have a wife and a young son," he said. "He's only four."

Billy cringed. If Parrish hoped to extract sympathy from Hugo Dorling, he was going about it the wrong way.

Billy and Hugo waited. Once Parrish began to gain control of himself, Billy asked, "When you say you didn't know about the other things until afterwards, what things are those?"

Parrish wiped his eyes with his sleeves. "All of it, I suppose. It started when Enos got to feeling bad about tricking the landowners and told Stella what we'd done."

"Enos told his sister about the mineral rights stuff?" asked Hugo.

Parrish nodded. "Yes, when Phil started making his threats, Enos told us it was because he had confessed to Stella, and Stella had told Phil. They were engaged to be married, you know."

"Yes," said Billy, "we know."

"Then when Phil died, Stella went crazy. She already had some sort of mind sickness, I guess. Sometimes it was more noticeable than other times, but Phil's death made it worse. Much worse. Enos said sometimes she heard voices and saw things that weren't there." He gave a little shudder at the memory of it.

"Did Stella realize you and Sloane had Pritchard murdered?" Billy asked.

Parrish blanched at the bluntness of the question. "I didn't know about Pritchard. I swear I didn't, not until afterwards."

"All right, all right," said Hugo. "You said that already. The question is, did Stella know Phil Pritchard had been murdered?"

Parrish nodded. "Enos said he'd never told her about it, but, yes, he was sure she knew. It might've been nothing more than a guess on her part, but she'd convinced herself Phil was murdered to keep him quiet about the minerals."

"Good guess, crazy or not." Hugo poured himself more brandy. "You want some of this, now, Billy?"

Again, Billy shook his head.

"That's fine." Hugo held the bottle to the light. "We look to be runnin' low anyhow." He took another sip and said, "The marshal who Nurse Waters hauled away told us Sloane bribed Thomas Reed to get Ben O'Dell acquitted of the murder of

Gwenfrei Faw. Why would Sloane do such a thing? Why did he care?"

Parrish set his glass on the table and dropped his face into his hands. The young, cocky bigwig Billy had so often watched strutting about town with his brother-in-law and mentor was no more. Scott Parrish was beaten. He was destroyed.

Billy felt a twinge of pity for the man, but it didn't last long. Maybe Parrish wasn't as culpable as Sloane. But he was a part of the plan to cheat the landowners, and even if he wasn't involved in Pritchard's murder, he helped cover it up. And Billy suspected Parrish played some role in Sloane's effort to run the Gypsies off. Maybe he was no more than a follower of Avery Sloane, but he was not without blame. Assuming Parrish could avoid the hangman, he would certainly go to prison, and he was smart enough to know it.

"I'm tired," said Parrish into his hands. "I don't want to talk anymore."

"That may be," said Hugo, "but you will."

Parrish shook his head no.

"Listen, Mr. Parrish," Billy said. "It's over now. Whatever you, Avery Sloane, and—" He stopped and swallowed away a small clump clogging his throat. "—and Enos were involved in, it's over. I expect all the truth will come out in time anyway."

Parrish sat silent. After a moment, he lifted his head, propped his forearms on his thighs, and laced his fingers together. "Confession," he said, "is good for the soul." It was not clear whether he directed his pronouncement to Billy, Hugo, or only to himself.

Regardless, it caused Billy some unease. He had killed several men over the course of this long, bitter day, and he hoped this notion of a "soul" was nothing more than an imaginary fantasy. If it was not—if a soul was something real that everyone possessed—Billy had concerns for his own.

For a while, all three sat in silence, and Billy pondered the notion of souls and confessions. After a moment, he cleared his throat and said, "I don't know for sure if what you said about confessions and souls is true. Smarter folks than me say it is, but who's to know, really. I do suspect, though, that as far as the *law* is concerned, giving a truthful confession might help you spend less time away from your wife and little boy."

Parrish looked down at his hands. The pause before he responded was a long one, but Billy waited, and, to Billy's surprise, so did Hugo.

"Despite what we told ourselves at first," Parrish began, "we never could control what was happening. Things got worse and worse, and we all kept getting dragged into it deeper and deeper. Even Avery. He wanted to fix things. That's all he wanted, was to get things back to normal. But no matter how hard we tried, there was no fixing it. No matter what we did, there was no *fixing* it. Getting things back to normal became impossible after the Gypsy woman was killed."

"Why *was* she killed?" asked Billy.

Parrish pushed himself up and placed his elbow on the arm of the sofa. He dug a fist into his hair and said, "I don't know for sure. I mean, I heard talk, but what I heard was hard to believe. The why of it was all too crazy. Insane."

"Did Sloane have Ben O'Dell kill the Gypsy, too?" Hugo asked, "or did that bastard do it just because he was mean?"

"O'Dell? No, Ben O'Dell didn't kill her."

"What do you mean he didn't?" snapped Hugo. "He told me his own self that he *did*. Connie Baxter told me he did."

In the last half hour, heavy, dark bags had formed beneath Scott Parrish's eyes. "No," he said. "It wasn't O'Dell. O'Dell was hired to drop the body on the trail to Gypsy Rock. He said what he did to you, because, by then, he'd been made certain promises should he be caught and charged. What he said to his woman was nothing more than the braggadocio of a small, stupid man trying to look tough or important or whatever it is his sort wants. Who's to know how Ben O'Dell's mind worked? In the end, our involvement with the O'Dells was among the biggest of our many mistakes."

He pulled his hand from his hair and dropped it into his lap. Looking across the table at Hugo, he said, "That Gypsy woman was killed by Stella Woodard. Stella shot her dead in the kitchen of her and her brother's home, not two blocks from where we now sit."

The more Scott Parrish talked, the easier it seemed to be.

"Right after Phil's death, Stella was inconsolable. She had a complete mental collapse. It was terrible. Frightening. She would go from screaming and raving to long hours—days—of total silence. She would barely eat or drink. Enos didn't know what to do. I guess she'd had similar episodes over the years. Enos had taken her to doctors from here to Denver without success. But none of those times had been anything like this. Sometimes it got better, but it would worsen again. Once when it was a little better, Stella met the Gypsy woman; after that, and to everyone's amazement, Stella became *much* better. She saw this Gypsy every week or so, and she continued to make progress. She really did. It was like magic." He lifted his snifter but didn't take a drink. "For a while, anyway."

"What happened?" asked Billy.

"All I know is what Enos told us. But I guess Stella started asking things of the old woman she wouldn't do—or couldn't do. The Gypsy made no bones about it. She admitted she couldn't do them, but Stella wouldn't accept the woman refusing."

"What sort of things was Stella wanting?"

Parrish appeared embarrassed. "It's so crazy, it's unbelievable," he said.

Hugo was fast losing the patience he'd shown earlier. "Get on with it, goddamn it."

"Stella had heard somewhere the Gypsies could contact the deceased. They could conduct séances and bring the dead right into the parlor. Of course, you'd *have* to be nuts to believe such a thing, but Stella did, and she demanded the Gypsy do it with Phil Pritchard—bring him back to Stella. I guess even the Gypsy thought it was crazy, because she wanted nothing to do with it."

It *was* crazy, but Billy was not surprised Stella, in her grief and instability, would ask it; and, considering the attitude of the Roms toward the dead, he was not surprised Gwenfrei Faw would refuse. The Roms avoided the dead because they believed the dead were angry at the injustice of death. Billy expected the Roms would feel the injustice was double-true when the cause of someone's death was murder.

"I don't know the circumstances for sure," said Parrish, "but I guess the Gypsy woman said 'no' once too often and Stella killed her."

"Damn," said Hugo.

Parrish went on without prompting. "Enos panicked. He found Stella standing over the old woman and still holding one of his guns. He begged Avery to help. Avery told Ben O'Dell to drop the body out toward Gypsy Rock, where the Gypsies would find her. We figured they might raise a bit of a fuss, but there was no way anyone could know who did it. When we found out Stella had been talking to the Gypsy about Phil, though, we were concerned the old woman might have told some of her tribe about the murder. But the Gypsies never said anything about it, neither before nor after the woman was killed. So for a while we breathed easier, figuring maybe that was going to be the end of it."

"But it wasn't," said Billy.

Parrish lifted his snifter and emptied his glass. "No," he said, "it was not, thanks to Ben O'Dell."

"I'm guessing he got drunk," said Hugo, "and for whatever reason, he told Connie he had killed Gwenfrei Faw."

"Knowing Ben," Billy said, "I'd bet he was in the middle of threatening Connie and he tossed in this business about the Gypsy woman to scare her even more."

"Sounds likely," agreed Hugo. "And he scared her enough she told me about it. Then, once you ran the damned fool to ground back in October, all hell broke loose for Mr. Parrish here and the not-so-clever-as-he-thought Mr. Sloane."

And Enos. Billy wasn't surprised Hugo didn't mention his friend. Enos's role in it all was a hard truth for Hugo to accept. Billy also found it difficult to accept. With Enos's wit and ever-jovial behavior, Billy never suspected what Enos was going through with Stella and Sloane and his guilt about what was happening. Now, though, from Enos's letters to the authorities and the things he said before his death, Billy knew Enos had spent the last few months of his life in turmoil.

"So what happened next?" Hugo asked.

"Avery promised Ben if he kept the truth to himself, Avery would do everything he could to get him off. And he did, too. Avery was a man of his word. He hired O'Dell the very best lawyer money could buy."

"And," added Hugo, "the best judge money could buy."

"It turned out not to be enough for O'Dell, though. Once he was acquitted, he wanted more. We got him a job where he was paid well for very little work."

"Still not enough," suggested Billy.

"No, he wanted cash money to keep quiet. Thousands. We didn't have access to that kind of cash. And even if we did, Ben O'Dell's sudden riches would have raised a lot of questions. Plus, Avery knew if we paid him once, it would never end."

Billy offered another suggestion. "So Sloane had Hank Green kill him. And since the Gypsies would probably be suspected anyway, you all decided to go out of your way to make it look like they did."

Parrish gave the briefest of nods. "We were still fearful the Gypsies knew about Phil Pritchard, and we hoped being suspected of O'Dell's murder would drive them off. But," he added, "it didn't."

Hugo made the next suggestion. "It didn't. So you hired Thatcher O'Dell to do somethin' that would drive 'em off."

"Avery," Parrish corrected, "not me. And he never told Thatcher to do what he did today. He would never order a massacre. Avery only wanted them out of here. He only wanted them gone."

Parrish turned his rheumy eyes away and looked out the front window into the darkness beyond the porch. "We just wanted this to end," he said in a whisper. "That's all any of us wanted. We just wanted it over."

Watching the sad, beaten man stare through the dark window, Billy knew now it *was* over. All his questions were finally answered. Even the one about why Sloane told Hank Green to stop Thatcher from drawing down on Hugo. The reason? Sloane knew Hugo would kill Thatcher O'Dell in a gunfight, and Sloane needed Thatcher alive to deal with the Gypsies.

Recognizing Hugo would make short work of Thatcher was the one thing Avery Sloane had gotten right. The bloody line of three bullet holes in Thatcher's abdomen was proof of that.

As for the Gypsies, maybe, as Scott Parrish said, Avery Sloane hadn't wanted them killed, merely run off; but as with everything else in this long nightmare, things had not gone as Sloane had planned.

There did turn out to be a certain justice to it all. The chain of events begun with the order of Pritchard's murder ultimately led to a parlor on Wolcott Street with Avery Sloane's lifeless body lashed to a chair.

CHAPTER THIRTY:
NO WAY TO EVER BREAK THE SAPLING

Once the last spade of dirt was thrown onto the last grave at the Young burial plot, the heavy pall covering the Gypsies, the town, and its citizens began to lift. The shame and sadness remained, but the overt signs of mourning and grief, which were so much a part of the Romani custom and culture, now could end.

Or at least begin to end.

Edith Baldwin stepped to the front of the three-hundred-plus crowd and clapped her hands to get everyone's attention. "We have food for supper set up in the barn. Everyone make your way back to the ranch headquarters. The families wish to wash before we eat, but we'll start to serve shortly, so don't dillydally. We have us a lot of hungry folks here." She nodded to Tasar Meche, and the two met at Mrs. Baldwin's phaeton, climbed in, and led the way back to the house.

The food was provided by the Gypsies and the Lutheran Women's League. The meal would be served in the barn, but even the barn was not large enough to contain the crowd, so additional areas were set up in the cookshack, bunkhouse, and most every room of the main house.

As good luck would have it, the day was very warm by late November standards, with, to everyone's surprise, no wind at all. Those who chose could eat outdoors next to the large bonfire Orozco had built in the open space beyond the corrals.

Wagons, buggies, and horses were available to haul folks back from the cemetery, but, the weather being as mild as it was,

Billy and Deya decided to walk.

"Things went well," Billy said. He had been nervous about the day's events. He'd never had so many people on the ranch at one time, and he hadn't known what to expect.

"Yes," Deya agreed. "The service was nice. Thank you for arranging it."

"No," said Billy, "I didn't have much to do with it. You have Mr. Teasdale to thank." Which was true. Teasdale had, of course, prepared the bodies. He had also rounded up a battalion of gravediggers, which was no simple task, considering the amount of work necessary in digging so many graves, especially when the first few inches of earth were frozen solid.

Billy had, though, approached the ministers from the town's various denominations who had been present at the Community Room the previous Saturday for the big meeting. He invited them all to preside at the funeral as a group. With embarrassment, they had agreed.

It didn't matter to the Roma if one or all of these men spoke at the service. Billy guessed if the Gypsies were forced to choose a specific Christian religion, it would be Catholic, but so long as words were said over the graves, it didn't appear to matter who said them.

Billy was not given the opportunity to ask Abner Sewell to attend. The powers in the local Lutheran church had suggested the Reverend seek another flock elsewhere. They also suggested he do so immediately.

Edith Baldwin was pleased with Sewell's departure. And, as Hugo was quick to point out, it meant she no longer had to undergo the rigors of becoming a Hindu.

"Are things still going all right with the group?" asked Billy.

"Yes," Deya said.

"Even Tasar?"

"Believe it or not, things are even going well with Tasar. She

278

took me aside this morning and said that I had always believed I was free to behave as a man. So, since I wanted to act as a man, under the circumstances, I might as well be our *Kapo.*"

"Was that a compliment?"

Deya smiled. "I thought so at the time, but maybe not."

They both laughed. Billy tried to recall the last time he and Deya had laughed together, but he couldn't remember.

"What have you told Hugo?"

"Nothing yet," said Billy. "I did visit with Rosco some."

"What did he say?"

"He's willing. Even eager."

"So there's no problem."

Billy shrugged.

"I had a long visit with your friend, Mrs. Baldwin, yesterday before the auction. She's nice."

Billy, Hugo, and the city fathers, under the leadership—to Billy's surprise—of Mayor Theodore Hart, had arranged to hold an auction of the Gypsies' belongings. The Gypsies, still in mourning, did not attend, but except for a few personal items each could carry, everything they owned had been sold. Also to Billy's surprise, a little over eight thousand dollars had been raised.

"Yes, Mrs. Baldwin is nice," said Billy. "What did you two visit about?"

"The woman who killed Gwenfrei. It's very sad."

"It is."

"Once when I was a little girl, we had a man in our group who heard voices. He would see things no one else could see. I remember being terrified of him. All of the children were. But as I look back on it now, we weren't afraid of him at first. He was a fine man. Smart. Funny. But sometimes the voices he heard and whatever it was he saw would frighten *him*. The elders tried to help. They did everything they could, but with time, the voices, the images, the way he acted grew worse. His anger and his own fear only got worse. And his strange behavior started to frighten the adults in our group as well as the children. Some—most, I suspect—believed the devils had taken him."

"What did they do?"

She hesitated.

"It's okay if you don't—"

"No, no. They never hurt him, not really. But our *Kapo* ordered the man to be tied to a sapling. A small one. Small enough that given enough time and effort, he could free himself. After he was tied, we rode off. I remember sitting in the back of the caravan as we rode away. I watched him struggle to break loose. He wept and screamed. He begged us not to leave him." After a pause, she added, "We were all the family he had ever known."

Billy started to say something but stopped himself. He had no idea what to say.

"I always wondered what happened to the poor man." She shook her head. "But, of course, there's no way to know."

"It sounds harsh, leaving him like that, but no worse than what we do, I reckon. Maybe not as bad."

"What do you do? What will happen to her?"

"She'll be locked away in an insane asylum for the rest of her life."

"And," Deya said, "with no way to ever break the sapling."

CHAPTER THIRTY-ONE:
WAITING TO HAPPEN TOO

At the depot the next morning, Deya took Billy's hand and led him to the end of the platform, away from the others. The Roma were waiting to board the train to Cheyenne where later in the day they would catch a westbound for California.

"I want us to have privacy," she said with a smile.

"Why?"

"Because, in a moment, I am going to kiss you goodbye. When I do, I want it to be a thorough kiss, and it can't be thorough with a crowd watching."

"Well," Billy said, trying his best not to stammer, "that sounds like a fine idea to me."

Despite Deya's pleasant promise, Billy did not feel well. The post-feast wake the night before had left him with a throbbing head, and he was anxious about the Gypsies leaving. Even though he was confident they would be fine, he could not stop fretting about them. "I wish," he said with honesty, "it didn't have to be this way."

Deya moved in closer and took the center button of his coat in both her hands. "Yes," she said, in a soft voice. "But we knew."

He had to agree. Even last week before the attack when they sneaked into the trees and kissed and held each other as tightly as possible, they both had known.

"I have never ridden a train," she said. "None of us have. We've never even been this close to one. It's very big, isn't it? It reminds me of the dragons from stories."

She had a unique way of seeing things, but Billy had to agree. Puffs of steam drifted from around the locomotive like smoke floating from the nostrils of a sleeping dragon.

They stood next to the engine, and with a sudden blast of its whistle, a burst of white steam shot across the platform. With a start, Deya jerked, and when she did, she ripped Billy's button from his jacket. Eyes wide, she held it up, surprised at what had happened. Billy laughed, and when he did, so did she.

Once their laughter trickled away, they stood in silence for a moment. "Thank you, Billy," Deya said.

"For what?"

"For so much."

"I didn't do much, Deya. If I had, things would be different. These bad things would've never happened."

"No," she said. "Bad things will happen. They are always there, waiting to happen."

Her perspective was dark, but Billy had to admit his own experience told him she was right.

"But," Deya added, "there are good things waiting to happen, too."

As she said that, a large crow swooped low across the platform, flew beyond the train's engine, and landed between the rails. With its sharp, black-crow eyes, it scanned the train, the station, and the waiting travelers. It then lifted its wings, rose into the air, and soared away down the middle of the tracks until it was no longer in sight.

"See," Deya said, with her beautiful smile, "sometimes good luck seeks us out."

Billy smiled, too. "What are you saying?"

"If a crow lands in the road you are about to travel, it's a sure sign of good fortune to come."

"It is, huh?" Billy was skeptical, just as he had been about the hoot of an owl.

"Yes," she said. "It is a well-known fact."

"Deya," someone called. *"Deya."*

They both turned to see Tasar standing next to the nearest passenger car. "Deya," she called again, motioning for Deya to come, and shouting in Romani.

Deya shouted something back, and Tasar frowned and climbed into the car.

"It's time," Deya said. She reached up and took Billy's lapels. She pulled his face down to hers and gave him a very thorough kiss.

With a mixture of joy and disappointment, Billy felt her pull away. She let out a soft sigh, touched his cheek, and started for the train car. After a half-dozen steps, she stopped and turned back to him. "Billy," she called, smiling another of her beautiful smiles, the one that always made his insides flutter.

Billy found her eyes, returned her smile, and waved.

When he did, she held up his button, kissed it, and tucked it into her pocket.

"Now, *that* is one pretty girl," shouted Hugo into Billy's left ear.

"Damn, Hugo, you scared the living bejesus outta me. What d'ya mean, sneaking up on a man like that?"

"I didn't sneak, boy. I've been here all along. You just weren't seein' anythin' but your little Gypsy gal, and my, oh my, she sure laid one impressive smacker on you. I bet it made your heart go pittery-pat, pittery-pat."

"Hush up, you old fool. What are you doing here, anyway?"

"Lookin' for you."

"Well, you found me. You're quite a detective."

"Yes, I am. A highly skilled professional." He pulled back his coat and exposed the star pinned to his vest.

"Finally started wearing your badge, I see."

"I did. It is official. I am once again a real-life United States Deputy Marshal."

"So you decided not to take the big job, eh?"

"I told you I wasn't takin' the marshal job the other morning at Scott Parrish's bail hearin'. I like bein' a deputy, 'specially now that I'm gonna get to spread the work out some. I spoke with Beau Burns about it not thirty minutes ago."

"How's the marshal doing?"

"Gettin' better by the hour. He's a tough one. I'll give 'im that. He likes my idea, too."

"He does, huh?"

"Yes, sir, he does. I told him I wasn't interested in bein' marshal. My old job was what I wanted, but I needed some help. The state's growin' fast, and one man all alone up here in the wilds of Wyomin' is not enough. It's time the marshal's office broke down and hired another deputy."

"He went for it, did he?"

"He did indeed. Under one condition."

"What condition might that be?"

"You. The condition is you, my young friend."

Hiring an additional deputy was not news to Billy. He and Hugo had talked about the possibility earlier, and if he could get the funds, Hugo wanted Billy to take the job.

"Did you run the idea by Rosco, yet?" Hugo asked.

"We discussed it."

"What did you say?"

"I'd mentioned to him earlier about my stepping back from ranching, so bringing it up again didn't surprise him."

"Did you get 'er settled?"

"Like I said, Hugo, we discussed it."

"Talkin' to you's like pullin' teeth out of a chicken." Hugo sometimes got his clichés mixed up.

"I told him I might be willing to sell the cattle operation. Not the land or buildings, just the cattle and equipment."

"And he could still run 'em on your ranch?"

"Sure. That'd be part of the deal."

"What did he say?"

"He's interested, if he can get the financing."

"Well, that won't be a problem. There's not a banker in the county who'd hesitate to front a man like Rosco. Not a one."

"I expect you're right."

" 'Specially if he's runnin' his cows on a lush hunk-a ground like yours. So is it a go?"

"I'm still thinking. It's a big step, Hugo."

"Why are you holdin' back, boy? I figure we could have us some fun."

"I fear a deputy marshal's life is not the life for me." There had been a time not so long ago when Billy believed it might be, but a great deal had happened since then. He had learned enforcing the law required things of a man that Billy questioned his willingness to provide.

"Not the life for you? Why wouldn't it be? It is a life full of excitement and adventure. It is a life of fine whiskey, pretty women, and fast horses. It is a life dispensin' justice to evildoers and helpin' good folks in dire times. Except for maybe bein' the king of England, what better life could any fella ever want?"

"It's a queen who's running England, Hugo, not a king. Don't you ever read a newspaper?"

"I rarely do, Billy-boy. The news tends to make me sad. And I don't like things bringin' down my otherwise rosy outlook and bubbly disposition." He nudged Billy with an elbow. "Let's get outta here and find us a saloon where we can talk about the fine art of marshalin'. What d'ya say?"

"A saloon? Hugo, it's barely nine o'clock in the morning."

"Is it that late already? Damn, boy, we'd better hurry." He tossed an arm around Billy's shoulder. "Come on. A beer would hit the spot. And," he added, "the good news for you is it'll be *my* treat."

Hugo must have suspected Billy was onto his wily ways because when Hugo said he would buy, he punctuated the offer with a sharp peal of laughter. Billy refused to share in the laugh, but with both a frown and a smile, he surrendered and allowed his old friend to shuttle him toward the depot's front doors.

ABOUT THE AUTHOR

Robert D. McKee has had a number of jobs, including four years in the military. He has also been employed as a warehouse worker, radio announcer, disc jockey, copy writer, court reporter, and municipal court judge.

After school in Texas, Bob settled in Wyoming, where he lived for over thirty years. He and his wife, Kathy, now make their home along Colorado's Front Range.

His short fiction has appeared in more than twenty commercial and literary publications. One of his stories was selected for the prestigious anthology *Best American Mystery Stories,* edited by Otto Penzler with the assistance that year of visiting editor Michael Connelly. He is also a recipient of the Wyoming Art Council's Literary Fellowship Award, as well as a three-time first-place winner of Wyoming Writers, Incorporated's adult fiction contest, and a two-time first-place winner of the National Writers Association's short fiction contest. His first novel, *Dakota Trails,* was awarded the 2016 Will Rogers Silver Medallion for Best Western. His second novel, *Killing Blood,* was a Western Fictioneers finalist for Best Novel.

When not at his computer writing, Bob can be found rummaging through antique stores in search of vintage fountain pens or roaming the back roads of Wyoming and Colorado.

The employees of Five Star Publishing hope you have enjoyed this book.

Our Five Star novels explore little-known chapters from America's history, stories told from unique perspectives that will entertain a broad range of readers.

Other Five Star books are available at your local library, bookstore, all major book distributors, and directly from Five Star/Gale.

Connect with Five Star Publishing

Visit us on Facebook:
   https://www.facebook.com/FiveStarCengage

Email:
   FiveStar@cengage.com

For information about titles and placing orders:
   (800) 223-1244
   gale.orders@cengage.com

To share your comments, write to us:
   Five Star Publishing
   Attn: Publisher
   10 Water St., Suite 310
   Waterville, ME 04901